find me

LAURA VAN DEN BERG

DEL REY

1 3 5 7 9 10 8 6 4 2

Del Rey, an imprint of Ebury Publishing
20 Vauxhall Bridge Road,
London SW1V 2SA

Penguin
Random House
UK

Del Rey is part of the Penguin Random House group of companies whose addresses can be found at
global.penguinrandomhouse.com

First published in the US in 2015 by Farrar, Straus and Giroux
First published in the UK in 2015 by Del Rey

www.eburypublishing.co.uk

A CIP catalogue record for this book is available from the British Library

Hardback ISBN 9781785031328
Trade paperback ISBN 9781785031335

Printed and bound in Great Britain by Clays Ltd, St Ives PLC

Penguin Random House is committed to a sustainable future for our
business, our readers and our planet. This book is made from
Forest Stewardship Council® certified paper.

'Laura van den Berg is the best young writer in America . . . earning deserved comparisons to Margaret Atwood and Kazuo Ishiguro. While it stands up to such fine company . . . van den Berg has a style, humour and grit that is all her own' *Salon* (Claire Cameron, author of *The Bear*)

'this elegiac debut novel . . . lingers and aches in the memory' *Guardian*

'pleasingly strange . . . impressively original dystopian novel' *The New York Times Book Review*

'she's a hot-shot short story writer, and her first novel is fascinating . . . A fresh spin on apocalyptic stories, *Find Me* beautifully evaluates memory loss and the stories we tell ourselves' *Huffington Post*

'spellbinding . . . *Find Me* is crafted to be consumed in small sips, though with a novel so full of mystery and surprise, the temptation is to gulp . . . a mesmerizing and emotional experience that invites readers to, like Joy, savour life' *O magazine*

'van den Berg's dystopian debut is a haunting exploration of loneliness' *Marie Claire*

'. . . a distinctive new voice. Her first novel is original – experimental, even – but written with remarkable clarity. Van den Berg blends the story of the strange plague with Joy's search for her lost mother into an intoxicating mystery' *BBC News*

'*Find Me* eases into itself, and the deeper we venture into it, the more glorious the book becomes in its embodiment of doubt and self-scrutiny . . . Van den Berg's dystopian debut novel blossoms into a timeless chronicle of self-discovery' *Time Out New York*

'marvellous' *Vanity Fair*

TO P.,

for never being afraid of the search

find me

Things I will never forget: my name, my made-up birthday, the rattle of a train in a tunnel. The sweet grit of toothpaste. The bitterness of coffee and blood. The dark of the Hospital at night. My mother's face, when she was young.

. . .

Things other people will forget: where they come from, how old they are, the faces of the people they love. The right words for bowl and sunshine and sidewalk. What is a beginning and what is an end.

BOOK 1

In a place far away from anyone or anywhere, I
drifted off for a moment.

—Haruki Murakami, *The Wind-Up Bird Chronicle*

1.

On our third month in the Hospital, the pilgrims begin to appear. They gather outside the doors, faces tipped to the sky, while our Floor Group watches at the end of the fifth-floor hallway. The windows have bars on the outside and we have to tilt our heads to get a good view. Sometimes the pilgrims wave and we wave back. Or they hold hands and sing and we hear their voices through the glass. Some stand outside for hours, others for days. We don't understand what they could want from us.

. . .

Early November and already the cold is descending across the plains. We can't go outside, but we hear about it on the Weather Channel and feel it on the windowpanes. We can tell from the pilgrims' clothing too, the way they come bundled in overcoats and scarves. The twins, Sam and Christopher, named the visitors, since the first one to turn up wore a black hat with a wide brim, like the pilgrims they learned about in school. I can remember the way the twins grinned as they offered this fact, pleased by the strength of their memories.

For hours I stand by the fifth-floor window and watch the pilgrims pace in front of the Hospital or use sticks to draw circles in the dirt. It's like observing wildlife.

When the sky darkens and rain falls for three days straight, I go to Dr. Bek and make a case for letting the pilgrims inside. His office is on the sixth floor, a windowless room at the end of the hallway, furnished with two high-backed rolling chairs— Venn chairs, he says they're called—and a desk shaped like a half moon. We all choose our dungeons: this is a saying I've heard somewhere before, though I can't remember the source, a nibble of worry. The one personal touch is a poster of massive gray cliffs, fog-dusted peaks, ridges veined with snow, on the wall behind Dr. Bek's desk. It's the Troll Wall in Norway, where he was born.

In Norway, there are half a million lakes. In Norway, the cheese is brown. In Norway, the paper clip was invented. These are the things Dr. Bek has told us.

Me, I know nothing of Norway. I used to live in Somerville, Massachusetts, on a narrow street with no trees.

Dr. Bek types at his desk. Manila files are stacked next to his computer. I look at the folders and try to imagine what's inside: our case histories, the results of our blood work, all the ways he is trying to find a cure. Dr. Bek is fair and tall, his posture stooped inside his silver hazmat suit, as though he's forever ducking under a low doorway. Behind the shield, his eyes are a cool blue, his cheekbones high and sharp. When he's angry, his face looks like it has been chiseled from a fine grade of stone.

The Hospital staff guards against the sickness with Level A hazmat suits, chemical-resistant boots and gloves, and decontamination showers before entering their quarters on the second floor. They need these precautions because they aren't special, like the patients are thought to be. When we came to the Hospital, our possessions were locked away in basement storage. "Why does our stuff have to stay in the basement?" some patients demanded to know, and Dr. Bek explained it was all part of releasing the outside world for a time, of releasing a life that no longer belonged to us.

Each patient was given a pair of white slippers and four sets of scrubs, two white and two mint green. Louis, my roommate, and I avoid wearing the white ones as much as possible, agreeing they make us look like ghosts.

All the patients have been assigned weekly appointments with Dr. Bek, to make sure our feelings don't stay in hiding. When our feelings stay in hiding, bad things can happen, or so we've been told.

I have no talent for following rules. I ignore my appointed times. I only go to his office when I have questions.

I sit across from Dr. Bek and tell him two pilgrims have been standing in the rain for days. They're shivering and sleeping on the ground.

"They could get pneumonia and die," I say. "Why can't we let them inside?"

"Joy, I take no pleasure in their struggle." Dr. Bek keeps typing. Every breath is a long rasp. The sound is worse than nails on a chalkboard or a person running out of air. "But we can't let them in. After all, how can we know where these people came from? What they want? What they might be carrying inside them?"

Disease is as old as life itself, Dr. Bek is fond of pointing out. An adversary that cannot be underestimated. For example, when cacao farming peaked in Brazil, mounds of pods amassed in the countryside, gathering just enough rainwater to create a breeding ground for the biting midge. From this slight ecological shift came an outbreak of Oropouche, or Brazilian hemorrhagic fever.

According to Dr. Bek, it only takes the smallest change to turn our lives inside out.

"It's my job to see danger where you, a patient, cannot." He stops typing and opens the folder at the top of the stack. I watch his eyes collect the information inside. "To protect you from the flaws in your judgment."

Dr. Bek is a widower, but not because of the sickness. His wife died many years ago, or at least that's what I've overheard from the nurses, who sometimes talk about him when they think they're alone. Dr. Bek tells us little about his life beyond the Hospital walls.

As for the pilgrims, I have no argument—there is plenty of evidence to suggest flaws in my judgment—so I leave his office. Already our group of one hundred and fifty has dwindled to seventy-five. During the first month alone, a dozen patients became symptomatic and were sent to the tenth floor. We didn't see them again.

Still, I feel a pain in my chest when I look out the window and find a pilgrim balled on the ground, his body pulsing from the cold. Before the rain, this man was pacing, and then, out of nowhere, he did one perfect cartwheel. I wish I had a way to talk to him, to ask why he came, to tell him no one is going to help him here. I don't think it's right to watch these people suffer, even if it's a suffering they have chosen.

Finally the rain lightens and the man scrambles to his feet. He stares up at the Hospital for a long time, and I wonder if he can see me watching. What kind of person he thinks I am. He turns from the window and staggers away. Another pilgrim calls after him, but he doesn't look back. It's still drizzling. The sky is charcoal and goes on forever. I watch his silhouette grow smaller, until he is just a speck on the edges of the land. We the patients are always dreaming about being released from the Hospital.

Sometimes it's all I can think about, the outdoor air rushing into my lungs, the light on my face, but I don't envy that man then.

• • •

The Hospital is ten stories high, plus the basement. The patients live on floors two through six. Each of us is assigned a Floor Group; each Group is staffed by two nurses. Louis and I belong to Group five. All floors amass for Community Meetings and activities and meals, but otherwise the Groups have a way of sticking together.

I call the basement the zero floor. On the zero floor, there is a door with a triangle of glass in the center, a small window to the outside, and beneath it the faint green glow of a security keypad. Floors seven through nine sit empty. All elevator service has been suspended. You can punch the round buttons, but nothing will happen. Dr. Bek believes in the importance of exercise, so the patients have free passage to the other floors by going through the stairwells, except the first floor, where the staff lives, and the tenth floor, where the sick patients go—both are forbidden to us, also guarded by keypads.

The Dining Hall has a keypad too, but the staff allows those doors to stay open. Whenever possible, they like to create the illusion of freedom.

In the beginning, there were thirty patients on each floor. Now, after three months, no floor has more than fifteen. But the staffing has not changed. There are still ten nurses and Dr. Bek. "Way to lighten your workload!" Louis and I sometimes joke, because laughter makes us feel brave. In the end, the patients might be outnumbered.

An incomplete list of the rules: each Floor Group has a job within the Hospital. The Common Room is located on floor five and it is the job of our Floor Group to keep that space neat and clean. Floor Group three is in charge of the library. Every other week, Group two rounds up patient laundry in canvas rolling carts. After meals, Groups four and six collect trash, stack the red plastic trays, and wipe the warm insides of the microwaves and the stainless steel buffet tables. The surfaces of the tables are dull, but sometimes I catch a smudged reflection as I move through the food line and think, Who is that face? Each floor is responsible for keeping their own hallway in order. "A busy mind is a healthy mind," Dr. Bek likes to say.

In the Hospital, there are no razors in the showers, just miniature bars of white soap that melt between fingertips, slip down drains. In the Hospital, there is nothing to drink but water. The plastic chairs in the Dining Hall are the color of tangerines. In the Hospital, we celebrate every patient birthday, knowing full well that it might be their last. In the Hospital, our meals come frozen in black trays, the plastic coverings fringed with ice, and we wait in line to heat them in the large humming microwaves. In the Hospital, there is no such thing as mail.

• • •

Before long the other patients lose interest in pilgrim spotting and go back to rummaging through the books in the Hospital library or watching TV in the Common Room or trying to sneak into the Computer Room on the fourth floor, yet another keypadded space, to check WeAreSorryForYourLoss.com, a government-maintained list of people reported dead from the sickness. We have supervised Internet Sessions every Wednesday and Friday, though of course we always want more.

When breakfast ends each morning, I stand on an orange chair and look out the Dining Hall windows. I turn my back on the maze of long tables, the clatter of the Groups stacking trays. The Dining Hall is on the fifth floor; the bars on the windows are thick as arms. I peer between them, searching for pilgrims. Sometimes it's the same people. Or a new one has arrived. Or there are no pilgrims at all, just a scattering of footprints in the brown soil.

I spend a lot of time thinking about why the pilgrims started coming here, how they even found us. The easy answer is that they think this is a safe place, that we might have a cure, but that reasoning has never satisfied me. I do much of this thinking in the library, sitting between the squat bookcases filled with dictionaries and encyclopedias, plus books on space travel and the Mayan empire and dinosaurs. Dr. Bek believes that even though our bodies are confined to the Hospital, there is no reason to limit our minds.

I think about how devoted the pilgrims seem, the way they stand out there in all kinds of weather, staring up at the windows. They don't bang on the doors and shout to be let inside; they don't demand to be included in our secrets. They just wait. Dr. Bek is always reminding us of our specialness. Do the pilgrims know we're special too?

For a while, the library is the space I like best. All the patient quarters are white-walled rooms with white twin beds and white rolling medicine cabinets—other things in the Hospital that are white: the sheets, the pillows, the hazmat suits of the nurses, the flimsy shower curtains, the towels that scratch our skin—and so the walnut bookcases and the round olive-colored rug make the library feel special, a portal to a place that is separate from the rest of the Hospital.

When I start reading about the dinosaurs and the Mayans, however, the things I learn disturb me. For example, the book on the dinosaurs is not about how big and magnificent they were, but about why they all died. There is no agreement on what happened. An asteroid, continental drift, an epidemic. In the book about the Mayans, the author says they were wiped out by a plague, that every so often "incurables" appear and civilizations are reset. When I discuss my findings with Dr. Bek, he says the sickness is not the result of some cosmic reordering. Rather it's the simple truth that the smallest alteration can create the perfect atmosphere for a new disease to emerge. "The world is a very fragile place," he tells me, another favorite line of his.

I've grown up knowing the world is fragile. No one needs to tell me that.

■ ■ ■

I stretch out in a hallway. I've been walking the Hospital for so many hours, I've forgotten what floor I'm on. I only know that I can't keep moving. I lie on my back, my arms pressed against my sides, and feel the cool on my spine. On the patient floors, the hallways are identical: long and white and fluorescent-lit, with an arched, barred window at one end. I think of the different Floor Groups standing at their window and watching the pilgrims at the same time, all of us mirrors of each other.

I gaze up at the lights and feel the burn in my corneas. I wonder how long I would have to look into them before I went blind. I feel the brightness in my cheekbones and inside my mouth. I feel it sinking into my skull. The floor stays empty. I begin to think no one will ever find me here. That I can lie like this forever, still and filled with light.

The voice brings me out. None of the patients have ever seen the Pathologist, but every day his voice crackles over the wall speakers. I sit up and rub my eyes, imagining a man alone in a room on the tenth floor, whispering into a machine. Sometimes he has practical things to say, like an announcement about meals, and sometimes he just talks to us.

Today he tells us what good patients we are. Meditations,

these are called, even though I've always been under the impression that meditating is something you're supposed to do in silence. REPEAT AFTER ME: YOU ARE WELL, YOU HAVE ALWAYS BEEN WELL, YOU WILL ALWAYS BE WELL. He says we're doing everything right. All we need to do now is keep breathing.

2.

Three things brought me to the Hospital. In my first month, in the library, I wrote it all out on sheets of paper and pretended I was telling someone a story.

Number one: the sickness itself. The first case was reported in June, in Bakersfield, California, when a fifty-year-old woman named Clara Sue Borden stumbled into the ER with a constellation of silver blisters on her face. She couldn't walk a straight line. She pressed a hand over her right eye, claiming everything she saw out of that eye had a funny look. She couldn't tell anyone her name or date of birth or where she lived or how she got to the ER. If there were relatives to call. She remembered nothing. "I am me," she kept saying.

For as long as I could remember, the weather had felt apocalyptic. Y2K fever and the War on Drugs and the War on Terror. The death of bees and the death of bats and radioactivity in the oceans and ravenous hurricanes. I thought the country was like a fire that would rage and rage until the embers lost their heat, but instead the sickness appeared and within two weeks it had burned through the borders of every state in America. It was everywhere and it was so fast. At first, the Centers for Disease Control thought it was a highly contagious strain of Creutzfeldt-Jakob. Autopsies showed prions eating through brain tissue, leading to sudden neurological collapse, but once they got everything under the microscopes, they realized it was something different, something new. We were awash in theories—biological attack, apocalypse, environmental meltdown—and no solutions. Our brains, our greatest human asset, were disintegrating. The president was moved to a secret location and the World Health Organization announced a Phase 5 alert. Our borders with Mexico and Canada were closed. For once, no one wanted to come in. And they definitely didn't want us coming out. By August, one hundred thousand people had died. By September, that number had doubled. Experts now say the toll could be worse than the 1918 influenza, which left half a million Americans dead.

■ ■ ■

When I was a child, I lived for a time with a boy I grew to love. One morning we were walking to school when we felt the ground shake. "Earthquake," the boy said, even though we'd never heard of an earthquake happening in Charlestown, which was where we were living, just north of downtown Boston. We saw smoke spiraling up in the distance and moved toward it. We forgot all about school.

On a city block, a building had exploded. Already the police had put up barricades and were rushing around in blue surgical masks, to shield their lungs from debris. The smoke was so dark and dense that if they moved too far down the street, they vanished into it. We stood behind the barricades and watched a woman rush out of the smoke in a beautiful gold dress, the scalloped hem falling just below her knees, and blue bedroom slippers. On the corner, she fell to her knees and released a scream that was shattering in its loudness. She kneaded her fists against her stomach. Her entire body quaked.

In the Hospital, on the news, I have watched people in emergency rooms beat their stomachs as they wail, have seen faces covered by those same blue surgical masks, and the memory of the masked police and the smoking emptiness in the middle of the block and the woman screaming in her fine dress seemed not like the result of a freak gas leak—the cause of the explosion, we would later learn—but like a premonition, a chance to witness the kind of world that was to come.

．．．

Raul used to be a hairdresser in Chicago. He's in our Floor Group and when he gets permission to give the patients haircuts, we line up outside the Common Room. I'm happy to have something to do besides pilgrim watching.

Louis and I have determined that there are two secrets to life in the Hospital:

1. Don't get sick.
2. Don't get driven insane by empty time.

The linoleum floors glow white under the fluorescent overheads. Sometimes it feels like we're standing inside a flashlight. I wait next to Louis. He's thirty, which to me seems young and old at the same time. He has the blondest hair and the greenest eyes and a dimple right in the center of his chin. He is a college graduate, handsome and solid, someone I never would have talked to out in the real world. I would have rung up his groceries, bagged his tomatoes and his eggs, handed him the coupons that printed with his receipt. We met on the bus that carried us to the

Hospital and were assigned to the same Floor Group, the same room. We are the only coed room on our floor. There were odd numbers of women and men, so Louis and I got stuck with each other, and Dr. Bek said the Hospital was placing extra trust in us, in our ability to handle being an exception to the rules.

On our first night, I did not sleep. I lay on my side, facing Louis, and watched the gentle rise and fall of his body under the sheets. I was used to aloneness, and it would take me days before I could drift off with another person in the room.

The Hospital looked like a fortress from the outside, so far from everything that went wrong, a towering structure rising from the absolute flatness of the plains. From the bus window, I thought at first that it was a mirage.

A brief history of the Hospital: It started out as a public psychiatric hospital, but state budget cuts shut it down in 2009. The building sat empty until Dr. Bek and his staff took it over during the sickness and made it into something useful again. I'm betting the people who built this Hospital, the people who lived and worked here, could never have imagined what it would one day be used for.

A red exit sign hangs over the stairwell entrance. The light inside has burned out. There are no working clocks, but my guess is Louis and I have been waiting for close to an hour.

"I only want a little off the ends." My hair falls past my shoulders in dark waves, lush and healthy-looking. It shines under the lights. No bangs, center part, showing off a high, smooth forehead. It's one of the few things I have found consistently admirable about myself, my hair. "Nothing dramatic."

"I don't want a haircut," Louis says. "Not from Raul, anyway."

"So what's your excuse?"

He's leaning against the wall, one leg bent, arms crossed. The hair on his forearms is as light and soft as corn silk. I want him to say that he is here, that he is standing in this line, because he would do anything to be close to me.

"I'm looking for Paige. Seen her?"

Louis has recently taken a special interest in Paige, a patient from our Floor Group and a former marathon runner from Seattle. I've seen him watching her in the Dining Hall as she props her heel on a chair for stretches or offering to time her when she practices sprints in the hallway.

I shrug. "Maybe she doesn't care about hair."

The twins emerge from the Common Room. Their hair has been trimmed at the crown, but left shaggy around the ears and napes. They look like a pair of elves. I avoid eye contact with Louis, but I can feel him smirking at me, at the flaws in my judgment, as the boys pass.

"Next!" Raul calls.

It's easy to picture psychiatric patients lolling around the Common Room, the air swelling with their cigarette smoke. A sour smell has gotten trapped in the dark blue carpeting. There are little holes all over the walls, rings of chipped white paint, evidence of what used to be there. The couch is long and the color of rust, the seat cushions indented with the impressions of bodies. The TV is an ancient black box resting on an equally ancient VCR. In Community Meetings, Dr. Bek has told us that he is suspicious of technology, of an overreliance on machines.

One morning a week, the nurses play a yoga video in the Common Room and patients from different floors bend and twist, form bridges with their bodies. On Saturday nights, the nurses select a movie to show. So far we have seen: *Sleepless in Seattle*, *Meatballs*, *Night of the Living Dead*, which gave half the patients nightmares, *The Maltese Falcon*, three installments of *Mission: Impossible*.

In *Mission: Impossible*, the masks made me think of the boy I used to live with, the boy I grew to love. That night, I lay in bed and mouthed his name. My private meditation.

When I first came to the Hospital, I wanted to know every-one. At Community Meetings and in the Dining Hall, I would go up to patients and ask them who they were and where they were from and what they missed. After the nineteenth person went to the tenth floor, a death for every year of my life, I stopped remembering names.

An orange Dining Hall chair stands in the corner, the metal legs encircled with mounds of hair. Raul waves me over with his scissors. A nurse from our Floor Group is sitting on the couch, supervising. We identify the nurses by the ID patches on the breasts of their hazmats. Hers is N5. She's reading a magazine, an old issue of *Newsweek*, from the library. A soldier in a mud-crusted combat helmet stares out from the cover, his eyes wide and vacant.

After the sickness broke out, people stopped talking about wars.

"This way." Raul's stomach is a small dome under his green scrubs.

I sit down, facing the wall. Despite the cleaning efforts of our group, there are scuffs on the floorboards. My slippers rest on a pile of hair. "Just a trim," I say to Raul, who has already started.

I watch dark clumps fall to the ground. Scissors graze the back of my neck. I tell him that I hope he's not getting carried away.

"You look like an old customer of mine." He digs his fingers into my hair, his hands warm and rough. His nails pierce my scalp. "You have the same kind of face."

I ask Raul what kind of face that would be, to describe this woman to me, but he doesn't answer and I wonder if this same-faced person has lost their memory, if they are dead. When he finishes, I pat my forehead and feel bangs.

"Do you have a mirror?" I ask.

"No, he does not," the nurse answers for him. She turns a magazine page.

Hair bits are stuck to my thighs. I brush them away. I stand and look at my hair spread all over the floor and try not to panic. In my head, I start a new list, because lists are what I lean on when I get upset.

In the Hospital, I have seen women with bangs that hang like curtains over their eyes and ends so split it looks like they've been electrocuted. I have seen a pixie cut that never seems to grow. In the Hospital, I have seen men with sideburns, men who only have swirls of hair at their temples, men with small bald spots on top of their heads, round and shiny as coins. There are all kinds of people in here.

Raul gives my bangs one last snip and calls for the next patient.

Louis is still hanging around the hallway. A few patients from other Floor Groups have wandered over and fallen into line. I rush past, sweeping hair from my scrubs.

"Sheepdog!" he shouts as I walk by. "Sheepdog, sheepdog!"

I hurry into our bathroom. In the mirror, my hair is short and thick, so it puffs out like a helmet, and heavy bangs blanket half my forehead. I lean closer and notice a black hair on the tip of my nose. I flick it into the sink and turn on the faucet.

"Fuck you, Raul," I say to no one.

• • •

One morning, near the end of November, I look out a Dining Hall window and there's just this one pilgrim, a woman. She isn't someone I've seen before. She wears a saggy black coat and her pale hair, which I envy immediately, falls past her waist. "Hello," I whisper. My breath makes a fog circle on the glass.

It takes me a minute to realize the pilgrim is barefoot. Her feet are white and delicate. The bare skin glints in the daylight, so it looks like her feet are made of crystal, like that part of her body is not quite real. I gaze through the bars and try to imagine what it would feel like to stand barefoot on that frozen ground.

Breakfast is over. Floor Groups four and six have finished cleaning the microwave trays with the smelly green sponges. I turn to call to Louis, to show him this barefoot woman, who must have some kind of death wish, forgetting that he's long gone, lured away by Paige, who needed a timer. After all, what is the point of running if there's no finish line? No audience? No one to tell you that you've won?

Louis and I used to have rituals. We sat across from each other at breakfast each morning. We kissed in the dark of the stairwells, his hands disappearing under my scrubs. I can still remember the wet, electric feeling of his tongue pressing into the hollow spot at the bottom of my throat. Now we are just roommates. Nothing more.

In Kansas, when it is not the dead of winter, there are lots of sunflowers. In Kansas, in the year 1897, in a city called Atchison, Amelia Earhart was born. Kansas is not the flattest state in America. In Dodge City, spitting on the sidewalk is illegal. The state insect is the honeybee. The people who live here are called Kansans.

I repeat my list about Kansas and keep watching the pilgrim, who—like everything else in the world—is unreachable through the distance and the glass.

■ ■ ■

Lights Out is at ten o'clock and to our room it brings the darkest night I've ever seen. It's not like city darkness, softened by streetlights and headlights, but thick and black as tar. Louis isn't in bed for Lights Out—typical ever since he took up with Paige;

her roommate was among the first to go to the tenth floor, so she can be counted on for privacy—but he returns not long after, in the mood to talk.

If your roommate dies, you remain in your room. There is no switching, no matter how lonely you get.

Tonight he's complaining about the food. In the Hospital, we have eaten lumps of breaded chicken drenched in a mysterious red sauce and partially defrosted peas and hard, stale dinner rolls, which Louis thinks taste like ash. At dinner, we pick up these rolls and make like we're going to clunk each other in the head.

"At least we're alive," I say. "When you're dead, you don't get to eat at all."

"Like *ash*," says Louis.

I stretch my legs underneath the sheets, into the cool space at the bottom of the bed. Our room smells like rubbing alcohol and Vaseline. Louis can talk about whatever he likes. I just want to keep hearing his voice.

In the beginning, I would climb into his bed and feel his hands move down my waist. The whole time, I told myself we just needed something that felt familiar, needed to prove that a part of ourselves still belonged to the outside world. But during our second month the routine changed. After Lights Out, I burrowed next to him, started kissing his chest. He sat up and shrugged me away. At first, I thought this was a symptom: the prions were attacking his brain, he was losing his memory, he no longer knew who I was. *Quick*, I remember saying to myself, as though there was something for me to do.

In the dark, he started talking about his wife. He told me about the tangles of hair he would find in the bathroom, like tumbleweeds, or the way she used to unroll maps on the floor of their travel bookstore and trace the blue lines of rivers with her pinkie finger. He was remembering perfectly well.

His wife died in the third week of July, at five in the morning, at the Penn Presbyterian Medical Center in Philadelphia.

They lived in Philadelphia, Louis and his wife, in an apartment above their travel bookstore. I lived in a basement apartment on a dead-end street, on the eastern edge of Somerville. I want to believe I can have a fresh start here, in the Hospital.

That night, after Louis stops talking, I concentrate on where I am, in a safe place, in the care of medical experts, but the truth is our Hospital is in middle-of-nowhere Kansas and it is very dark. There aren't even shadows on the walls.

When he starts to snore, I crouch beside his bed and watch him sleep. A hand rests over his heart. His eyelids flutter, and I wonder if he's dreaming.

In the Hospital, I can't get away from the idea that sleep is preparation for death.

I slip out of our room and down the hall. The arched window looks beautiful and foreboding in the night. The floodlights illuminate the ground outside and it's a relief to be away from the deep dark of our room. I look for the barefoot woman, but don't see anything except falling snow, the flakes fat and drifting sideways. I've been told that in this part of the country, once the snow begins, the cold will be endless.

I remember the perfect cartwheel the pilgrim did before he wandered out into the plains. I lose my slippers and run down the hallway with my hands over my head. Step, reach, kick. Soon I'm dizzy. My brain rocks back and forth inside my skull.

Here is a dream I keep having about my mother: We are sitting at a round table, a glass of water between us. She is faceless, but I know it's her. We are both staring into the glass. There's a gold coin in the bottom. We want to get it out, but don't know how.

I fall four times, knees and elbows smacking cold linoleum, before I get one right. No one has ever called me a fast learner.

3.

For most of my life before the Hospital, I was an orphan. As a baby, I was left on the steps of Brigham and Women's Hospital in Boston, in the winter. A nurse found me wrapped in a white T-shirt and rolling around in a cardboard supermarket box, the kind of thing you put oranges in. I was in the early stages of frostbite.

From my first group home I remember: sleeping on mattresses with springs that time had turned flat and hard; a hole in the staircase that was a portal for winged roaches; sandwiches made of Wonder Bread and grape jelly; a communal bathroom with snot green walls and a ceiling dotted with mold. In this bathroom, all the sinks dripped. In this bathroom, I found tampons, heavy with water and blood, clogging the shower drain. The light was always flickering off, usually when someone was in the shower. The girls at the home started spreading rumors about a ghost in the bathroom, when we all knew the ghost could be any one of us.

This was in Roxbury. Back then I dreamed of the countryside:

fields with mazes of tall grass, graceful rivers, climbing trees. Nearby there was an overgrown lot surrounded by a chain-link fence, and sometimes I would slip through a hole in the fence and walk through the dead grass, ignoring the shattered glass and the shadows of crumbling buildings, pretending I was free.

Once a fire alarm tore open our night. Eighteen girls raced down the staircase, led by our overnight counselor, a woman who wore white knee socks with sandals and her hair in a thick braid. Eighteen girls scattered across the front lawn. Some had thought to pull on shoes and some, like me, had just run. It was September and already there was a sharp chill in the air. I could feel a splinter settling into the arch of my foot. I stood on one leg. The night was dark and still. A grease fire had ignited in the kitchen. We watched smoke blacken the windows as we waited for the howl of the sirens, waited to be saved.

The kitchen was scorched long before a fire truck came, an early lesson in exactly how much the outside world cared about us.

I didn't know anything about my real mother until the sickness. That was the second thing that brought me to the Hospital.

During the sickness, a company called Last Rites was formed. For a fee, they got the dying whatever they wanted. The first person they kissed. A vintage arcade game. A jar of sand from a foreign beach. In the early days of August, I got a call from a Last Rites representative who said my aunt wanted to see me. When I told them I didn't have an aunt, didn't have any family at all, they said I did. Her name was Christina. My mother's sister. She was at Mass General. If I ever wanted to see her, this was my chance.

I was exhausted. I hadn't been sleeping. The nights were a long scream of emergency. I'd started seeing orange spots in the air, small discs that slid through the streams of dust and light in my apartment—a symptom, I was increasingly sure, of something incurable. The T was closed. There were no taxis or buses. I hadn't been outside in days, surviving on soup cups and lime

Jell-O and getting stoned on cough syrup. My apartment felt like a tomb, the door a seal—would I ever get out? The representative's voice had a hypnotic effect on me. I couldn't tell if it was a man or a woman speaking. They told me to wait ten minutes and then go outside.

The street was scattered with flyers warning people to stay in their homes and refuse contact with the sick. There was a drawing of a man peering out a window, one arm around a woman, the other around a child. Some flyers lay in the gutter, the paper a black pulp.

On the corner an aluminum trash can had been overturned. A thin brown dog trotted up and licked the metal edges. The dog ran away, howling. The sky was clear and bright.

At first, the black town car was a spot in my periphery. I looked down the street and watched it grow larger, turn into something real. The driver wore an orange hazmat suit. A nozzle connected mouth to body. A thin sheet of glass separated the backseat from the front. Inside the car reeked of bleach. The smell made my eyes run and my nose itch.

The streets stayed empty. We passed telephone poles papered with flyers and yards wild with vines and yellow grass.

HUMAN SACRIFICES someone had spray-painted on the concrete side of a municipal building in dark, oozing letters.

It felt strange to be in the car, to be the one on the inside.

As we drove through Cambridge, I thought about Mount Auburn Cemetery, to the west of Harvard Square, and imagined the land swelling with bodies. I thought about the shop across the street from the cemetery that sold headstones. They were displayed outside, smooth hunks of gray and blue marble, made taller in the winter by ridges of snow. There was a condominium building next door, and I thought about what it must be like for the people who lived there to stare down at their eventual destiny. I thought about the supermarket a little farther up Mount Auburn and the jigsaw of abandoned shopping carts that always filled the parking lot.

All these signs of the end. How could we claim to have been caught by surprise?

We crossed over the Charles River, empty water.

At Mass General, a hazmatted doctor showed me to a quarantine room, where a suit of my own was waiting, hanging from a hook on the wall. A chair and table stood in the center of the room, parts of the hazmat—neon yellow boots, blue rubber gloves—laid out on top. First, an inspection. The doctor searched my body for silver blisters and then pointed a little flashlight in my eyes.

"Dilated pupils," he observed.

"It's the Robitussin," I said.

How much Robitussin and do you take it all the time? he might have asked.

So much, all the time, I might have said.

Instead the doctor clicked off the flashlight, unfazed. Dilated pupils were not a symptom of what he was tasked with finding.

I had to sit in the chair and do a coordination test where I placed my hands on my thighs and turned them over thirty times in a row.

"A beautiful brain," the doctor said when I finished. He lifted the suit off the wall and carried it over to me.

I worked the suit on, one leg at a time. The boots and gloves followed. The air tank on my back was the size of a small fire extinguisher. The doctor secured the sleeves and legs with thick tape. He pulled the hood over my head and sealed me inside.

I followed him down a beige hallway. In the suit, my steps were clumsy and slow, as though I was moving underwater, and my heart felt like it was beating outside my body. I counted the heavy thuds.

Christina's bed was encased in a clear plastic tent. Machines surrounded her, screens and monitors that beeped and growled and sprouted white tubes. Her cheeks were collapsing into her face, as though the interior structure, the bones, were melting away. Her hair was a pale swirl on the pillow. She had a silver sore in the center of her forehead like an extra eye.

An epidemic of forgetting. That much is known. First: silver blisters, like fish scales, like the patient is evolving into a different class of creature. Second: the loss of memory. The slips might be small at first, but by the end the patient won't remember the most basic details of who they are. What is a job? What is a staircase? What is a goldfish? A telephone? A spoon? What is a mother? What is a me? Coordination deteriorates. Vision goes strange. The patient falls into a coma and never wakes.

This woman, this Christina, stared blankly through her tent. Even in the suit, I was afraid to get too close. I wondered if a mistake had been made.

The doctor lingered in the doorway, watching us, until shouting broke out in the hall and he was called away to another disaster.

"I'm Joy," I said, taking a step toward her, trying to be brave. "Joy Jones."

I was named Joy Jones by the nurses at Brigham, who got tired of calling me 6212, my hospital ID number. The symmetry of the name has never suited me.

Christina's mouth was molting silver. Her lips smacked at the air.

A doctor's stool stood in the corner and on that stool sat an envelope, my name written across it. Inside I found a square of paper with an address, a street in the South End, and a key. On the other side of the paper, there was a note:

Joy—
Look under the bed.
C

"Is this for me?" I pressed the envelope against the tent and the plastic shuddered. I felt a burn under my skin, like my nerve endings were catching fire. "Is this where I'm supposed to go?"

She squeezed her eyes shut, her lids clay-colored and sagging. Her right arm began to twitch on the bed.

In the end, the muscles spasm. Patients cannot swallow or talk and are fed through tubes or not at all. Those who are not being properly monitored suffocate. In the end, sight betrays them. They see things that aren't there. The once solid world dissolves like a brick of sugar left out in the rain. In the end, the patients shit their beds. Touch is agony. They cannot sleep. They lie rigid under the sheets, a corpse in the making, somewhere between conscious and not.

The doctor returned and pumped morphine into her IV. Her eyes were the color of milk. Three hours later, she was dead. From the corner of the room, the envelope stuck between my gloves, I watched her body go still and stiller, and even then it did not look restful, like sleep. I never got to ask how she found me or who my mother was or why she left me at Brigham. I never got to ask what was so wrong with her, or with me.

On my way out, the doctor stopped me in the hallway, his gloved hand brushing my shoulder, and told me the address was the last thing she wrote before her memory disappeared.

I entered a small, dark room where people in hazmats were waiting to scrub my suit with neon white paddles frothing with a liquid that looked like water but was not water. The suit was part of the Last Rites package, forever mine. Outside, the town car was waiting to take me to the address, a brownstone on Warren Avenue.

The key unlocked an apartment on the first floor. I followed a carpeted hall into the bedroom. Framed photos of people I did not know had been arranged on the wall in a shape that looked like a puzzle on the verge of completion. The suit made a cracking sound as I knelt and reached under the bed.

I found a white shoebox. I pulled it out and raised the lid: a single photograph surrounded by curls of paper. A Polaroid, the edges worn soft. In the photo, a woman stood on a ship deck, the sunlight caught in the brown sheen of the wood. She wore khaki pants and a white blouse, turned translucent by the light, so I could make out the tan bra straps pressing against her collarbone. She was holding a pair of binoculars and looking straight into the camera, as though the photographer had just offered her a challenge. Hair the color of coal poured over her shoulders. Her eyes were stuck deep in her skull. Her lips were parted slightly, and there was a tiny oval of darkness between them. Behind her I could see the blue expanse of water.

I started reading the strips of paper, the details Christina must have tried to preserve before she started forgetting.

Scorpio, allergic to raw apples, afraid of not very much.
She kept you one month before—
Her first and only love is water.
She made it through childhood without vomiting once.
We have not spoken in seven years.
Hates heights, likes to be low, close to the earth.
She has no patience for anything!
You are her only child.
Regrets—we have many.

I flipped the photo over. *Your mother,* 1997 was written on the back. This was shot two years after I was born.

I took the photo with me. I left everything else behind.

I slipped into the backseat of the town car and the driver peeled away. I unzipped my hood. Warm, bleachy air gusted into the suit. I always imagined my mother only glimpsed me at birth, only held me for a minute or two, my body still slick with her insides, before handing me over.

According to Christina, I was wrong: she had a life with me and, after thirty days, she decided that she did not want that life.

The sun was coming through the back window. No matter how many people died, no matter how far the sickness spread, there was always the sun, a fact of our existence that seemed both miraculous and chilling. I looked again at the photo. If I concentrated very hard, I could remember one detail about my mother. A scent, something close to fresh-cut grass. Now there was an image to fill in what memory had failed to catch. All I was missing was a name.

■ ■ ■

Two days after Christina died, a man knocked on my door. He was dressed like a pallbearer underneath his hazmat: a black suit with a red carnation tucked into the lapel. His hair was shorn close to the skull. He carried a black briefcase. He was the third thing.

This man had come to invite me to the Hospital. He said I was among the small portion of the population who, despite exposure to the infected, didn't get sick. That I, and others like me, had a resistance. I might be in possession of a genetic abnormality that could lead to a cure; the formula could be waiting right there in my blood. He pointed a gloved finger at my chest as he said this. When I said I didn't think I was the kind of person who could help with such a thing, he told me Louis Pasteur cured rabies by injecting the virus into the brains of mad dogs.

"All avenues, no matter how unlikely, must be explored," he said.

My basement apartment was warm and dark. Trash collection had been suspended and black garbage bags were piling up in my little galley kitchen, swollen and reeking. Outside I could hear a police vehicle rolling down the street, an announcement being made through a megaphone. The hazmat suit was slung over the couch and I had started to think of it as company.

Sometimes, at night, I would put the suit on and walk around my apartment and listen to the peculiar sound of my breath. Or watch reruns of *The X-Files* on my laptop, which always left me wishing for a partner in crime. I've never liked the things girls my age are supposed to.

In my favorite episodes, a virus caused by aliens takes over human bodies and a death row inmate with psychic powers channels the ghost of Scully's father and in a suburb called Arcadia a monster eats people who break community rules about lawn decorations. In the suit, I felt like not a person but a creature, the kind of thing that could turn up on an episode of *The X-Files*.

The man told me the sickness usually killed within seven days, but in rare cases there was a lengthy incubation period, so the deal was a ten-month stay in the Hospital, long enough to be sure I wasn't infected, and then I would be released. People like this man were knocking on doors all across the country and offering 149 other Americans the same plan. Not a single person refused.

It was true I touched one of the infected, back when the sickness was still new. A neighbor wobbled into the backyard. From my doorway I watched her plop down and grab at her eyelids. I called 911. I went outside. We didn't know much about the sickness then, didn't know it could be spread through any human contact. I asked if she wanted to go home and she looked at me and said, "Where is a home?" She reached for me and her fingertips, rough with the silvery beginnings of blisters, grazed my wrist.

When the ambulance came, paramedics in rubber gloves and gas masks shooed me back inside like I had committed a crime.

The man snapped open his briefcase and passed me a thick stack of papers. He pointed to a paragraph with tiny font, marked by an arrow-shaped sticker. "As you can see here, your primary role in the Hospital is to simply exist, along with daily examinations, to ensure there are no signs of infection."

"Sounds like the beginning of a horror movie," I said.

"More horrifying than what you've already experienced?" The man took a fountain pen from his briefcase and placed it next to the papers. "I sincerely doubt it."

How would *he* know what I had already experienced?

I won't even pack a suitcase, I decided then. I would go in the clothes I was wearing, my mother's photo in my pocket. I bent at the waist. My hair fell over my eyes. Blood rushed to my skull. I had my own reasons for wanting out of Somerville.

Here were the facts of my life: I worked as a cashier at a twenty-four-hour Stop & Shop, graveyard shift. My basement apartment had no windows. I slept through the daylight hours and never left for work without drinking at least four ounces of cough syrup. I stole fresh bottles from the Stop & Shop and I knew one day I would get caught and be fired, but did I care? I did not care.

It was at the Stop & Shop that I started with the cough syrup. I got the idea while restocking shelves in Health & Beauty. I tried Creomulsion, Boiron, Mucinex, but cherry-flavored Robitussin, maximum strength, was my favorite.

"I already have a suit." I pointed at the hazmat draped over the couch, almost proud to be so well prepared.

"That won't be necessary." He smiled, showing off long incisors. "In the Hospital, you will be safe from germs."

It wasn't much longer before I boarded the bus and we rolled through Connecticut, Pennsylvania, the Midwest, picking up patients along the way. The trip took two days. I remember the swaying power lines and the thin blue sky and the light contracting and expanding along the horizon. At the Hospital, I watched a hazmatted nurse seal the photo in a plastic baggie and imagined the day of my release, my mother being handed back to me.

I do not know her name or where she lives or if she is still alive. Even so I have developed an attachment. I smell grass everywhere. I dream about her. In a different one, we are swimming in the ocean. No land is in sight, but we are not afraid. The water is calm and glistening. We can hold our breath for hours. When I wake in the Hospital, I wrap my hands around my head and try to remember the things she said to me.

Who else do I have to listen to?

4.

Every morning, a nurse comes for our examination. Their face shields are narrow rectangles, so we can't see anything but scrunching foreheads and darting eyes. Dr. Bek is the only member of the Hospital staff with a proper name and a fully visible face. I know all about psychological tricks: he wants the patients to believe he is the only one we can trust with our lives.

Today I sit on the edge of my bed and gaze through N5's shield, in search of something human. The gold flecks around her irises. The lash that has fallen out and stuck to the bluish skin under her eye. Some mornings I want to shake her white plastic sleeve and beg her to tell me what is going to happen to all of us.

Here is what she measures: our blood pressure with cuffs that squeeze and hiss; temperature with an ear thermometer that makes a clicking noise inside the canal; sight with a flashlight we have to track back and forth, up and down; coordination with the Romberg's test, where we stand straight and still, our feet pressed together, then shut our eyes and hold the pose.

Do the Romberg! Do the Romberg! I imagine a dance with steps I never learned.

"That doesn't seem so hard," I said the first time I did the Romberg, and N5 said try doing it with holes in your brain.

I stand and she uses the same flashlight to check my skin for blisters. She examines my scalp, her rubber fingers pushing aside my hair, so close I can feel the sound of her breathing nest inside my lungs.

Three times a week, she draws blood. My arms are dappled with tiny purple bruises, like a piece of meat beginning to rot, and the sight of a needle sliding from its casing makes me shiver. I watch the needle slip under my skin and red velvety fluid fill the vial.

"Healthy as a hummingbird." She turns to Louis, big and slow in her suit. From the far end of a hallway, in a certain kind of light, I sometimes think the nurses look like enormous white birds. The air tank underneath is a hump between her shoulders. During our first week in the Hospital, she used long Q-tips to take cultures from our throats. I remember the cotton end of the Q-tip disappearing into my mouth, the brief sensation of choking.

"Hummingbirds have a very short lifespan." Louis extends his arm for the needle. "Three years, max."

"Good memory trick." N5 ties a rubber tourniquet around his biceps and the bright tip of the needle appears. Louis doesn't flinch when his blood is drawn and I wonder if he is still able to register feeling. "Now where did you learn about hummingbirds?" We are encouraged to recite whatever facts we know, to make sure we aren't forgetting.

"Costa Rica was a bestseller at the store," he says. "I lived my life surrounded by travel guides, but I never went anywhere."

In her suit, N5 makes a noise that sounds like approval. But how do you know he's telling the truth? I want to ask. In the Hospital, I can feel myself growing more and more suspicious.

After our exams, she crosses off the date on the countdown calendar tacked to the wall between our beds. The week is a row of black *x*'s. Our calendar has a bird theme. December's is the African gray parrot—prehistoric claws gripping a branch, a beady eye I can feel following us in the night. We have seven months until we can leave, until we know for sure if we have the sickness, if we are going to stop remembering.

I look around at the four white walls of our room and ask Louis what else he knows about birds. He's lying on top of his sheets and flexing his arm. I want to go to him, to touch his knee, to press my hands against the bones in his chest.

I stay sitting on the edge of my bed.

"Hummingbirds can fly upside down." He rolls onto his side and slides his hands under his cheek. He closes his eyes, already bored with this entire conversation. "The macaws in South America have a scream that will shatter your heart."

The inside of my arm throbs. I press my thumb against the fresh needle mark. Blood seeps from the hole.

"Today is a very special day," N5 says as she packs up her kit, a red duffel bag with a white cross on the front. "Today Dr. Bek is going to look inside your minds."

■ ■ ■

After breakfast, the patients stay in the Dining Hall for testing. We fill the long tables, facing a portable projector screen. The nurses give us paper and tiny pencils with no erasers. I'm sitting with my Floor Group, across from Paige and Louis. The red trays are stacked on the buffet tables. The faces of the microwaves stare out at us. I can smell our last meal, breakfast meatballs, a category of food no one in our Floor Group has ever heard of before, rising from the green garbage cans in the corners of the room. Shadows slip around on the tables. Paige is doodling flowers on the edge of Louis's paper.

We are supposed to write down the story of what we think is happening in the slides. The lights go out and the first slide is a black-and-white image of a house in a winter landscape. The windows are pale smudges and something is rising behind the house—large, dark clouds that cast strange shapes on the snow. Ridges of ice stick out of the ground like a creature's spine. The more I look at the slide, the more I think the house is about to be consumed by the weather.

House getting eaten by winter, I write.

By now we the patients are used to Dr. Bek's tests. In our first month, each of us got an electroencephalogram, a test that measures electrical activity in the brain. In Dr. Bek's office, I sat in a chair and wore a helmet made of white electrodes. At the base of the helmet, long wires connected me to his computer. The office was silent. Dr. Bek watched the screen. Halfway through the test, I started to feel like I was going to explode. I couldn't sit still any longer. I crossed and uncrossed my legs. I tapped my fingers against the seat. My bladder was suddenly full and I didn't think I could hold it in.

"What is this doing to me?" I finally shouted, and Dr. Bek looked up from his screen and explained that it wasn't *doing* anything; it was simply measuring, presenting him with data, helping him figure out how to keep me well.

Later we were given written personality tests where we had to answer yes or no to statements like "The best decision is the one that can be easily changed" or "You value justice more than mercy." This test seemed like a trap, because the right response to nearly every statement—"It depends"—was never an option. Where he sees science, I just see something new to pass the time.

The next image looks like a tunnel, some kind of shadowy underground place. I put my head on the table and listen to the other patients scratching out their replies. I wait for the click of the slide changing. In East Somerville, I would wake in the dark of my basement apartment and think for a moment that I had fallen asleep in a cave. That this was where I had brought myself to die. The third image is blank. At first, I think it's a mistake, but then I notice other patients writing away. Louis pinches his pencil between his fingers, tilts his head in concentration. I don't see anything there, but I recognize a feeling.

■ ■ ■

I stand in the mouth of my bedroom closet and run my hands over the scrubs. I watch the white ones sway on their wire hangers, as though invisible bodies are occupying them. I go into our bathroom and turn the sink water on and off. The floors are cool tile. The shower curtain is a wisp of white plastic. This faucet does not leak.

In the bathroom, I hear another one of the Pathologist's meditations. WITH OPEN HANDS I WELCOME THE CONTINUATION OF LIFE.

I sit on the bedroom floor and poke myself in the knee, numb with boredom.

I thought I knew about boredom in my old life, but I was wrong. I knew about lulls in the action, stretches of stillness, but I did not know what it was like to feel time become a wet, heavy thing. I did not know days so long and familiar, you find yourself holding your breath until you're dizzy and flushed, all for your own amusement.

There is no cough syrup in the Hospital, nothing to soften the borders of the mind.

A nightmare becomes a nightmare when you start to believe

it will never end. In our contracts, there is an ending, but sometimes, when I'm lying awake at night, I wonder.

I'm saved when the twins come to see how I did on the test. The boys live in the room next door. They are ten and their parents are dead. They have no other family. They are orphans, signed away to the Hospital by a social worker.

The summer before the sickness came, they went to Hawaii with their parents. Now all they want is to go back. They draw maps—patchworks of blue and green, with black cones to mark the volcanoes—and get the nurses to hang them on their walls. They make leis from toilet paper and request pineapple rings in the Dining Hall. For hours they watch the Discovery Channel in the Common Room and sift through the encyclopedias in the library, in search of anything to do with Hawaii.

The twins have taught me that Hawaii, with so much water between its islands and the rest of America, has the fewest cases of the sickness. Hawaii is the only state that grows coffee. Astronauts trained for moon landings on the hardened lava fields of Mauna Loa. The island of Molokai used to be a leper colony. The oldest Catholic church in America stands in Honolulu.

In East Somerville, I would go to the evangelical church near my apartment and stand on the sidewalk and listen to the people singing inside. The sign above the door was in Spanish and there was an image of a cross draped in white cloth, except the cloth looked more like flames.

"Did you know all the answers?" Christopher says.

"I don't think it was that kind of test."

"I wish there were questions about Hawaii," Sam says. "Then we would have known the answers for sure." Their haircuts are still growing out and their scrubs are too big. The sleeves fall to their elbows and they're always pulling at their waistbands.

"Who knows what Dr. Bek does with all these results, anyway," I say.

"He wants to make sure we don't have zombie personalities," Sam says.

The boys love to pretend they're zombies. I'll hear a groaning in a hallway and find the twins staggering around, arms raised and straight, mouths open wide. I'll tell them to stop, that they're being creepy, but they just call out *"Garrr!"* and chase me down the hall.

"If he's checking for zombie personalities, you're both in trouble," I tell them.

"We didn't just come here to talk about the test." Christopher closes the door. He drops his voice to a whisper. "We have something to tell you."

"Yes?"

"We're digging a tunnel in our room."

I stand and swing my arms in circles, to get the blood flowing. I don't often use my body in the Hospital. Regardless of taste, I eat everything at every meal. My stomach is as soft as a sponge.

"What do you mean a tunnel?"

The boys smile, baring their front teeth. They have round eyes and sprays of freckles on their throats.

I follow them to their room. In the hallway, Louis is timing Paige. As she runs, the arms of her scrubs flap like wings. There's a flush in her cheeks; I can see tendrils of muscle in her neck. So healthy, so alive. Louis is holding the wall clock he poached from a storage closet. The hour is wrong, but the second hand works for timing. He cheers as she blows past me and the twins, raising the clock over his head like a trophy. A cluster of patients from our Floor Group applaud.

In their room, Christopher rolls away the white medicine cabinet, the wheels squeaking, and peels back a square of linoleum. The thin, pink skin between his fingers turns translucent in the light. The three of us kneel by the site. The matter underneath the linoleum is brown and sticky, artificial dirt. In the center, the digging has already started, the opening as wide as a coffee saucer.

Christopher explains the next step is peeling up more linoleum and widening the hole. He has a tiny mole on his upper lip, the only way a stranger could tell the boys apart. "Eventually we'll hit an air-conditioning duct."

The boys know an unusual amount about building structure. Their father was an architect. They grew up surrounded by blueprints and scale models, compasses and triangles. Instead of a fairy tale, their father would unroll a set of plans and tell them the story of how a building is constructed.

"And then?" I imagine big silver ducts curled inside the Hospital like snakes.

"We'll have what we need."

"For?"

"To go to Hawaii. Of course."

I look at the drawings lined up on the wall. In one, there's an outdoor movie screen with cars parked in front. A headless, footless figure, drawn in thick red crayon, hovers nearby. According to the boys, this is a drive-in theater on Waialae Avenue, the most haunted place in Hawaii. A ghost lives in the mirror in the women's bathroom and drives people insane from the terror of checking their own reflections and finding a ghost in the glass.

"What are you going to do with all the dirt?" Hawaii is too absurd to even address. In Kansas, we are thousands of miles away.

"We're flushing it down the toilet," Sam says.

The bathroom door is shut, and I think I hear a gurgling inside.

"Bad idea," I say.

The twins press the linoleum square back into place and roll the medicine cabinet over it.

We hear shouting in the hallway, the thumping of fists on

walls. As the months progress, as the land around us gets colder, that sound is becoming less and less unusual. We stay close to the hole. We wait out the danger. When the shouting stops and we go back into the hall, into the shock of light, there are no patients, no running Paige, no sign at all of what might have caused the disturbance.

5.

That night, I walk the hallways, even though we only have thirty minutes until Lights Out. I go up to the sixth floor, where the hall is empty and I can hear patients rustling behind closed doors, and back into the dark stairwell and down to my floor, where the twins are zombie-walking. They sway and gurgle, their pale fingers wiggling. From the end of the hallway, I watch their approach. N5 appears from behind a door and herds them into their room. "Lights out," she calls through her suit, like a train conductor announcing the next station.

On the speakers, the Pathologist is telling us how well we have done today. GOOD TEST, he purrs. Does it seem strange that we've all accepted the voice of this man we've never seen? Does it seem strange that we don't look up at the speakers and say, Who the fuck are you to be talking to us?

At night, his voice is like a lullaby.

I wonder what the nurses and Dr. Bek do after the patient floors go dark, after they have been rinsed and stripped of their suits, become recognizably human again. Maybe they perform the tests on themselves and try to see inside their own minds. Maybe they lie around naked and relish the feeling of being bare-skinned and free.

In the Common Room, Olds and Older, the two oldest patients in our Floor Group, are sitting on the couch, watching the news, their heads mops of gray from the back. They have a tai chi routine they practice in the hallways. Good for the circulation, they claim, and anything good for the circulation is good for the memory. I stand in the doorway and listen.

For months, the news has been a misery. The death toll climbs. People are starving to death and giving birth and killing each other in their homes. In hospitals, beds are jammed into hallways and stairwells and waiting rooms. In hospitals, doctors are passing out from exhaustion. If there are flaws in the decontamination protocols, the doctors become infected. There is a black market for hazmat suits. Trash has not been collected in months; it sits like small mountains in driveways, leaks into streets. If you call 911, nothing happens. Gangs of people, made crazy by the waiting, are setting fire to city parks. I have watched fire move like an orange wave across Golden Gate Park in San Francisco. When they were finished with Grant Park in Chicago, the streetlamps and walkways were black with ash, a volcanic aftermath. In some neighborhoods, all the streetlights have gone out. At night, these people wait and freeze and hope in perfect darkness. I have watched a helicopter swoop over a hot zone and the National Guard collect citizens wandering an empty Times Square, the mammoth billboards flashing behind them. In that footage of New York, a place I have never been, a place I might never get to see, the streets and skyscrapers glistened from a recent rain. Always I look for that boy I grew to love, who would now be a man, and my mother in the crowds.

Tonight the news is different.

From the studio, a reporter tells us that no new cases have

been recorded in seventy-two hours. Behind him an electronic map of America tracks the progression of the sickness. Whenever a certain number of new cases are reported in a state, the borders turn neon red. Just last week Arkansas and Ohio were pulsing with alarm.

I step into the Common Room. My slippers sink into the carpet. Is it possible the sickness, which came from nowhere, could vanish back into nowhere? According to this reporter, that's exactly what happened with the 1967 Marburg outbreak in West Germany. The hotter the virus, the faster it burns out. Olds points the remote at the TV and raises the volume higher.

The news spreads throughout the Groups. Patients start rushing down from their different floors. They amass in front of the TV, our oracle, and gaze at the screen in wonder. They rub the top of the box, the sleeves of their scrubs swaying, as though to encourage it to keep giving us the kind of information we crave. The lights stay on, which means Dr. Bek and the nurses have become aware of our discovery. The only skeptic is a man from our Floor Group, Curtis, who used to be a cop in Cleveland. His roommate is dead. We stand on the edges of the Common Room.

"Hope is a seductive thing," he says. "Hope can make people lose all sense."

I don't like Curtis. He never does his fair share when we're cleaning the Common Room. He'll stand by the window with a spray bottle and a rag and never actually touch the glass. Still, I have to admit that I don't disagree.

■ ■ ■

Our wonder doesn't last long. When Dr. Bek enters the Common Room, all ten of the nurses trailing behind him, the patients go silent. We stand with our Floor Groups. Mine is huddled by the door. From this angle, the bars on the windows remind me of skeleton ribs. Group three takes over the couch, like they always do. Dr. Bek stands in front of the TV, the nurses fanning out around him. The sound of their collective breathing scratches at the air.

I know the questions we are all burning to ask. Is the world really getting safer? Have our contracts changed? How much longer do we have to wait until we are free?

Dr. Bek takes the remote from Olds and mutes the volume. On TV, a different reporter, a woman, is wandering down a street. The sky is dark, but a news truck has turned the street electric. All the houses are heavy with snow. In her white hazmat, standing in a front yard, the reporter looks like she's in camouflage. The camera moves across doors and windows, waiting for someone to emerge, for some sign of life.

"You are the danger now," Dr. Bek tells us.

He keeps talking. I watch the floor. After Raul finished his haircuts, our group swept and vacuumed, but I keep finding strands, some light, some dark, stuck inside the carpet.

First, he explains, there's no way to know how safe it really is out there, at the start of this alleged recovery. Twenty days must pass before it can be called a recovery at all. Second, if the sickness has vanished, it's more important than ever to make sure we are not infected, to let the incubation period run its course. To hold tight to our memories. He says now is the time for skepticism and questioning.

"Every day in the Hospital progress is made." Dr. Bek presses a button and the reporter vanishes. "But still there is so much to be done."

I can feel the Floor Groups looking at each other. We have all swung from excited to confused. Outside I hear a winter wind moving over the Hospital. I imagine it prying open the bars and the windows and trying to get at what's inside.

Dr. Bek can sense our hesitation. He has more to say. Do we

know the story of the flight attendant who carried the AIDS virus from Africa to the West? The index case. How much time do we spend considering the reactions of our actions, the way one disaster can give way to another, like mud sliding down a mountain in springtime? He pauses and makes a diving motion with his gloved hands.

"What a calamity it would be for you to go *out there* now." He points the remote at the window. "You could reinfect the entire population. You could ruin our chances of finding a cure. Do we want America to be just as helpless if the sickness returns? No. We want her to be able to help herself next time. Isn't that what we want?"

None of the patients say anything. "Well, isn't it?" Dr. Bek presses.

"Yes," some of us mutter in reply.

"I thought so." He nods at the white wall of nurses behind him, as though he's just given them a lesson in how to handle us. Behind the shield his teeth are like tiny polished stones.

Dr. Bek reminds us that Lights Out was over an hour ago and it's time for us to be on our way.

• • •

When darkness comes, I lie awake and picture patients flooding out of the Hospital, into the snowy land, and drifting back to wherever they came from. I'm left standing outside, looking east and west, unsure of where to go.

I try to see something different: Louis and I walking out of the Hospital and across the frozen plains. Catching a bus and watching the white landscape roll by. His hand on my cheek. Our fingertips on the cold windowpanes. It's all going beautifully until I hear Paige's feathery voice and realize she's on the bus too, sitting right behind Louis, her hands on his shoulders.

I get out of bed and go to the Common Room. The space is dark and quiet. I sit down on the couch and turn on the TV. Another news truck moves through a suburb and catches people cracking open doors and peering outside. This is in California, where the sickness started. The sky is a violet haze. When a truck passes a blue gingerbread house with a white fence, I see a family standing in the yard. They're wearing gas masks. They even have one small enough for their little girl. The truck casts a net of light over the mother as she kneels and rubs the dirt. The father holds the child. The girl waves her tiny finger around like a wand. The mother and father look up and raise their fingers too. The girl lifts her hand higher. They are all pointing at something in the sky.

■ ■ ■

I'm on a highway in Boston, passing through the Sumner Tunnel. I'm riding in the passenger seat. The driver is a heavy shadow. Is he wearing some kind of mask? The tunnel has turned the radio music to static. I am feeling very curious about the glove compartment. The car speeds past the tile walls and the tracks of white light on the ceiling. There are doors in the tile. Where do they lead? There is no traffic.

"Wake up, Joy," I hear Louis say. I feel myself blinking. I'm sitting up in bed. I don't know how long I've been back in my room.

"You're talking in your dreams again." I listen to him roll over, his voice thick with sleep.

He's wrong, or maybe half-wrong: I wasn't awake, but I wasn't dreaming either.

6.

0–6. Group home, Roxbury.
7–9. Foster with the Carroll family, Allston.
10–12. Group home for children, hundred-acre farm,
   Walpole.
13–14. Foster with Ms. Neuman, Charlestown.
15–17. Group home for teenage girls, Mission Hill.
18. Over and out.

· · ·

If someone (my mother?) asked me to account for how I've spent
my life, the Years is one place I could start.

· · ·

Massachusetts Safe Haven Law, definition: "Voluntary abandonment of a newborn infant to an appropriate person at a hospital, police department, or manned fire station shall not by itself

constitute either a finding of abuse or neglect or a violation of any criminal statute."

For years, I did not think it was right that what my mother did to me could not be called a crime.

■ ■ ■

At the Stop & Shop, some people bought very strange things in the middle of the night. Chicken in a can, glow-in-the-dark condoms, fish guts wrapped in brown paper, baskets filled with little round tins of Ant-B-Gon, baskets filled with chewing gum, baskets filled with enough birthday candles to light the world's largest cake, one whole coconut.

Once a man came in and said he was lost and asked me to draw him a map that would lead him to where he wanted to go. I drew one on a folded-up shopping bag and hoped my landmarks were clear. Once someone wanted to buy five shopping carts and the manager said, "No way." The person gave up and left and the manager told me, "My price was a hundred dollars. I would have let them go for that." More than once people brought us sagging bags of loose change, wanting cash in return. More than once I found a woman weeping in the Frozens section.

For a while a bagger with tattoos on his knuckles worked nights with me. He used to be in jail. When there was nothing else to do he would count and recount the numbers of each item on the shelves—thirty-five bags of hot dog buns, seven cartons of egg substitute, fourteen jars of grape jelly—and sometimes I would follow behind him and ask what he was doing, which I knew he found annoying, and he would say, "There is no enemy like time."

After he left I worked with another guy who was always trying to play a joke where he snuck up behind me and put a plastic bag over my head, no matter how many times I told him that I did not find this funny at all.

If there were no shoppers, I would slip into the bathroom and sip a little more Robitussin and when I came out, the light was soft and running down the walls like rainwater.

Things I saw in the homes that made me frightened of real drugs: a boy who collapsed in a field, blue from the neck up; a girl who frothed at the mouth like a wild dog; a girl who got stabbed in the shoulder during a buy; countless zombie shuffles. Still, I envied the empty-headed place they went to, where nothing mattered and nothing hurt. Cough syrup, those hits of dextromethorphan, seemed like a not unreasonable way to manage my life.

I had a case manager, but I kept skipping our appointments. At these appointments, we were supposed to be getting me signed up for emotional wellness classes and college prep at Bridgewater State, even though I did not want to do any of those things.

"How can we be expected to help those who will not help themselves?" I can hear my case manager saying. I was never able to explain that the help I needed was a different kind.

The Stop & Shop was never robbed while I was working there, but it happened one night, at three in the morning, when the cashier who was always trying to put plastic bags over my head was on shift. The robbers wore stockings over their faces and packed the money into black JanSport backpacks, the kind high school students carry. They were very professional. They were out in under five minutes and it wasn't until after they had disappeared into the night and the police had been called that the manager found this cashier collapsed in Paper & Plastics, a roll of paper towels clasped to his chest.

After that, people knew the Stop & Shop as the place where a cashier was killed in Paper & Plastics. A heart attack was the official cause of death, but we all knew fear was what got him.

. . .

On the way home from the Stop & Shop, the bus passed a construction site where a metal skeleton was rising slowly from the ground. A doctor's office with a billboard ad for the flu shot: GET THE FLU BEFORE IT GETS YOU! Laundry World, a Laundromat with pool tables, and Beauty Island, which sold hair extensions called the Cinderella and body lotion with glitter inside. In East Somerville, we passed the evangelical church and a check cashing service and a discount store for maternity clothes.

At my stop, I would see the same man holding a newspaper over his head, even when it wasn't raining. At my address, I would see the same woman smoking on the fire escape in a Celtics T-shirt and sweatpants, even after the cold began to settle in. I felt both soothed and suffocated by these routines.

In winter, in Harvard Square, nets shaped like gold stars hung between buildings.

Once I got on the wrong bus. I was not awake and not asleep and when I looked out the window, I was in Kendall Square. The bus stopped. I got out. The sky was a bruise. I was unsure of the time. I stood outside the Microsoft building and watched a boy on a skateboard cut through a barren park. For a second, I had crazy ideas about going inside and demanding a job that had to do with computers, but instead I decided to cross the Longfellow Bridge. I thought I would stand on the bridge and look out at the river and the downtown lights and the Citgo sign beaming out from Kenmore. I would walk down Charles Street and look in the shop windows and up the steep cobblestone hills, observing all the lives that could never be mine.

But when I reached the bridge, it was closed for construction. I followed detour signs through a tunnel, a long concrete tube stained with graffiti. I was alone and the tunnel was dark. The longer I walked, the longer the tunnel seemed.

Sometimes the same thing happens when I walk the Hospital halls: the white path seems to stretch on, the stairwell door moves farther away. The echo of my breath grows louder. We believe what we see, whether it's real or not.

In my basement apartment, where it was dark regardless of the time, I would take more Robitussin and get into bed in my Stop & Shop uniform and hope for sleep. On the nights where the cough syrup failed to turn my brain to sludge, I would stare up at the ceiling and remember.

My second foster, Ms. Neuman, lived in a yellow house on Ferrin Street, between the water and Bunker Hill park, where an obelisk, a monument to battle, rose above the trees. The day I came, she was waiting on the curb, in a pink sweatsuit and flip-flops, her toenails painted gold.

"Joy, Joy, Joy," she sang as she walked me up the driveway, her hand on the center of my backpack. White Christmas lights blinked in the windowsills, even though it was August. She smelled of cigarettes and rosy perfume. "Will you fill our house with it?"

In the living room, a boy in a werewolf mask was sitting on the orange shag carpet. The black rubber face was bearded with fur. The eyes were red and hungry. The mouth was open in a roar, the teeth long and yellow.

"Say hello to Marcus," Ms. Neuman said, as though we were already supposed to know each other. She pulled a pack of Virginia Slims from the waist of her sweatpants, lit a cigarette, and drifted into the kitchen.

"How long?" I asked the boy from the edge of the living room, still wearing my backpack.

"Six months." The wolf ears on the mask were small and pointed, like they once belonged to a gentler kind of animal.

"And she hasn't killed you yet?"

"Does secondhand smoke count?"

Secondhand smoke did not count.

The boy told me he could read my past and my future. I sat

facing him, my backpack heavy on my shoulders. The carpet was soft. The fangs on his mask were as long as fingers.

"How?"

"Let me see your hands."

I held out my hands and he started rubbing my palms. His skin was warm and soft and I knew I should have been disgusted or afraid, but instead I felt calmed. He pressed the lumps of bone at the base of my thumbs and the rough swirls on my palms. He asked me to cup my hands and peered into them like I was holding something precious.

"Your right hand is what you have when you're born," he said. "Your left hand is what's been given to you."

On my right hand, the heart and head lines were straight and smooth. On my left, those same lines were broken and wavy.

Soon I would learn that Marcus always wore masks. The Grim Reaper, the Incredible Hulk, Richard Nixon, Michael Myers, Ronald Reagan, Darth Vader. Monsters and dead presidents were his favorite.

One night, he showed me why.

We were in the bathroom, sitting in the tub, the shower curtain printed with cartoon bears closed around us. We sat with our knees pulled to our chests, our toes touching. He asked if I wanted to see and I said that I always wanted to see. He peeled away the werewolf mask and I saw the shriveled eye, the lid drooping, the iris peeking out like a raisin. On this eye, there were no lashes. It didn't blink like the other eye did. The skin around it was a thick, puckered swirl.

I wanted to touch, but I kept my hands in my lap. The tub was smooth and white. The fat bar of soap in the dish smelled of lavender.

"The cat got me," he said.

As a child, he was left alone in an apartment in Dorchester and his father's cat, Annabelle, attacked him. The cat was named after his own mother, or the Biggest Bitch That Ever Lived. His father would go for days without feeding her. She pissed in sneakers. She stood on her hind legs and ribboned the wallpaper with her claws. He was three when it happened. He remembered the heavy heat of her body, the needling teeth. His parents found him wailing and blood-wet. The scars on his face reminded me of the whorls on tree bark.

"Fuck that cat," I said in the bathtub.

Ms. Neuman was not married. She worked as a receptionist in a dentist's office and was always home by five. She bought us new clothes at Bunker Hill Mall and we would wait months before snipping off the tags, the evidence of their newness, of how much she was willing to spend. She painted our nails a shade of electric blue called Aruba. She gave us a weekly allowance, twenty dollars each, and we did not have to do anything in return. She had cupboards filled with chocolate cupcakes, the rich insides stuffed with cream, and Kool-Aid, which looked like red dust in the bottom of the glass.

We went to school at Clarence Edwards Middle. That year, there were presidential elections and scientists invented a vaccine that protected patients against five different diseases with a single shot. That year, the building exploded. That year, we learned about exponents and fractions and the Latin words for "happy" and "nothing" and "I run." For the first time in my life, I did my homework.

After school, Marcus and I went to a drugstore and bought hair dye called Chocolate Cherry. Ms. Neuman was particular about cleanliness, so we squeezed on the color in the backyard. We put on the plastic shower caps that came in the box and sat under a tree, our scalps itching. We were both thirteen, on the cusp of teenagehood. Our bodies were still thin and hairless, but I knew mine was starting to change. Just six months before, on the farm in Walpole, I woke in the night with a dreadful pain in my stomach and blood on the insides of my thighs. Marcus had a white tuft at the top of his hairline, soft as animal fur; it had been with him for as long as he could remember.

We rinsed our hair with a garden hose. We took turns bending over and shutting our eyes and feeling the cold splatter. Marcus stood with his legs parted, the water rushing between his feet. The dye turned our hair the color of grapes and stained our fingernails.

"That," Ms. Neuman said when she saw us, "is not a color found in nature."

That was the point, we wanted to tell her. We were in camouflage, both of us hoping to pass undetected by the world we knew before.

Marcus is the closest thing I have ever had to a real brother. I knew him just long enough to love him. I have not seen him in many years.

One night, Ms. Neuman woke us at four in the morning and brought us downstairs. All the lights were out. The TV was blaring. She sat us down in front of it. The local weatherman was talking about the highs and the lows, the chance of rain. He was wearing a pinstriped suit and a black toupee.

"Do you see him?" Ms. Neuman bent over and tapped the screen. Right then the man grinned and pointed at the weather map. A cartoon sun winked at us.

Marcus and I nodded. Our hair still smelled like ammonia and it looked like we had dirt under our nails. We could see the lacy edges of her slip peeking out from underneath her bathrobe. Her collarbone was raised and spotted with tiny moles.

She tapped the screen harder. "Would you believe I used to be married to this man?"

I looked at the man on TV, his fake hair slipping around on his head, and felt glad he wasn't living here anymore.

From then on Ms. Neuman did this once a week, always the

same routine, like she thought we would forget about whatever happened in the night.

· · ·

In Allston, on the western edge of the city, my first fosters, Mr. and Mrs. Carroll, both worked as security guards at an art museum. We lived in a brick house on Park Vale Avenue. At night, I would sit on the stairs and listen to them talk about all the strange and useless things they were tasked with guarding, like sculptures made from plastic sticks of butter or giant balls of string.

"The secret to life," Mr. Carroll liked to say, "is to do whatever stupid-ass thing you want and call it art."

I always thought it was funny, what they said about their jobs, because the neighborhood they'd spent their lives in was named for a painter, Washington Allston, or so I learned in school.

Allston was isolated, pushed away from the rest of Boston by Brookline, split in two by the Mass Pike, blocked from Cambridge by the Charles. The Horace Mann School for the deaf was nearby and sometimes I would see buses filled with deaf children roaming the streets. They had a particular way of looking out the windows, a slow, deliberate turn of the head, as though if they could see deeply enough, sound might follow.

The Carrolls had a son. He was in his thirties and lived near Fenway. He was a psychologist. The word "psychologist" made me picture the big-breasted school counselor who wore reading glasses on a lanyard and broke up fights, but when I asked Mrs. Carroll if her son worked in a school like mine, she laughed and told me that he worked at a university, that he was the owner of an advanced degree. There were framed photos of him in cap and gown all over the house. He was never looking right at the camera, like his attention had been captured by something just beyond the lens.

One day the son moved back home, into the second bedroom upstairs. Next to me. Something had happened with his job, something that couldn't be helped by his advanced degree, but no one wanted to talk about it. I would press my ear against the wall and listen to him moving around in his room. I learned that he liked songs sung in Spanish. He never had anyone over. His cell phone never rang. He watched action movies late into the night; I could hear the explosions of gunfire through the wall. In the mornings, when I was getting ready for school, I would find him in the kitchen, eating a bowl of sugar cereal without any milk. He wore square glasses, his eyes brown dots behind the lenses, and his teeth seemed crowded in his mouth. He wore polo shirts in different shades of blue. "The colors of the sea," he would say, plucking at the collar of his shirt. At first, it was okay having him around.

We were alone one afternoon and he invited me into his room, which had been his since childhood and was preserved in his absence. I'd never been in there before. Posters of cities with cathedrals overlooking cobblestone squares were taped to the walls. Towers of books with linen spines filled the corners. He had a little contraption set up: two white electrodes hanging from thin wires, the wires connected to a laptop. He told me to sit on his bed. He put a white circle on each of my temples. Neurofeedback, he said this was called.

"Do you know what this does?" he asked me.

I shook my head.

"It lets me read your thoughts."

I was seven and I had all kinds of thoughts I didn't want anyone to read.

He sat in front of his laptop and pressed a button. I felt a tiny pulse on my skull.

"What am I thinking right now?" I asked.

"You're scared," he said. "Don't be scared."

There is a period of time in Allston, the eighth year of my life, that I still cannot remember. One day I was nine years old and away from Park Vale Avenue, living on the farm in Walpole. One day I was sitting at a school desk in a renovated barn and sleeping in a cottage dorm that overlooked a green field. I can't remember arriving there or leaving Allston. It was like waking up from, or into, a dream.

7.

At the end of December, I turn twenty. A new decade, but of what? When our Floor Group cleans the Common Room, we keep the TV on, so we can hear about the recovery. As a result, we don't spend much time cleaning. We stand around the TV with our sponges and spray bottles and brooms, watching. The windows are streaked with fingerprints, dust has settled along the floorboards, but the world around us is coming back to life. The president is in the White House. Hospital populations are shrinking. Garbage trucks are rumbling down streets. Snowplows are clearing roads. On TV, they make a noise that sounds like thunder.

We watch blue salt scatter across sidewalks. We watch a city bus dock by a stop; we watch the doors snap open. We watch a subway car bolt through a tunnel. We watch people line up outside a grocery. This is somewhere in Michigan. The grocery is surrounded by a lake of milky ice. In the line, there is an energy; I can feel it coming through the screen. It connects one person to another, like they are all holding a long rope.

These people belong to the same category now. They are the survivors.

The divide between us patients and the outside world has never seemed greater. Watching the recovery is like watching a new TV show play out: the narratives of the characters evolve, branch in new directions, while ours stays the same.

"Outside! Outside!" a patient shouts in the hallway.

During an Internet Session, I look at photos of abandoned places. There's an empty power plant in Belgium, where the walls spiral up like a giant snail shell, slick with neon algae. A hotel in Colombia that sits high on a mountain, overlooking the Bogotá River, a lush garden growing on the roof. An underwater city in Shicheng. Michigan Central Station in Detroit, where rivers of rubble and silt flood the hallways. Holy Land USA in Waterbury, Connecticut, where tiny buildings are packed onto ridges, the eyelike windows looking out at the vines climbing walls and the crosses crumbling into the earth.

These places were not created by the sickness, just as the gap in my own memory was not created by the sickness. This was all done long before.

"Time is passing," N5 says on the morning of my birthday, sucking blood into a syringe. "The world is moving on."

"*We* aren't moving on," I say.

"That's right," says Louis. "We're getting left behind."

After she's gone, Louis stands on his bed and starts jumping up and down. The mattress bobs. The frame shudders. "Happy birthday to you," he sings.

I often wonder what Louis was like before the sickness, if he was a good husband, if he was faithful to his wife.

I climb up and jump beside him. I can almost touch the ceiling. I think the bed is going to come apart. For a few glorious seconds, I feel our togetherness return and believe we are going to be launched far away from here.

At breakfast, a cupcake topped with a white curl of icing is waiting for me in the Dining Hall, sitting on one of the long tables. All the Floor Groups have crowded around the table, along with Dr. Bek and the nurses. They applaud when Louis and I walk in. I play my role. I give a little wave. N5 hands me a plastic fork.

"Go ahead," she says.

I take a bite. The center is still frozen. The icing is cold and sweet and hurts my teeth. The twins come over and present me with a toilet paper lei. I bend down and let them loop it around my neck. Dr. Bek stands beside me, a gloved hand on the point of my shoulder. I see a flush in the high ridges of his cheekbones.

I don't tell anyone that my birthday is a guess made by a doctor at Brigham. The month is right, but the date could be a fiction.

Dr. Bek fails to mention the last birthday the Hospital celebrated, back in October, was for a man who became symptomatic a week later and died. Instead he leads the patients in a round of "Happy Birthday." The nurses join in, the lyrics a rumble inside their suits, followed by the patients. I'm stuck inside the tornado of sound, trying to look happy to be alive. As the room swells with our voices, I think about how, if I'm carrying the sickness inside me, I will one day forget Dr. Bek and all these singing people. I will forget the meaning of the words "birthday" and "patient." I will forget how to use a fork. I take another bite of the cupcake and wait for the party to end.

■ ■ ■

I spend the rest of the day alone in the Common Room, passing time by looking out the window. There are no pilgrims, too cold now for even the most devoted. The plains gleam with ice. I know the world around us is changing, but the view from the window is the same.

On my last birthday, I worked a double at the Stop & Shop and got a free M&M's cookie from the bakery and stole an extra bottle of Robitussin. I drank half of it in the bathroom, which seemed like an okay thing to do because it was my birthday, and I spent the rest of my shift in Produce, standing beside a pyramid of lemons and feeling the rapid twitch of my heart.

During my first week in the Hospital, my blood pressure was jumpy and I sweated rivers under my scrubs. I kept thinking about the time Ms. Neuman found out about me stealing from a neighborhood kid, the time I took a girl's red barrettes and lied about it and her mother called. "You can be any kind of person you want," Ms. Neuman told me in her kitchen, kneeling in front of me, an unlit Virginia Slims behind her ear. "Why would you choose to be this?"

Which was exactly what I thought on my last birthday, standing in Produce, my skin dewy from the vegetable misters: Why did I choose to be this?

GOOD HEALTH IS CONTAGIOUS AND YOU HAVE CAUGHT IT, the Pathologist says on the speakers, his latest meditation.

I turn on the TV. A show called *Mysteries of the Sea* is just starting on the Discovery Channel, the twins' favorite station. A woman stands on the deck of a white fishing boat with a navy blue hull, speaking into a walkie-talkie. I hear wind and static, a tumble of voices. The railing is dotted with orange lifesavers.

A scattering of birds in the sky. They cross over, white wings flapping, disappear from sight. The camera pulls away and for a moment the boat is just a spot on the water. A voiceover says it's spring in Las Tumbas, Cuba.

This woman is wearing a baseball cap that says AHOY and a blue jumpsuit and black boots, the laces pulled tight. On the deck, she discusses coordinates with her chief engineer. I hear official-sounding words like "dew point" and "barometric pressure." The captain keeps her eyes on the water, even though there is nothing around them except dark, undulating waves.

She is slim, but her sleeves are cuffed and I can see the muscle in her arms. Her hair is an inky knot at the base of her neck. She points the walkie-talkie antenna at something off in the distance. The chief engineer nods.

This captain, she is striking, serious. The more I look at her, the more I can't stop looking.

I get on the floor, on my hands and knees. A primal feeling takes hold and I move closer to the TV on all fours. The paper lei swings from my neck. I get close to the screen, so close I can feel static on the tip of my nose.

There are things aging changes and things it preserves. It's like looking into a mirror and having my future self projected back at me. Still, it takes me the entire episode to believe what I am seeing.

8.

In an hour of TV, here is what I learn about my mother:

Her name is Beatrice Lurry. She is an underwater archaeologist, a member of the Institute of Nautical Archaeology. A ship detective. She is the person who is called in after a ship has gone missing and the coast guard has failed in their pursuit. She has a special talent for searching.

A special talent for searching, for finding, but not for holding on. I am proof of that.

A Russian ship, named after an old film star, that vanished on its way to the Dominican Republic—recovered by my mother off the coast of Newfoundland. A cabin cruiser that disappeared in the Gulf of Mexico. That vessel had a unique gravity weight, was designed to be unsinkable, but my mother discovered that it did in fact sink, as did the yacht that went missing in the Indian Ocean, drowning its sixteen passengers.

Of course, it's not every day a ship goes missing. When she doesn't have a live case, she searches for the wrecks, the long lost—the cruise liner that disappeared in the Arctic Ocean a hundred years ago; the merchant vessel abandoned in the South Pacific in the fifties. The wreck that made her famous was found near the Wallabi islands: in the hold she uncovered a mass grave, the casualties of a mutiny.

She got her start on the wrecks, but it's the live cases she loves best, the urgency of the search.

In that hour of TV, I learn about her first expedition, when she was part of a maritime team looking for a steamship that sank in Lake Michigan a century ago, during a storm. They found the ship nearly intact, thanks to the freezing lake water. She was one of the technical divers, in charge of taking photos. She dove two hundred and fifty feet below the surface.

Once she was down that deep, she never wanted to leave.

I learn that she takes medication for migraines. When she is struck by one, she has to lie down in a dark room with a wet towel over her eyes. When she's not at sea, she lives on an island called Shadow Key, just beyond the coast of Key West. The only way to reach the island is by boat. There are images of a red houseboat with porthole windows docked in a still harbor. She can't sleep in a regular house, can't sleep in anything that doesn't float.

"Water is neutral," my mother tells the camera. "It doesn't have wants."

On this voyage, she has a live one: *The Estrella*, a freighter that vanished en route from Miami to Argentina, an episode filmed when a memory-destroying epidemic was still something that existed only in the apocalyptic corners of our imaginations or didn't exist at all.

The Estrella was last spotted near Las Tumbas, in the Gulf of Mexico. When the vessel never reached its destination in the Argentine province of Santa Cruz, the cargo and the crew unaccounted for, including the captain's wife and teenage daughter, my mother got the call.

On the ship deck, she watches the sky and I notice the long

grace of her neck. In the Common Room, I extend my neck, feel the muscles in my throat stretch, and search for resemblance. Midway through the episode, a storm blows through and the clouds shimmer with lightning.

During the storm, my mother works in the lower cabin, a tiny wood-paneled room. Black cords snake across the floor and around the metal legs of a desk and a chair. Graphs are tacked to the walls. A cot with a white pillow and a yellow blanket is pressed along one side of the room. A seaside painting hangs above it. In the center of the room, a marine radar beeps; a green circle flashes on the screen. My mother takes off her AHOY cap and shakes out her hair. Her roots have been bleached auburn by the sun. I see the familiar middle part, the high forehead. My inheritance.

How strange it is to watch her past become animated, to no longer wonder where and how her life was unfolding, but to know.

She sits hunched over a notebook. A circular clock, the hands shaped like oars, and a map of the Atlantic hang on the wall behind her. Points in the water have been marked with black pushpins. The clock slides back and forth as the boat rocks on the ocean. The low light brings out the shadows in her face and for a moment, that grass scent comes back to me. She switches on a tape recorder and starts talking about microbursts. I consider the way the start of a bad feeling feels, that little pop of dread— microburst, what a perfect name for that feeling, even though I know my mother is talking about things that don't have to do with the body but with the sea. Her voice is soft. There is the hint of something troubling her in the back of her throat. Her knuckles are red and splitting. Her fingernails are cut past the quick.

I wonder if she ever thinks about me. What she remembers. If she dreams of finding the captain's daughter alive and well, floating in a lifeboat in the middle of the sea.

■ ■ ■

As the weather gets colder, as the recovery progresses on the outside, Floor Groups four and six become harder to control. It starts when a patient from six, a young guy from California, has a dream. In the dream, he wakes in the night to find a Native American man standing at his bedside. His skin is crusted with dirt, like he's just been dug up from a grave. He's wearing a big headdress with feathers and tiny animal skulls. He leans over this patient and breathes breath as hot as death in his face and tells him to wake the fuck up.

"And I did," this guy tells us during morning yoga, when we're all supposed to be in Child's Pose. "I woke up."

Now this man is claiming Floor Groups four and six are doing more work than the other patients; he has become a representative. In a Community Meeting, he asks Dr. Bek if he has any idea what kind of crap the patients leave behind in the Dining Hall. Is he aware that under the tables they find crumpled paper napkins and plastic forks, the tines crusted with food, and corn niblets that have been smashed like bugs? Is he aware that microwaves leach the nutrition from our food? That cleaning microwaves three times a day could expose them to carcinogenic radiation?

"Don't we," he says in the Common Room, his chest puffed under his scrubs, "deserve to simply enjoy a meal?"

"Perhaps you are familiar with the old Norwegian saying *'Det kjem inkte steikte fuglar flug jande i mun'*?" Dr. Bek replies. "Or, 'Birds do not fly into our mouths already roasted.'"

At dinner that night, this guy walks over to where Group three is sitting, picks up a tray, and throws it on the floor. Peas scatter like marbles. A roll slides under a table. A water glass overturns. The clatter echoes inside the Dining Hall. The patients drop their

plastic forks and look toward the noise. I stop chewing. My teri-
yaki beef is a soft lump on my tongue. Dr. Bek and the nurses,
who are always in the Dining Hall during meals but are never
seen eating, stand along a wall, underneath the windows. They
don't say anything. They don't move. They wait to see what will
happen next.

He throws another tray. The patients from Groups four and
six rise from their tables. They begin picking up trays and throw-
ing them too—first their own, then others. The other Groups do
not join in. There is an old Kansan saying that goes "Not our
Floor Group, not our problem."

They pull trays away from patients who are still eating. Limp
green beans stick to the white linoleum like slugs. Ketchup
splats across the floor. Under the lights it takes on the color and
texture of blood. Louis and I watch from our table, frozen in our
orange seats. The falling trays sound like a string of firecrackers
detonating.

On my plate, there is a pile of mashed potatoes, molded into
a little volcano and filled with peas. This is something Marcus
and I used to do at Ms. Neuman's. In the Hospital, I find myself
reverting back.

"I'm still hungry," I call across the Dining Hall, holding the
edges of my tray, but it doesn't do any good.

When they come for our trays, we don't resist. I let go of mine,
and we watch the red rectangles rise from the table and crash
against the floor.

Finally Groups four and six walk out of the Dining Hall,
leaving behind a swamp of gooey red footprints. The staff doesn't
move. They breathe with monstrous slowness. The trays stay on
the floor. The microwaves go uncleaned.

That night, the nurses play *Carrie* in the Common Room. A
girl with very long hair gets soaked in pig's blood at a high school

dance and uses her paranormal powers to burn the school to the ground. In the dark of the Common Room, I find myself wishing for powers like that. The lights go out at the usual time. Two Groups have broken the rules, but nothing seems to have changed.

In the morning, the Dining Hall is somehow spotless and the patient from California is not at breakfast. No one in his Floor Group knows what's happened to him. He was there when his roommate went to sleep; he was gone when the roommate woke. The staff tells us nothing. I walk the hallways and the stairwells, looking, like a dog on the trail of a funny scent. Not our Floor Group, not our problem, but still I don't like the idea of people disappearing.

In three days, he's returned to us. At his first meal back, he sits by himself. He eats withered blueberries one at a time. He stacks trays. He snaps on cleaning gloves and fishes a green sponge from a bucket of water and wipes all the microwaves. He looks like himself, but acts like a different person—how can we be sure who he is? He never says anything about his dreams again.

■ ■ ■

In my next Internet Session, I sit down and go right to WeAreSorryForYourLoss.com. As I scroll through the names, I get hot and itchy and keep sending the cursor in the wrong direction. It's possible I will find my mother's name on the list and everything will go back to the way it was before.

My list of worst mothers includes mothers who drugged their daughters with heroin and taught them to shoplift and used them to make porn and sold them and poured hot sauce in their eyes and buried them in the woods. This a list I keep to remind myself that there are worse things than leaving.

I scroll down to the *l*'s. I check three times. I do the *b*'s too, just to be sure. Her name is not there. It is on another list, on the list for the living, that I find her.

. . .

One morning I wake later than usual, because no one has come for our examination. My mouth is dry and sour. Louis is still in bed, his white sheets tangled around his calves. I go into the hall, into the tunnel of fluorescence. The door to the twins' room is flung open and I see N5 swatting at their floor with a mop. Sam and Christopher are standing in the corner, barefoot, their pale toes curled like animal claws. Their floor is coated in water.

"What's going on?" I ask from the doorway.

"Our toilet is overflowing," Sam says. He swallows, and the freckles jump around on his throat. "We don't know how to make it stop."

I can make out N5's body, her human body, heaving inside the suit. The shield is fogged. I can barely see her eyes. She keeps pushing the mop around. When she notices me standing there, she tells me to go find N6, the other nurse assigned to our floor.

I wander down the hall, past the bright white walls. There's no one at the window, nothing but snow to see outside. I find N6 at the opposite end of the hallway, completing an exam.

"There's a flood," I tell him. "In the twins' room."

A patient, a gemologist from Santa Fe who knows the name of every kind of stone, sits on a narrow bed. Her bare feet are pressed against the floor and she's rubbing the crook of her arm, so I know N6 must have just taken her blood.

"A what?" N6 says, squinting at me through the face shield, like I might be playing some kind of prank.

"A flood," I repeat. "Like water. Like Noah's Ark."

N6 takes a mop from the supply closet and hustles down the hallway. The nurses mop and mop but the water keeps coming, a thin stream seeping from the base of the toilet and expanding into a clear pool on the bedroom floor. It's rare to see something appear in the Hospital that the staff cannot control.

Finally N6 does something to the toilet that makes the water stop. He orders me and the twins to the Common Room until everything has been cleaned up.

"We want to stay," the boys protest, their toes curling tighter.

The nurses point the ends of their mops toward the door.

Don't you ever wish you could tell us your real names? I know better than to ask.

In the hall, the twins explain the program they saw on the Discovery Channel about rising sea levels. A chart showed Hawaii being covered in water. The Kohala volcano is gradually submerging. Hilo is shrinking 2.3 millimeters per year.

"Hawaii is sinking," Christopher says.

"It'll take a hundred years for Hawaii to sink," I tell them. We pass the Common Room, where patients are coiled up like children on the floor, asleep or pretending to be. "You'll be dead by the time Hawaii sinks."

After I say "dead," they go silent. They shrink inside their scrubs. We walk by two women holding hands. They aren't from our Floor Group. I can't remember their names. They don't look at us as we pass. We the patients are like a chain of islands: occupying the same water, but isolated from one another.

"I'm sorry," I tell the twins. "But it's true."

"The fact remains," Christopher says.

"We started digging faster," Sam says. "What will happen if they find our hole?"

I roll my eyes. "I told you dumping dirt in the toilet was a bad idea."

"Shut up," Christopher says.

■ ■ ■

In the next *Mysteries of the Sea*, my mother tells us about the painting above her cot, a print by Winslow Homer called *Rowing Home*. Outside the Hospital, night is already spreading. As the light from the barred window dims, the TV grows brighter. In the painting, there are three figures, dark and obscure, in a small boat. A red sun bleeds color into the sky and into the stormy waves. My mother says no one captures sea light like Winslow Homer. No one makes water look more alive. It took him a week to paint the oars alone. She says she looks at this painting every night—the falling light, the small act of three men rowing, set against the vast motions of the sea—and it helps her find her place in the world, to feel at peace.

■ ■ ■

I wonder if I will ever know what it's like to feel at peace.

9.

On Thursdays, there was free admission to the museum where my first fosters, Mr. and Mrs. Carroll, worked. One afternoon, I rode the T to the waterfront.

In the station, a flyer for a missing girl, taped to a concrete post, stopped me. From the date of birth, I knew I was around the same age. The girl even looked a little like me. She had been missing for six years, a span of time that made the flyer seem more like a memorial than a way to search. I stared at the hotline number and imagined what it would be like to look at a flyer and recognize your own face, to realize you had once been someone else, that people were out there looking for you.

At the waterfront, the buildings were ragged with construction. I passed lots with long trash Dumpsters behind orange safety fencing. An office chair, the seat torn open, on a corner. I walked through a tunnel of scaffolding, smelling fish and brine. I saw a green rubber glove on the ground—a sign, I would later think, of the Hospital that lay in my future. The fingers were splayed; gray pebbles had collected in the palm. When I emerged, back into the light, my arms were sticky with sawdust. The side-walks were damp from an early morning rain. All week I'd been feeling cold and restless. I thought maybe I was coming down with something.

That morning, I had woken up in my Stop & Shop uniform, in the dark of the basement apartment, and couldn't go back to sleep. I felt the itch of the black spot in my memory and decided to go looking for Mr. and Mrs. Carroll. I had questions about their son.

I passed a man in a red sweat suit walking down the sidewalk very slowly, a pace I didn't like. If you walk slowly in a city it means you don't have an internal destination in mind. You are just waiting for something to come along and that something could be me.

The museum looked like a spaceship teetering on the edge of the water, a huge glass box supported by an intricate system of smaller glass boxes. Inside I got my ticket and started looking around. Some guards sat on stools, limp with boredom. Some skulked from room to room, hunting for open beverages and cameras with a flash.

As I wandered the museum, I counted the things I remembered. He bought his reading glasses at the drugstore. In his bedroom, he had a whole drawer of them, the frames large and square. He had an old white Honda with broken windshield wipers. In the rain, he took the bus. He did not put milk in his cereal because he was allergic to dairy. Once I brought up the way a boy from the deaf school who lived in our neighborhood drifted through crosswalks, like he was moving on a different wavelength. How at the playground he stood on the swings instead of sitting, how he kicked around the mulch. The Psychologist pointed out that if the boy could not *hear* the rules, it would take him longer to learn how to follow them, and I remember thinking he sounded wise. For a brief time, he went out with a woman who worked at the deaf school. She came around the house once, in a cardigan and a jean skirt, and then I never saw her again.

In the Hospital, I do not tell anyone that this list is the memory trick I practice when I'm alone at night.

I couldn't find Mr. or Mrs. Carroll. I even asked Information and the woman at the desk said that wasn't the kind of information she was available to provide. I ended up in a dark, curtained room on the top floor, watching a video. No one else was up there. I sat down on a bench. On the screen, a woman stood in a green room with a pair of antlers on her head. I heard ocean sounds: a rushing tide, a gull's cry.

The scenes began to change. There was a field and the damp bottom of a stairwell and a train racing through the night. The woman in the green room, sitting on a bench like the one I was sitting on, and staring into the camera.

Why didn't I just go to the Carrolls' house? I remembered their street in Allston. I could see the brass numbers tacked above the entrance. Over a decade had passed. They could have retired or gotten new jobs. Was this even the right museum? When I thought back to Allston, it was like being able to see all of a room except for one little corner. What was that dark spot hiding.

The video played on a loop. I kept watching. I imagined myself stepping into the screen and sitting next to the woman. I imagined wearing my own set of antlers and staring out at the empty room. I saw myself turning to the woman and asking what it would feel like to not carry such division within, because to look inside yourself and see so much mystery is the worst kind of loneliness.

For me, the woman had no answers.

10.

In the New Year, I start keeping a list of all the nautical terms I've heard on *Mysteries of the Sea*. It's like learning a new language, my mother's language. Abaft. Aft. Hull down. Brails. Doldrums. Scud. Sextant. Beaufort scale. Windward. Windlass. Lee side. Absolute bearing. Bower. Magnetic north. Whitecaps. Starboard. Vanishing angle.

. . .

I have watched my mother roll over her deck railing and into the water below, dark and seal-like in her diving suit. A light splash, a crown of bubbles—the only evidence that she came from land. She carried an underwater flashlight and the white circle grew fainter the deeper she swam, until there was only a ghostly glow. I have watched her curl up on the cot during a migraine, a white washcloth draped over her eyes like a convalescent in an old war movie. I have watched her hand cut the air as she made a point to her chief engineer, the gesture of a person convinced of her own rightness.

After seeing all this, after watching her become not a dream but a person, I can't stop myself from imagining my own abandonment.

Here is one version. She wraps me in the white shirt and lays the box on the steps with care. She shivers, pulls her coat sleeves over her hands—how long will it take for someone to find me? She looks into my wide, wet eyes. She strokes my cheek. She kisses my hair, leaving behind a string of spit, a bit of her. She can't decide what her last gesture should be. What to leave me with. She feels her heart turn into a fist as she walks away. She is certain she will never do anything harder.

Here is another. The shirt is sour with milk. She sets the box down and I whimper and she makes no move to comfort. That list of things a mother can do that are worse than leaving? She can see herself being capable of something like that. She breathes in the cold and looks at the fat pink thing squirming in the box and waits to see what she feels, if she feels anything. She leaves without tears and once the hospital is out of sight, she is light with relief.

After one of these imaginings, I wander over to a window. We're a week into January. Time has never moved so slowly. I look up through the glass, expecting to see something icy and pale, and am startled to find a dark and terrifying sky.

■ ■ ■

A blizzard, the first to come this winter. The snowfall gets so thick, I can't make out the flat fields surrounding us. That afternoon, there is no sunset. There is only gusting snow and hissing wind and dark slivers of sky through the bars. We are plunged straight into the deepest night. On the speakers, the Pathologist summons the Floor Groups to the Common Room, where Dr. Bek and the nurses have gathered.

Dr. Bek reviews our inclement weather protocols. If we lose power, the emergency generators will come on. If we lose power, we should congregate in our communal spaces and keep each other warm with the heat of our bodies. We should stay away from the windows. We should not go wandering into hallways and stairwells. This is not the time to get lost.

The patients glance at the Common Room window with nervous eyes. Through the bars the sky looks like black paint being mixed around in a can.

In Massachusetts, I have seen snow that falls as heavy as a driving rain and drifts as tall as me. I have seen winds that shred power lines and uproot trees. I think I am prepared.

Dr. Bek asks if we have questions. Hands grab at the air.

"Are we going to die?" a patient from Floor Group three calls out.

He blinks rapidly, like he has something in his eye. "No one is going to die," he says.

■ ■ ■

We lose power in the middle of dinner. The lights flicker and flicker and then go out. We sit in darkness, our trays in front of us, our food growing cold, and listen to the windows rattle behind the bars. We hear a humming and the lights come back on, but they are not the lights we are used to. They are a dull gold and they shine out from the corners, so some tables are trapped in a bubble of light, others shadowed.

We finish our dinner, our fingers moving dumbly in the partial light. I wrap my fist around a plastic fork and poke at a kidney-shaped piece of chicken. I can hear the staff breathing on the borders of the room. Floor Groups four and six leave their tables and begin collecting trays. Our table is cloaked in shadow, so they forget all about us. After dinner, the patients stay where they are, afraid to leave the enclosure of the Dining Hall. The faces around me are dark glimmers.

I'm sitting across from the twins. They have started a word association game, where they take turns calling out things that have to do with Hawaii. This is the memory trick Dr. Bek has invented for them. Whoever can keep it up the longest wins.

"Magma!"

"Lokelani!"

"Sugarcane!"

"What does the winner get, anyway?" I ask after Christopher wins for the fourth time in a row, clearly in no danger of forgetting.

"The distinction of having superior knowledge," he says.

I hear the clank of a tray falling. Somewhere in the Dining Hall a patient is laughing. On the speakers, the Pathologist is making a sound that reminds me of the ocean noises on the video I watched at the museum.

What was I really looking for that day?

I overhear Olds say that when she was growing up in Michigan, they called weather events like this "silver storms." I let that phrase linger with me. I imagine icicles hanging like tentacles from power lines and trees.

■ ■ ■

Once a thunderstorm knocked out power at the Stop & Shop. An emergency generator switched on, but the electronic lock on the manager's office failed. A cashier went in and stole the manager's computer and never came back to the store. If only that had been my shift. In the Dining Hall, I start to get ideas.

No one notices when I slip away from my Floor Group, into the cold hall. Faint lights run along the sides of the ceiling. My footsteps sound like falling rain. I'm halfway to the stairwell when I hear a scream spill out of the Dining Hall. I am afraid of what patients might become willing to do in the near dark.

An incomplete list of things that make patients scream in the Hospital: nightmares, needles, bad memories, fear of death, homesickness, rules, rage, boredom, lack of sunlight, each other.

In the stairwell, I go down five flights of stairs, all the way to the basement, the zero floor, where the air is frigid and damp and I can hear the storm whirring. I dart around a corner and down another hallway, lit by floodlights. I pat the walls, the cold stinging my palms, and search for the storage room door. I think about how my life before the Hospital prepared me for dark underground moments like this. Consider the pattern of transferring T lines: through a narrow tunnel, up stairs, down stairs, through another narrow tunnel, all of it done underground, the thumping sound of footsteps above, the walls vibrating from passing trains. Consider the journey through the dark of my basement apartment, from bed to toilet and back again, in the middle of the night. The graveyard shift at the Stop & Shop. The city was training me and I had no idea.

In the storage room, the keypad is dark. I lean on the door and it gives. Inside, the generator lights are a sickly yellow. Metal shelves are built into the walls; each shelf holds a row of gray rubber tubs. Every patient has a tub, their last name written across the bottom in black marker, the letters large and blocky. I try to un-see the names of the patients who have died.

Inside my tub I find my jeans and my black sweatshirt, all neatly folded. Three crumpled twenties are still a wad inside the front pocket. I press my sweatshirt against my mouth. It smells like the outdoors. I imagine my clothes have feelings and are glad to see me.

I lift out the sneakers and reach for the plastic baggie beneath. The photo is just like I remembered. The thin white blouse, the sliver of blue visible over her shoulder.

Since finding my mother there have been moments where I've doubted my own memory, my own sight. There have been moments where I've worried the woman on TV might not be my mother at all, but a careful copy, designed to trick me. The photo, my proof of her, is the only way to be sure.

The dark gloss of her hair is just the same. So is the teardrop shape of her cheekbones, the hard lines of her jaw. Her eyes. There is something slightly different about the angle of her nose. Her skin has paled with age. These alterations are to be expected: the body shows the impressions of time.

"Beatrice," I say, touching her lips.

I tuck the photo into the waistband of my scrubs. I fold up my clothes, slide the tub back on the shelf. I leave the cold of the basement and go up and up, back to the fifth floor, the muscles in my thighs pulsing. The Dining Hall is still full. The patients are still sitting at their tables. On my way back to my Floor Group, I step in something wet. I brush against the shadowed body of a patient. Fingers skate across the small of my back. In one corner of the Dining Hall, I catch a white hazmat trudging through a wedge of light. A nurse, though I can't tell which one.

I sit down at my Floor Group table, where the twins are still playing their word association game. I rub my thighs. I squeeze out the soreness. My breathing slows. I feel alive with secrets.

"*A hui hou*," Christopher says. "I win again."

■ ■ ■

It takes twenty-four hours for the power to come back on, for the Hospital to return to being warm and fluorescent, for the Internet to be restored. The TV service is a different matter.

In a Community Meeting, Dr. Bek explains that a power line fell during the storm. He clicks on the TV to demonstrate and the screen pops with static. He turns up the volume, so we can hear the buzzing, so it has a chance to dig inside our brains. The nurses are clustered by the window. The patients crouch, wanting to get away from the sound. They shut their eyes and scratch at their ears.

"How long will it be out?" I shout over the static, not wanting to see these gray worming lines on the screen but my mother's face.

Dr. Bek doesn't say anything. He doesn't lower the volume. He just stands there in his suit and watches his patients kneel on the floor. He watches them tuck their heads under their arms or between their knees, trying to escape the noise. If a stranger appeared in the doorway, I wonder if it would look like we were engaged in some peculiar form of prayer.

■ ■ ■

I use my next Internet Session to research my mother. I tell myself that I am working on a very special project, that I, like Dr. Bek, need all the data I can get. She is famous enough to have her own Wikipedia entry, which says she was born in 1968, in Nova Scotia, and raised in Belfast, Maine, where her parents owned a seafood restaurant. She went to college in Connecticut and was a champion swimmer. There's a photo of her in a bathing suit, hair slicked back, medals heaped around her neck. Water is beading on her chin. Her lips are pale, her pupils wide and dark. She is not smiling. She has been once married and once divorced. I don't see anything more about family.

I find a video of her in a minisubmarine that looks like a giant orange egg. The video lasts two minutes and forty-three seconds. I replay it thirteen times. Her figure is miniature inside the machine.

I watch the submarine move gradually into a stream of light. The camera tilts upward and I see the outline of the cave, black and yawning, like the open mouth of a giant. As she passes through the entrance, the light shifts, becomes translucent.

I listen to the supervising nurse breathe in a corner and think about all the staff does not know. I don't want to share my mother with the Hospital. She is one of the only things in here that feels private, that belongs to me.

I want to edit her Wikipedia page, even though online we're only supposed to observe, not communicate: check the weather, check the news, check the death list. No e-mails, no status updates. For our safety, Dr. Bek has assured us. Our security.

Under Biography I could type: *In 1995, a daughter, Joy Jones, was born.*

Her daughter grew into a fine person, maybe even a *special* person, despite her mother leaving her *outside* in *winter*. Those are just some of the things I could write.

I close the window.

No one will ever write a Wikipedia page for me.

■ ■ ■

In another session, I find my mother's phone number, the one for her headquarters on Shadow Key: Rescue, Inc. I stare at the number, the ten digits linked by dashes, until it has been committed to memory.

■ ■ ■

After the blizzard, the snow does not stop. It keeps falling, hiding the plains behind a curtain of white, and a patient from Floor Group two turns symptomatic. During her morning exam, a nurse discovered a shoulder pocked with silver blisters. I imagine a gloved hand raising her scrubs and finding a shoulder blade turned to quartz. When they asked about the season, she smiled and said, "Summertime." The nurses called for Dr. Bek and didn't mark another day on her calendar. By breakfast she was on the tenth floor and I wanted my brain to be filled with ice.

In the Common Room, I stand by the window and remember winter in Boston, how in January the ice would become thick and permanent and items would get trapped inside: a penny, a cigarette butt, a Coke bottle, a pen. On one of those raw winter days, I looked down at a frozen street corner and saw my own face looking back and imagined the ice had gotten me.

Later, in the Dining Hall, I wander around with an empty red tray. It's lunchtime, but for once I don't feel like eating. Louis is sitting alone at a table, apart from our Floor Group. Thunder booms outside and I wonder if another storm is coming and all of a sudden I'm not in the Hospital anymore. I'm back on the bus that brought us here. I'm looking out the window and seeing a sneaker lying in a ditch, the shoelaces black with mud, and then I'm back, standing next to Louis, who is dissecting a burrito with his fork.

"Shit," I say.

"Don't you wonder who'll be next?" he says without looking up. "We should start taking bets."

I've hidden my mother's photo in my pillowcase. When I'm alone, I take it out and will myself not to get sick.

"I wouldn't bet on you," I say. "You're going to live a very long time."

"How would you know?"

I smile, no teeth. "Assholes live forever."

He does not smile back. I sit down next to him. He slumps in his chair. We don't speak for a while. I slide my empty tray back and forth on the table.

"Will you cut that out?" Louis smacks the table, glaring.

I let go of the tray. His hands are cupped around his eyes. I want to touch every finger, to kiss every knuckle, like I used to when we first came to the Hospital and weren't afraid to act like we needed each other.

"What's the matter with you? Besides the obvious, I mean." The obvious being the country getting razed by forgetting and then coming back to life and all the while we stay stuck in here, getting sicker.

"Paige doesn't want to see me."

"Oh," I say. "Did she give you a reason?"

His hands fall into his lap. He looks out at the patients bent over their plates and sawing open burritos with plastic knives. "Do I really need to tell you, Joy? This is a hopeless place, for hopeless people. Not a place for romance."

"I don't know about all that," I say.

I touch his shoulder and feel heat rising from his body, proof of his aliveness. I want to tell him to not give up, that Paige only loves running, that she was never going to love him, that there are other kinds of people in here.

There is, for example, me.

"Well." He rubs the fine hair on his arms. "It's not like I was madly in love."

"Oh," I say again. "So you don't miss her?"

"What I miss is living."

I keep my hand on his shoulder. I feel his skin grow warmer under my palm.

Across the room, I catch the twins sitting under an empty table. Their legs are bent and pulled to their chests. They're facing each other, chins resting on knees, and whispering. They go unnoticed by the patients walking past, by everyone but me.

■ ■ ■

I walk the Hospital for hours that afternoon. In the third-floor hallway, I pass a spot where the paint has bubbled. I touch the lump, troubled by the anomaly, by the image of tumors multiplying inside the building and pushing their way through the walls. The cold coming up through the floor makes the bones in my feet ache. Afterwards I visit the Dining Hall and then do a slow pass through the Common Room, where Curtis is trying to get the TV to come on.

"Any luck?" I ask him. How I miss seeing my mother's face.

"Nope." He kneels behind the black box and fiddles with a nest of yellow wires. During the blizzard, a patient snuck into the Common Room and pissed in a corner. Our Floor Group treated the stain with powdered carpet cleaner, but there's still a dark, tangy splotch.

In the days between our Internet Sessions, we worry about what might be happening. If life on the outside is still getting better or if it is getting worse. We know how quickly things can change: one day the sickness does not exist; one day the sickness is in California; one day it is everywhere; one day it is starting to disappear. The scheduled Internet Sessions are like sips of water in a long hot desert, and we want more to drink.

Curtis gives up on the TV and starts grumbling about Dr. Bek's lack of progress. "Why should we keep waiting around here to die?" he says, dropping into the battered couch, not quite talking to me.

11.

I start to hear a scraping sound coming from the twins' room at night. It's a soft clawing noise, like they're using their fingernails to scratch through the floor. I roll away from the wall and shut my eyes, but I can't stop listening. I imagine miners pickaxing their way through a cave, archaeologists excavating ruins, explorers drilling through the earth's crust and mantle and into the deepest core.

∎ ∎ ∎

Some nights I don't listen to the twins at all because I am tangled up in a net of remembering. I think about the stories Marcus and I used to tell each other in Charlestown. Real-Life Ghost Stories, we called them. Here's one.

On my first night in Mission Hill, I was brushing my teeth in the bathroom and when I looked up, an older girl was in the doorway. She was tan and wide. Pink jelly bracelets were stacked on her wrists. She smacked the toothbrush out of my hand. It

clattered against the floor. White foam ran down my chin. I felt
the bathroom shrinking. She smacked me in the face. I crashed
into the wall, banging my head on the sharp edge of the paper
towel dispenser. She cornered me and did it again and again—
fast, open-handed slaps. My face was scorching. My mouth was
filling with blood. Her last slap knocked loose a tooth, a molar,
and I swallowed it whole.

. . .

In the Hospital, I worry the gap in the back of my mouth with
my tongue.

. . .

Here's another. After I had been with Ms. Neuman for a year, I
woke to find Marcus sitting on my legs in his Frankenstein
mask, the rubber bolts sticking out of his temples. He told me he
had a dream. We needed to go downstairs. In the living room,
we found Ms. Neuman lying on the carpet, in the glow of the
TV, her ex-husband talking about stationary weather fronts in
his toupee. Her slip was hiked up. She was still holding the remote. A stroke, not the killing kind, but she couldn't take care of
us anymore, my case worker would tell me later, after I was gone
from the yellow house on Ferrin Street, gone from Marcus, after
I was spitting blood into a bathroom sink in Mission Hill and
wondering how he knew.

12.

At the next Community Meeting, Dr. Bek informs us that the patient from Floor Group two has died. He tells us about the silver scales on her fingertips, about her forgetting. He tells us the last thing she said, "Oh," and I imagine her lips rounding and her eyes growing large. I wonder if that "Oh" was a sudden recognition, a final moment of remembering.

He tells us her name, Marie.

In the Common Room, Floor Group two collapses into itself, knees bending, arms folding across stomachs, a structure dissolving into dust. They are the ones who will see the absence in her bed and in their hallway and when they push around the laundry carts. Each time a Group is reduced by a single body, a single voice, every member feels themselves grow smaller.

The nurses are a mass in the doorway. I can hear them breathing behind us, the rustle of their suits. Floor Group three sits on the couch and stares at Dr. Bek like a row of inquisitors. The standing patients sway between the white walls. After this Community Meeting, our Floor Group will do our best to clean away the palm prints from the walls, the greasy outlines of fingers that always make me think about the residue of ghosts—if ghosts leave anything behind.

There is no mention of what has happened to Marie's body. Late at night, in our room, Louis and I have agreed there must be a large incinerator somewhere in the Hospital.

Dr. Bek looks around the room, the silver head of his suit turning back and forth like it is moving independently from the rest of him. "Believe in your own wellness. Right here in this room, feel every cell in your body grow stronger."

The patients are not in the mood for meditations.

What we want is answers to our questions. Has he made any progress? Is he closer to a cure? How much longer until you are standing up there and talking about my death? That is the question we are all really asking him.

"Next time" is Dr. Bek's answer. His head stills and his suit shudders, like something very strange is happening inside his body. "We are treating you. We are getting closer. That's why you are all so important. For the next time."

He holds out his gloved hands, palms turned up, as though he is about to give us a blessing. "In times of sadness, it is important to not give in to negative feelings. To not be afraid."

I think about how the Psychologist in Allston, with his little white electrodes, was the last person who told me to not be afraid.

"What if there wasn't a next time?" Curtis shouts, his voice tearing through our Floor Group. He's standing right in front of me, and I can see the flush climbing his neck. He breaks away and moves closer to the front. Group three scrambles up from the couch, still staring.

Olds and Older are right next to me, wild-eyed and rubbing their palms together and telling everyone they don't want to die in here. The twins are lost in our Floor Group, in the rush of adult bodies, but I can hear them going on about the TV, how we need it, how it should be working, and others start taking up their cause.

The room gets loud and hot and my memory tips back to summers in Boston, when the hair on my neck was always damp and the standing fans in my basement apartment churned around the warm air. At the Stop & Shop, every time the doors opened the heat would find its way in. I would escape to Frozens and press icy bags of peas against my forehead. On the T, the heat swarmed the bodies slouching in seats, the bodies wound around the poles, the bodies holding the straps like children who had tired of standing. When the cars rose aboveground and clacked across the tracks, the sun burned through the windows and I felt the burn in my cheeks just like the one I'm feeling now, in the Common Room.

Patients stomp and chant. Some are chanting for hazmat suits and some are chanting for a new TV and some are chanting for our release and some are shouting, "Cure! Cure! Cure!" The mantras spread like fire. The exception is the guy from California, the one who led the rebellion in the Dining Hall, who is looking at all of us like, Oh no, not this shit again.

I sink into the crowd. Green and white figures spread across the Common Room like a wave. I lose sight of Dr. Bek. The patients spill over the couch and around the TV, still chanting. The nurses have vanished from the doorway, leaving Dr. Bek to face us on his own.

Me, I'm not chanting for anything. I just want the noise to stop.

"I can't breathe in here," I say to Louis. I swat at my chest, swat at his arm, looking for something steady.

The heat, the noise, it swells like a balloon. We are too much for this space to hold. We are about to blow it apart. Dr. Bek bolts up the side of the room, a silver flash shooting into the hall, and then everyone starts to run.

Dr. Bek races down the white hall. The fluorescents hit the edges of his hazmat, framing his body in light. All the patients follow. The fifth floor is filled with the thunder of our footsteps. The patients in the lead reach for Dr. Bek, their fingers long and pale. What will happen if we catch him? Will we tear off his suit and rub our hands all over his face and say, You are one of us now?

Patients fall and claw their way back. Those who can't run as fast, who are abandoned by the group, throw themselves against the walls and scream. I feel a hand grabbing at my ankle, digging nails, and I nearly go down, but Louis takes me by the elbow and pulls me up.

We are falling behind, Louis and me, but that doesn't mean we aren't still a part of it.

"*Garrr!*" Sam and Christopher call out.

The halls pass in a white smudge. When Dr. Bek reaches the Dining Hall, he taps a code into the keypad and darts inside. We hear the doors lock behind him, the heavy click.

Patients kick the doors. They slam their bodies against them. There are two small round windows in the doors and Dr. Bek stares out at us through one of those windows, so still that he looks like he could be part of an exhibit, an astronaut frozen behind a sheet of glass.

A plan is devised to break into the Dining Hall. No one knows the code, so patients raid the supply closets for brooms and mops and beat the doors with the long wooden handles. The tools the Hospital has given us to fulfill our duties, to maintain cleanliness and order, are now being used in the name of chaos. Broom handles bash the round panes, but the glass appears unbreakable. Dr. Bek's face recedes from the window. I imagine him shrinking into a dark corner of the Dining Hall, breathing fast inside his suit.

When the doors do not open, the patients try to guess the code. We try the date of the first reported case and the date of our arrival at the Hospital and random configurations of numbers. After each wrong entry, the keypad turns red and bleats with disapproval. Some patients throw down their weapons and say they will wait for as long as it takes, but after a few hours most of us grow bored and listless and abandon the scene of our crime.

■ ■ ■

A small group of patients insists on guarding the Dining Hall. Others wander back to their rooms or the Common Room, where they sit in front of the blank TV, awaiting further instruction. Others travel down to the basement, hoping to figure out the code, but then they look through the triangular window and see the white ocean outside and go back upstairs. In the Hospital, we are far away from everything.

I'm walking the third-floor hallway when I hear a sound coming from the supply closet. I open the door and find N5 sitting there.

She's pressed into a corner, next to a plastic caddy filled with cleaning supplies. Behind the shield her eyes are bloodshot. She's holding on to her shins and I can see the shapes of her knuckles through the gloves. She blinks at me. Each breath is long and gasping. I look down at her and wonder what the consequences of abandoning Dr. Bek will be.

"It's over," I say. It's strange to see a member of the staff looking so small and vulnerable, so human. "Everything is calming down." I am surprised by my desire to help.

"I don't understand why you're doing this to us," she cries.

Her lids disappear. Her eyes grow wide. "We're not even real doctors."

. . .

The patients give up their rebellion when they realize nothing works in the Hospital without Dr. Bek and his staff. The Dining Hall stays locked. There is no other place for us to get food. There is no Lights Out. The fluorescent overheads burn through the night. The few patients intent on guarding the Dining Hall sleep on the floor and wake feeling cold and hungry and stiff. In the morning, they go back to their floors, to their rooms, and wait for their morning examinations. No one comes.

Louis and I drink water from the bathroom tap. We knead our aching stomachs. We give each other an exam. Louis pantomimes administering a shot. I sit on my mattress. His fingers form an imaginary needle. He takes my arm and nudges the delicate purple skin, a fake needle looking for a real vein.

"This won't hurt." He frowns at my arm. "Hold still. Let us help you."

A sure sign it's going to hurt? The more a person tells you it won't, the more you can be certain it will.

"Owww," I say.

We peek beneath scrubs and down throats. His throat is a dark moist tunnel. When I look under his scrubs, I see the flat white of his stomach, the soft blond fuzz. We palm foreheads and peel back eyelids. We do the Romberg. It feels good to be close to him.

Once we are touching each other, how can we be expected to stop? Soon I am flat against his bed, my scrubs around my ankles. My legs are parting and then he is on top of me, pushing. It's daytime and there is no lock on the door, so we are quick, but I will never forget the feeling of blood flooding my body or our hot grasping hands or the way his eyes rolled back as we slipped into a place where time has no meaning, where we forget all about hunger, where we are so completely alive it seems impossible that we will not live forever.

■ ■ ■

All day the staff remains invisible. The patients are silent and drifting. The Dining Hall is still locked. We have not eaten in twenty-four hours. There are no meditations. I go back to the third floor and look for N5 in the supply closet, but there's just the caddie stuffed with rags and spray bottles. I begin to worry they have left us for good.

From the Common Room window, I watch the sky go dark. I can still smell Louis in my hair and on my fingers. I can't stop wondering where my mother is right now.

Is she happy? Is she alone? Is she glad to be alive?

You might think we the patients would band together and make our own kingdom. You might think we would figure out a way to leave the Hospital, to trek into the closest town, La Harpe, or at least find a way into the Dining Hall. In December, when Floor Groups four and six threw around the trays, there was a leader. This time around, the patient from California is holed up in his room. He wants no part in leadership and no other leader has emerged. Still, there are seventy-four patients, the better part of a hundred. Isn't this what we wanted, freedom from the rules? Why aren't we doing anything useful with that freedom? What is wrong with us?

The longer the staff stays missing, the more patients I see curling up in corners or wandering aimlessly under the lights. Everyone starts taking on the same blank expression, the look of a child who has been left behind in a shopping mall, the look that knows there are all these people here but they are not the *right* people—where have those right people gone? How can I get them to come back?

Under the hallway lights, I read the twins' palms in the way that Marcus taught me. From their thumbs, I can tell them about the division between will and logic and that they both fall on the side of will. The fingers of Saturn are longer than the fingers of Apollo. I can't find Sam's life line and instead of the truth I tell him his is as strong a line as I have ever seen.

That evening, the Pathologist's voice washes over the floors. I look up at the speakers, hopeful. I remember the evangelical church in Somerville and wonder if this is what it feels like to be called by God, to hear a voice and peer into the lights above and know at once what it is you're supposed to be doing with your life—which is, in my case, to proceed immediately to the Dining Hall.

In the Dining Hall, I find patients lining up for red trays. The line is straight and slow. There is no pushing, no laughing or screaming, no accusations of cutting. The windows are dark. Dr. Bek and the nurses stand against a wall, silent, watching. They have nothing to say to us. Already I can see our Floor Group cleaning the Common Room, erasing the evidence of what we've done.

Louis is there. He touches my hip. Together we fall into line.

I don't tell him what N5 said to me in the closet. Her words are too large and slippery to make the journey from thought, from memory, to speech.

The staff left us alone just long enough for us to imagine a life without their oversight, a life of hunger and bathroom tap water and an endless wait for spring and maybe even cannibalism. I read all about the Donner Party in the Hospital library: I know what hungry people can become capable of. We thought time moved slowly before, but it was nothing compared to the way time moved without exams and meals and activities and testing.

If you have no way to mark the hours, no variance in the days, time will open its mouth and swallow you.

· · ·

After Lights Out, I hear the same scratching sound next door, but this time I get out of bed and investigate. In the twins' room, I find the boys by the hole. Sam is holding a flashlight. Christopher is pecking at the ground with a big metal spoon, the kind of serving spoon I've seen before in the Dining Hall.

"Where did you get *that*?" I whisper.

"We stole it," the boys whisper back.

The medicine cabinet blocks the bathroom entrance. Linoleum squares are piled nearby like shed skin. Sam points the flashlight at the hole and I am astonished by the size. The opening is as large as a car tire. I move closer and feel grit on the bottoms of my feet and think about how long it's been since I've touched the outdoors.

I remember: snow in my eyelashes, grass sticking to my elbows, dirt on my knees.

The boys are crouched like rabbits around the hole, wide-eyed and pale. The freckles on their throats look like a spreading rash. Christopher holds the spoon in midair. I can hear their quick, panting breath. Sam shines the flashlight in my eyes and they become hidden behind a bright white wall.

"You can't leave." I raise a hand to block the glare. For starters, no one knows the keypad codes. For starters, the weather. The light stays on me and I try to find the boys in it.

I'm imagining a means of escape that is only passable by children, a path that gets tighter the longer you crawl, so what I really mean is: you can't leave me.

"We found our way out," Christopher says.

They lower the light. Translucent circles slip around in my

vision. I blink them away. From the sound of metal striking earth, I know the twins have gone back to digging.

• • •

In the middle of breakfast, we hear that familiar voice on the speakers. We let our plastic spoons sink into our oatmeal, gray and gummy from the microwave, and look up toward the noise.

THERE WILL BE NO MORE TV, the Pathologist tells us, and I know right away that this is not a meditation. Apparently the weather has made it impossible to fix the lines. He pauses, and there's a gurgling that is something like a cough or a growl or a person quietly drowning. AND BESIDES, he continues, DID YOU REALLY THINK THERE WOULD BE NO PENALTY FOR WHAT YOU'VE DONE?

Not one patient complains, or at least not out in the open. We're fearful of what else might be taken away.

13.

In the year before the sickness, Marcus began haunting the Stop & Shop. I don't know how else to explain it. He was no-where and everywhere at the same time, which is how I imagine ghosts to be.

At first, I worried something had happened to him, that this was a sign from the Beyond, and so in the break room at the Stop & Shop I sat down at the computer and entered his name into all the search engines. I looked for accidents and news articles and obituaries and I found nothing to suggest he was anything other than alive.

The haunting started around Halloween, when the masks we stocked at the Stop & Shop made me think only of him. When there were no customers to check out, I walked the Halloween aisle and looked at all the monsters staring back. One night I stuffed a vampire mask into my coat pocket and took it home.

On the bus, I kept a hand on the rubber face twisted up in my pocket. I watched the people sitting low in their seats and leaning their heads against the windows, sick with exhaustion, giving in to it. Others passengers played their music so loud, lyrics spilled from headphones, into the open air, like they were trying to shock themselves awake with sound. I listened and sometimes I liked what I heard.

My favorites: Michael Jackson, Madonna, David Bowie, Ghostface Killah.

In my bathroom, I took a few capfuls of Robitussin and put the mask on. The skin was green, the eyebrows tiny black pyramids, the tips of the teeth red with blood. I tied a black sheet around my shoulders and in the mirror I watched the movement of the thing that was no longer a sheet but a cape. I bared my fangs at my own reflection. I stuck out a hand and said, "Pleased to meet you."

When I was out on my own, I could have gone looking for Marcus, but I didn't. I let the purple grow out of my hair, like a snake shedding its skin, and tried to forget. I told myself that I was used to impermanence, that attachments would get me exactly nowhere, but then some people stay with you in ways you don't expect and you try to shake them out, shake them away, but your memory won't let you.

In my apartment, I wore the mask and drank Robitussin all through winter.

In March, there was road construction. I had to take a different route, multiple buses. We passed an abandoned warehouse, the walls charred with weather and age, and I remembered the new construction I used to see through the bus window, the silver skeleton rising from the ground.

A string of teenagers on bikes, standing up on the pedals and leaning over the handlebars, calling to each other. How I admired the looseness in their posture, the freedom. In Chinatown, neon yellow signs with indecipherable red lettering and a restaurant with a fish tank in the window. Steam rose from the manholes.

The bus growled behind a sluggish line of cars, in a gray swirl of exhaust.

Downtown I had to change buses. I was sitting up in my seat, my Stop & Shop apron folded in my lap, my nametag pinned to the neck string, when through the window I saw a man in a lion mask on a street corner. He was standing tall, his hands behind his back. The mask had a plastic wave of golden mane, a black nose, a pink tongue. I turned in my seat. I pressed my palms against the window. When the bus stopped, I rushed outside. I did not go to my next stop, but back to that corner in Chinatown, which was empty except for the rising steam and the silver fish darting around in the window across the street.

■ ■ ■

The last time it happened we were on the edge of spring. I remember the slush, the tentative green, the break in the bitter cold. At work, it was two in the morning and my manager was on a smoke break. A cashier had called in sick. I was the only one on the floor and I hadn't checked out a customer since midnight. For hours the same half-dozen pop songs had been playing on a loop. I didn't want to know the words, but was remembering them anyway.

I walked around Produce and petted the rough fur of coconuts and squeezed kiwis and examined items I had never eaten before, like kumquats and kohlrabi. The kohlrabi was a green bulb. I thought about stealing one and eating it like an apple in my apartment. I was pinching a kumquat when I saw a person swoop around a corner and down Canned Goods. There was something strange about their face. I followed them.

We went down Canned Goods and up Dry Packaged Goods and down Condiments & Sauces. I kept some distance between us, squeezing the kumquat. This person didn't stop and examine the shelves. They weren't pushing a cart or carrying a basket. They didn't appear to be shopping for anything. They were just walking.

Each time they rounded a corner, I caught a glimpse of their face. The skin was unnaturally smooth and white, the expression vacant, like the mask of a horror movie villain I was having trouble placing. I should have been scared, should have taken this masked person as a sign of an impending robbery or worse, but instead I followed them through Baking Supplies and Cereals and Health & Beauty. There was familiarity in their posture, their gait.

I lost the person in the cold labyrinth of Frozens. "Marcus," I said at last, testing the possibility. I let go of the kumquat and it rolled across the white floor. My palm smelled of citrus. I ran around the store, checking all the aisles and the bathrooms. I went outside and stood under the lights that attracted fluttering clouds of moths. The parking lot was empty. The person was gone.

At home I drank enough Robitussin for me to pass out in my bathroom. I woke in a puddle of vomit that had hardened into a sour glue on the floor, my brain thumping inside my skull.

■ ■ ■

The last time I rode the bus, I sat across from a woman with a Seeing Eye dog. The dog had a golden coat and wore a bright yellow vest. He sat perfectly still, like he rode in buses all the time, which I suppose he did. When we passed the evangelical church, the dog started to lick my hand. The woman gave the leash a little yank, but the dog kept on licking. Summer was here; the days had gotten long again. I had stopped seeing signs of Marcus and tried to think as little as possible about what that might mean. I did not know that in a few weeks, the sickness would be all over the news and a hazmatted man with a carnation in his lapel would come to tell me about the Hospital, the first time I had ever been chosen for anything that could be called special. That my life would soon be burned down to a stub. Now I wonder what Clara Sue Borden was doing while I was riding that bus, a dog licking the salt from my arm with its long, rough tongue. Had she already started to feel a strange roughness on her skin, a fuzziness around the edges of her memory?

14.

I wake to voices in the hallway. The pitches shoot up and down. In my half-sleep I see a heart monitor screen and neon lines jumping around from LIVING to DEAD. I stare up at the white ceiling and listen. I roll around and get trapped in my sheets. When I hear Dr. Bek, I kick my way out of bed. He is rarely on the fifth floor in the mornings.

"Louis, wake up. Something's going on."

He sits up and his pale hair falls across his forehead in a way that makes my heart pound.

"Something's always going on," he says, yawning wide.

We go into the hall. The overhead lights are bright white. The door to the twins' room is open. Dr. Bek is in there, questioning the nurses from our floor. I look at the three of them standing by the beds, large and huffing and helpless. Next to them is a small tower of linoleum squares and a dark, gaping hole. "Have you looked in the basement?" he's asking, his blue eyes flitting around behind the shield. "Have you checked all the storage closets?"

Right away I know what's happened. The twins are gone.

. . .

An Emergency Community Meeting is called. All the patients are broken into pairs and each pair is assigned a part of the Hospital to search. Our Group gets floor eight. No one gets floors one or ten. There is no mention of the hole.

The eighth floor is residential, like ours: the long hallway, the arched window at one end, the smooth white walls, the row of closed doors. But since the eighth floor is unoccupied, the knobs on these doors don't turn. Faces, ashen from months spent inside, don't peek out into the hall.

I don't like this ghost version of our floor. I don't like the emptiness, the reminder of what the Hospital will be like after we are gone, dead or released from our contracts. I touch the walls as we pass, imagining I'm leaving my DNA behind. On the speakers, the Pathologist is calling the boys' names. Other patients are opening the doors to the supply closets and rummaging around inside.

Louis and I go into every room. All the beds have been stripped, leaving behind metal frames and green rubber mattresses. White sheets are folded on the mattresses, like patients have just departed or the Hospital is expecting imminent arrivals. On our countdown calendar, the bird for January is the snowy egret, which has feathers that spring from its body like a long fringe, but there are no calendars on these walls. In the bathrooms the little motes between the shower tiles are thick with black mildew, the mirrors bordered with rust. We shout "Sam!" and "Christopher!" and our voices refract back at us in a way that makes me sick with fear.

I don't think the twins are here, on this floor, but they are just kids and they have to be hiding out somewhere. We have more rooms to search. We keep going.

At the very end of the hallway, we find a room that has been turned into some kind of storage area. A hospital bed in full recline is parked in the corner. Brown boxes, the cardboard tongues flapping, have been pushed underneath. Tall rolls of plastic sheeting lean against walls, ready to be unfurled into the casings that surround the sick. Empty IV bags hang from metal stands like withered organs. Clear tubes are coiled on the ground and on the mattress and on top of the boxes. Death requires a lot of equipment, we are learning.

I remember Christina, the beeping of her monitors and the squares of flesh-colored tape holding the needles in her veins and the long pauses between her breaths. Her ransacked memory. The years of silence and secrets.

We lived in the same city and she never once thought to claim me, not until she was almost out of time.

Louis and I step into the room. We close the door behind us. This is the last place we have left to search; there is no sign of the twins here or anywhere else on this floor. I see us retreating downstairs and hearing all about how another patient found the boys in the basement or in the library, reading up on the Hawaiian alphabet, or in some remote corner of the Dining Hall.

Behind the door, against another wall, we find a tall tape recorder with two circles that stare out at us like eyes. Louis and I sit in front of it. There are rows of buttons and dials. I press a square button.

Static, Dr. Bek reciting a date, a woman's voice. The voice sounds familiar, like a voice we used to hear around the Hospital, but it is not one I hear anymore and so I know this woman must be dead.

Tell me a memory, Dr. Bek says on the tape, and the woman answers, *One morning, he stared at me for a long time and said, "You look like a woman I used to know, maybe from the grocery," and I said, "What do you mean 'used to know' and what do you mean 'gro-*

cery'?" and he said I looked so familiar, he was sure I'd been bagging his groceries for years, if only he could remember my name. After two decades of marriage he said these things. That's when I knew he was forgetting.

These are the intake interviews we did when we first came to the Hospital. I did not know we were being taped.

I remember this thing I read in a magazine, the woman continues. *It was about a village in Greenland where all the residents have dementia. They go to the grocery and feed birds in the park and go to the theater. They get lost and miraculously there is always someone to help with directions. They are being watched all the time, but they have no idea. They have no idea they are stuck in a very pleasant kind of trap. I remember looking at my husband and wishing there was a place like that for us.* She pauses. I hear the sound of papers being shuffled. *Is that where we are now? In some sort of pleasant trap?*

Louis and I haven't been together since that morning in our room, haven't talked about how it felt, if we want to do it again, but being in this strange room with him reminds me of our early days, when we traveled the floors and halls together. It reminds him of something too, because under the lights he clamps an arm around my shoulder and I feel the damp of his mouth along the hot curve of my ear.

After we fucked, I didn't shower for days, desperate to keep the smell of him.

I'm startled to hear the twins' voices. I look around, thinking for a moment that they're somewhere in the room, but then I realize they've just taken over the recording, already going on about Hawaii, about the birds they will find there, Christopher talking over his brother. *The starlings*, he is saying. *The nightjars. The bitterns.*

"Why Paige?" I pull away from Louis. This is the question I've wanted to ask him since the fall, but I didn't and I couldn't because I was scared of the answer. I expect him to say there was always something about me that seemed defective. "Why not me?"

He looks down at the patch of white linoleum between his legs. "I liked the way she ran, I guess. I liked that she was doing something instead of waiting around here like the rest of us."

He does not know about my mother, about all the work I have been doing in my mind.

"I'm planning to do a lot," I say.

When I hear my own voice on the tape, I go to turn off the recorder, but Louis stops me. Before the interview, I stayed in motion. I drank my Robitussin. I refused to absorb all that had happened. The sickness. Christina, memoryless in her plastic tent. My mother. There was something about Dr. Bek's dark little office and the wheeze of his hazmat and the Venn chair and the sea cliffs poster that put everything into focus. It was like running into a wall. My life was a wreck, had been seething with a sickness that was beyond what any doctor could cure, and I had agreed to spend ten months in a Hospital and I might live or I might die. During the interview, you can only hear Dr. Bek's questions—*Don't you have memories, Joy? Do you remember what a memory is?*—and, if you listen closely, a woman sobbing. During that first meeting, I wasn't able to say a word.

■ ■ ■

We drift back down to the fifth floor. Some of the patients have congregated in the Dining Hall, even though it's not a mealtime. They are sitting at the long tables or on the floor under the windows, in pale cones of light. They have all finished searching their assigned areas. No one has seen the twins. Nightfall is slow to come to the Hospital. From the window, the eventual moon is fat and white and sunk behind banks of cloud. I want to run through the Hospital shouting: Come on out! Everyone gets found eventually.

. . .

The twins do not get found. They stay missing.

That night, in our beds, we hear the sound of the nurses moving up and down the hallways, and in the morning the pairs of patients are sent to look around the Hospital once more. This time Louis and I get the library. I comb the pages of the encyclopedias for clues. I examine the book on space travel.

The nurses venture out in the Hospital vans and search the land around us. Our Floor Group stands by the arched window and watches two vans move like white bullets over the snow. We all find nothing and more nothing. After the twins have been missing for three days, Dr. Bek calls a Community Meeting and explains that he has contacted the local authorities in La Harpe and they are doing what they can from the outside. They are searching too. Dogs are getting involved.

He tells us that we are not giving up on finding the boys, but not all questions have immediate answers. Life in the Hospital must continue on.

I feel Dr. Bek's breath travel down my skin. I feel something in the Hospital tilt. The possibilities, the rules of what can and cannot happen to us, are being rearranged.

The nurses stand by the window, facing away from the Floor Groups, so we can only see their humped backs. I imagine they are still looking.

Every patient has a theory. In our Floor Group, they include: falling through frozen ice; getting lost on the plains and maybe they are still out there, wandering through winter; they made it to La Harpe and were taken in by a townsperson; they made it to La Harpe and were abducted off the street; dematerialization;

bears; they never left the Hospital, they are trapped somewhere inside; Hawaii.

What each theory reveals: how much hope the theorizer has left.

Raul says that maybe the twins were never here, maybe we have been driven mad by winter and started seeing things and then stopped seeing those things. Maybe something inside *us* has gone missing. I know this theory is the most untrue—how do you explain the hole and the drawings on the walls?—but the idea of our minds playing such a powerful trick scares me.

"Hawaii," I whisper when I'm alone.

An absence, an unanswered question, is not the same as a death, not the same as what happened to Marie, and I'm starting to think that in some ways it's worse. A death without closure.

I spend most of my time by a window, any window, waiting to see the boys emerge from the land.

As the days pass, word about the twins' hole gets out. It moves through our Floor Group and despite the KEEP OUT sign that has been taped to their door, I start seeing white and green bodies slipping in and out of their room. I find faint trails of dirt leading into the hall. In the eyes of the patients, I detect a new kind of aliveness. An unspoken question spreads like a germ through the air: is it possible for *me* to leave too?

■ ■ ■

After Lights Out, after Louis has fallen asleep, I listen for the sound of the twins digging next door, but of course there is nothing. The wait for morning becomes unbearably long.

One night, I catch a different kind of sound through the walls—a strange buzzing. I get up and go to the twins' room. The air in the Hospital is still and yet the edges of the KEEP OUT sign flutter.

The hole has been covered with a black tarp. The beds have been stripped, white sheets folded on green mattresses, like the vacant rooms on the eighth floor. The drawings are still hanging on the walls and I'm glad it's too dark for me to see the ghost of Waialae Avenue, who has nothing better to do than drive women insane.

The buzzing sound is coming from the hole. I kneel in front of it and push away the tarp. The floor is covered in grit. There's dust and darkness and a metallic smell—not the earthy scent of dirt, but chemicals. The silver body of the air-conditioning duct snakes below the opening. If I reach into the hole, I can almost touch it. Warm air gusts onto my face. The buzzing is even louder up close, like construction is happening somewhere in the Hospital.

Could that one theory be right? Could the twins still be trapped in here?

"Sam?" I say into the hole. "Christopher?"

The buzzing gets louder. It opens a door in the side of my head and walks right into my brain. I wonder if the twins heard this sound when they lowered themselves into the tunnel, if it became unbearable as they moved through the duct, if they still had the noise ringing in their ears as they ran out into the snow.

15.

One morning, in the first week of February, I look out the arched window and see a pilgrim standing outside the Hospital. He is the first person to come since the start of winter. He is standing on a bank of ice. His face is wrapped in a black scarf. Only his eyes are visible and I am too far away to tell what kind of eyes they are. His hands are covered in mittens so thick, they look like bandages. He reminds me of the photos I have seen of men trekking through distant deserts, their heads swathed in cloth to protect them from the sun.

This pilgrim is holding something in his arms. This something looks long and heavy.

I squint. A swirl of human hair, a bare foot.

He is holding a body. He is holding a child.

"Nurse," I hear myself say, but I can't move from the window. I touch the glass and feel the burn of the cold.

Other patients come to the window. The faces around me are pale blurs. They press their hands against the glass and look and look and then one of them runs away shouting, "Let him in let him in let him in!"

I watch nurses in hazmats pour out of the Hospital. They trudge through the snow, their white arms flapping. The pilgrim skids down the bank of ice. One of the nurses takes the pilgrim by the shoulders and another touches the body and then they all start rushing back toward the Hospital. In the arms of the pilgrim, the body is still in a way that lets me know the child is no longer alive. Everyone, even the pilgrim, disappears inside.

I imagine a chill moving across a person's skin and into their veins. I imagine the veins delivering the chill like poison to the lungs and spleen and heart. All those soft squishy places that want to stay warm. The person runs and sweats, a comfort until the wet fabric turns to ice on their ribs and they forget how exactly running is supposed to work. They can feel their body temperature dropping, a machine shutting down. They think about going back, to the place where people do experiments with blood, where they know they will be welcomed, because they still have blood to give. They turn around, look at the endless white field behind them, and realize the way back has become a mystery. They are getting very sleepy. They lie down under a tree. They imagine the tree is a house and they are climbing through a window and getting warm by a fire or a stove or a bearskin rug with the head still on and the mouth open like this rug has been waiting its whole life to eat someone. *Hawaii*, they keep saying to each other, trying to ignore the hungry bearskin rug, until they can't feel anything, not their tongues drying up in their mouths, not their slowing hearts, not their eyes that flicker like a wild, trapped animal until they stop.

In the hallway a patient screams and it takes me a second to realize the screaming person is me.

16.

I run straight into our room. I shut myself in the bathroom. Get in the shower stall and turn the water on. Listen to the water beat the tile. Sit on the floor in my scrubs and feel the cold spray. I turn my body into a tight ball to keep everything from shaking loose. I want to drown out the sound of me.

From the window I was too far away to know if the body should be called Christopher or Sam.

. . .

I don't know how long I'm in the shower before Louis pulls back the curtain and turns off the water and tries to get me to come out. At first I won't break the tight ball of my body, because I am afraid of what will happen if I do. He sits next to me in the shower stall and touches my wet knee. The toes of his slippers are soggy.

He starts explaining about how I missed the Emergency Community Meeting, missed Dr. Bek saying that they have no choice but to admit the pilgrim to the Hospital, that releasing him back into the world was not an option. I missed the way the meeting broke up, with Dr. Bek turning away from the patients, toward the window, and releasing a long and shuddering sigh, a rare admission of defeat.

The pilgrim was carrying Sam. He died from exposure. He was killed by the weather. I think of the slides Dr. Bek showed us, of the house that was being eaten by winter. Christopher is still out there and this pilgrim is the only person who knows where he is.

Right now the nurses are conducting a full examination in the basement. They are preparing him to meet us.

In the shower, my palms are fixed to the wet floor and there is an awful pressure in my chest.

"Joy," he says. "Can you hear me?"

My hair is dripping. Everything is dripping. My scrubs are stuck to my skin. It sounds like he's speaking to me through a wall.

I shake my head. I feel the cold of the tiles on the back of my scalp, taste the salt of snot.

"Joy." He lets go of my knee. "The pilgrim is coming upstairs."

■ ■ ■

The patients clot in the fifth-floor hallway. I listen to the coughs and sniffs, to the slipper soles scratching the white floors. Some patients stand in the middle of the hall, their arms crossed, others lean against the walls. Patients from Group four take turns punching the dead elevator buttons to pass the time. Louis and I keep watching the stairwell door, the unlit exit sign. We are in a fog of disbelief. No one from the outside has ever been let into the Hospital before.

It takes a long time for the nurses to bring the pilgrim up. We whisper and nudge as he emerges from the stairwell, into the blistering fluorescent light. He pauses under the exit sign, starts moving toward us.

He's wearing slippers and scrubs like the rest of us, like he's never been anything but a patient, except he smells of the rankest part of nature. The nurses trudge behind him, a white hissing mass. The pilgrim hunches inside his scrubs. His slippers drag against the floor. His hands have been unwrapped, revealing slivers of pink oozing skin. His fingernails are black crescents. Matted gray hair coats his arms and the back of his neck. His eyes are beady and dark. Reptilian.

Louis is standing next to me. I hold on to his arm. The lights pour down on us, bleach out our skin. The ends of my hair are still damp.

The patients part to make room for the pilgrim. We don't say anything. We step aside. He stops in the middle of the hall, the nurses breathing on one end, Dr. Bek breathing on the other, the patients all around him, flashes of white wall visible between our bodies. He looks very tired, but he does not look afraid. A red cut pulses along the side of his throat.

He knows what we want to know and before we can even ask he starts telling us about finding the boys lying together in the snow, in the shadow of a tree. Icicles hung from the branches like rows of teeth. Their eyes were closed. Their bodies were wrapped in white sheets, their feet in pillowcases. Their hair shone with ice. At first he thought he was hallucinating—from a distance they looked like mummies—but then he touched their cheeks and they became instantly real. He checked for breath and found only the worst silence. These children were wearing scrubs and he knew they must have come from the Hospital, the very place he was trying to find.

"I tried to bring them both back to you," the pilgrim tells us. He stretches out his arms like that second child, that left-behind child, might appear in the empty space. "But I could only carry the one."

17.

Without the twins, life in the Hospital feels stiller, quieter, like a creature that's been stunned. The nurses are silent during our morning exams. They forget to mark the days on our calendar and we don't remind them. They rush through the Romberg. The needle is not a gentle slide, but a jab. N5 never brings up what she said in the closet and I don't know how to ask.

I start to cry one morning as she prepares to take my blood. My veins are swollen and throbbing. You're taking too much from us, I want to tell her, but instead I just say, "No," and hide my arm behind my back like a stubborn child. She takes my wrist and straightens my arm. She ties the rubber around my biceps and the needle finds its way in.

With the pilgrim's guidance, two nurses drive out into the plains in search of Christopher. I imagine the nurses leaving the van and creeping through the land in their hazmat suits, the careful crunch of their steps, the echo of their breath slipping around the trees. Their long, strange shadows. Will the animals see them? What will they think? From the arched window, our Floor Group watches the van make its way back to the Hospital. The windshield gleams. The black tires spin on the snow.

The nurses unload a small blue body bag from the back of the van. Olds and Older whimper, clasp their hands to their mouths and turn away. Dense cottony clouds loom in the sky.

The patients stop asking questions at Community Meetings. No one shows up for morning yoga or Saturday night movies. The nurses turn on the videos at the appointed times and end up sitting on the empty couch, watching the hero charge through a blaze of gunfire or yoga people twist their bodies in ways that would be impossible in the suits.

Not a single patient continues to entertain the idea of escape.

The pilgrim is named Rick and he came all the way from Eugene, Oregon, to find us. He is assigned to our Floor Group.

Curtis has an empty bed in his room, so he and Rick become roommates. Curtis tells us that in the mornings he finds Rick not in his bed, but asleep on the floor, bundled up in his sheets. He's caught him pissing in a corner. He saw his bright white ass. Once he woke in the night and Rick was standing at the foot of his bed. He was just looking at Curtis. And whistling.

"Whistling what?" I ask.

"I don't know," Curtis says. "Country western, it sounded like."

It is the afternoon. Our bellies are full from lunch.

"The point here is that to be a cop means to be an excellent judge of character," Curtis tells our Floor Group. "And that guy is not right at all." He points at Rick, who is standing alone at the other end of the hallway, staring at a white wall.

We have to show Rick how to use the microwaves in the Dining Hall. Without our help, he finds these machines confusing. When it is time for us to clean, we have to show Rick how to wipe the handprints and scuff marks from the Common Room walls. At first, we talk to him as little as possible, because we can't look at him without seeing Sam's body in his arms.

I try to focus on my mother, on leaving the Hospital and finding her, but that lost feeling is creeping back. I walk the Hospital until my feet are numb, hoping the numbness will spread. I keep to the lit hallways. I stay away from the ghost floors and the basement. I keep visiting the hole at night and stay long enough for the buzzing to make my eardrums burn. I feel on the brink of seeing the Hospital's inner machinery, its lungs and guts and heart. Its secrets.

One night the light from the hall splashes on the wall, on the drawing of Waialae Avenue, and I see the red headless figure floating toward me.

In my room, I pull my mother's photo from my pillowcase and find myself in the slight droop in the corners of her eyes and in the curves of her nostrils. During an Internet Session, I watch a video of her standing on her ship deck, explaining an electrical phenomenon called St. Elmo's fire, not uncommon on ships before a storm. In the video, St. Elmo's is why all the antennae on her ship are glowing blue. I pause on an image of my mother standing near one of the antennae. Her head is tilted back, showing off the elegance of her neck. Her mouth is open and dark. Above her the bright blue end of the antenna looks like a hot poker or a magic wand.

■ ■ ■

At dinner, Rick sits with our Floor Group because he is supposed to be one of us now. I tell Rick that I've never been to Oregon before and ask what it's like there. He says it's big and empty and filled with rivers and forests and wild animals and rain. I think it sounds beautiful and frightening, Oregon.

I watch him eat rice and beans covered in a thick black sauce, and wonder how this compares to what he's been eating outside the Hospital walls.

We listen to stories of Rick's travels. He's slept on roadsides and in fields and in barns. He's been soaked with rain and waded through waist-deep snow. He's killed fish with sticks and eaten them raw, felt their flesh shiver in his throat. He's hitchhiked with people who let him sleep in the backseat and people who wanted to talk through the night and people who wanted to steal.

"Do you want to know the Laws of the Road?" he asks us, and then keeps going before anyone has a chance to answer.

I want to know about these laws.

The Laws of the Road include: Never turn down food or water. Lose your shame about what you are willing to eat. Never underestimate the usefulness of a towel. Lose your shame about where you go to the bathroom. The older the car, the better your chance of hitching a ride. Solo hitchhikers have better odds than those in pairs or groups. Avoid vans. Believe in your ability to keep walking forever. Lose your shame about where you sleep, but never fall asleep around strangers. Only sleep when you're alone.

I want to know more, but other patients are less interested in the Laws of the Road. They cut in and ask Rick why he came here, how he found us.

Rick frowns. "Don't you know about the chat room?"

We shake our heads. We know nothing about a chat room.

According to Rick, there is a chat room devoted entirely to the Hospital, to the special ones who have been hidden away for study. In this chat room, people share stories about the early days of the sickness, a person in a hazmat coming to their neighbor's door and that neighbor disappearing—not dying, but going to some other mysterious place. In this chat room, there are rumors about a state psychiatric hospital in Kansas that has found a use again.

We lean back in our chairs, absorb this new information.

"I didn't get sick," Rick explains. "I knew this place was where I belonged."

"But the sickness is over," I say. "This isn't the only safe place anymore."

Rick laughs, his tongue black from the sauce.

"Nothing is over," he says.

The Pathologist's voice seeps into the room. A meditation. BREATHE DEEPLY THREE TIMES AND SAY I AM DOING JUST FINE.

All the patients in our Floor Group rest their hands on the table and take three breaths. Even Rick plays along.

"I am doing just fine," we all say to each other, like that part of church where you turn to the congregants and say *peace be with you*, though I am starting to wonder if the Hospital is doing us about as much good as church—which is to say not much good at all.

. . .

I decide to start keeping my mandatory appointments with Dr. Bek, the ones I have been ignoring since the fall. I am drowning in questions. From the doorway of his office, I tell him that I want to start coming to my appointments, but first I want him to promise me something: no more electroencephalogram, no more tests. I just want to talk.

Dr. Bek is sitting at his desk. Behind him the Troll Wall rises through the fog.

"You don't think talking is a test?"

He doesn't look up from his computer screen. He moves the mouse around on a black pad. I wonder if he knows about what N5 said to me in the closet.

"I know things about this place," I say.

"I'm aware you *think* you know things," Dr. Bek says.

Finally he looks up and sits back in his chair. "Do you remember the appointment time you were given when you first came here? The one you have chosen all these months to ignore?"

I nod. "After lunch on Thursdays."

"Come back then," he says, and returns to looking at whatever is on the screen.

18.

After lunch on Thursday, I go to Dr. Bek's office. I sink down into the Venn chair. There is no sign of the electroencephalogram. He folds his gloved hands on his desk and begins in Oslo.

"In Oslo, there is a hospital that sits on a hill. It overlooks the water, the inner Oslofjord. In 1985, I was a much younger man. That year, Arne Treholt, a Norwegian politician, went on trial for spying. He had smuggled classified materials to the KGB and the Iraqis—not enough to sell our secrets to just one country. In the break room at the hospital, the trial was always on the news. I was fascinated by the case because Arne Treholt looked just like my father."

I can't imagine what all this has to do with our Hospital.

"What happened to him?" I ask.

"He was sentenced to twenty years, out in a decade. He moved to Cyprus and started writing books." He leans forward in his chair, his suit groaning. "If you are asking about what happened to my father, that is a story for another time."

I didn't mean to ask about his father; I always think of mothers first.

Dr. Bek tells me about other things that happened that year in Norway. Parliamentary elections were held. A volcano on the Norwegian island of Jan Mayen erupted. He seems to enjoy talking about Norway, about home.

Jan Mayen has a nice sound to it. Maybe one day I would like to live in a place called Jan Mayen.

"I've never seen a volcano before," I tell Dr. Bek.

"I know." His mouth stays open and I see the damp mass of his tongue.

In 1985, he was thirty years old. In 1985, he got married and went to work at this hospital. It is not, however, the year when the most important part of this story takes place.

• • •

"The hospital on the hill was not a place where people went to get well," Dr. Bek tells me during our next appointment. It was a hospital for people with troubled minds, troubles that could not ever be cured. He had been working at the hospital for seven years when a young woman with Creutzfeldt-Jakob was admitted.

In the beginning, this woman noticed herself stumbling more than usual. The toe of her shoe was always catching on the bottom stair or on patches of uneven sidewalk. When she woke, she was stiff as an old lady. All day the muscles in her legs twitched. She stopped sleeping. She grew confused. She tried to go to the grocery store in the middle of the night. At the bank, she could not remember her own address. Her speech turned thick and slow and she screamed at her husband, accused him of getting her drunk. She was admitted to an emergency room after she collapsed in a museum.

It was fall in Oslo, the season for picking berries and mushrooms, the season when the waters of the inner Oslofjord protect the city from the cold.

In the emergency room, the doctors performed a spinal tap and discovered the 14-3-3 protein, which suggested Creutzfeldt-Jakob. The diagnosis was supported by an MRI. One doctor described her diseased brain as a spider web where the threads were being pulled apart until they snapped. No one knew the cause: it wasn't hereditary, as a small amount of Creutzfeldt-Jakob cases are, and infection by contamination, like a medical procedure or tainted food, was unlikely. She had never had an operation. She had not left Norway in fifteen years. It was sporadic Creutzfeldt-Jakob, where the cause is a mystery.

After the diagnosis, she was sent to this hospital on the hill to die, which was expected to take four to eight weeks. She was twenty-eight years old, and there was nothing anyone could do for her. At least in this hospital, the nurses could roll her wheelchair to a window and she could look out at the water, if she was still able to remember what water was.

"She spent her days in bed or in the wheelchair, parked in front of the window, her arms trembling," Dr. Bek tells me. "One eye drooped shut, and it looked like she was winking. She went days without speaking and when she did speak, her speech slurred like a drunk's. "Sleep" sounded like "Shhheep." "You" sounded like "Fooo." I had not the faintest idea what was happening inside her mind, what she remembered, and by then I had been married to this woman for the better part of a decade."

I hold tight to the arms of the Venn chair.

One day another doctor at the hospital, a man in a senior position, took an interest in his wife. As a young man, he had studied psychosomatic medicine with a famous German doctor, who would ask a patient with a broken arm why he no longer wanted to have use of his arm or ask a patient with a flu what he hoped the fever was going to sweat out. He believed the body followed the orders of the unconscious mind.

If your unconscious mind wishes you to be well, you are well. If it wishes you to be sick, you become sick. If it wishes you to die, you die.

"If a patient's unconscious mind has turned against her, the patient must turn it right back around," Dr. Bek tells me.

This doctor asked permission to apply the treatments he learned in Germany. He said doctors had been studying psycho-somatic medicine since the Middle Ages and even though the contemporary medical community was skeptical, he for one took comfort in practices that had lasted so long. He started coming to check her vitals, her coordination and reflexes; at first the re-sults were dire and unchanging, but he insisted that wasn't im-portant: what was important was his wife believing she was being treated, that there was the possibility of a cure. He mas-saged her hands and feet daily. Her room was divided by a thin curtain. On the other side, a man was dying of Alzheimer's. She was moved to a room where, on the other side of the curtain, a man, one of the few patients who would ever leave this hospital, was nearly recovered from a bout of cholera. A private nurse was assigned to his wife, a pretty young woman in a white uniform who sat with her and told her how healthy she was starting to look, how she would soon be well. With a warm washcloth, the nurse kept her skin moist and clean. She trimmed her fingernails and brushed her hair. In the wheelchair, she took her for long outings all around the hospital.

In the winter, Dr. Bek expected to bury his wife, but the snow began to fall in Oslo and she was still alive. The treatments continued. The senior doctor was pleased. She began saying one or two words daily. Her sagging eye peeped open. One afternoon, when Dr. Bek stopped the wheelchair in front of a window, she raised a hand toward a distant ship and said, "Sail." Her arm trembled, but her voice was clear.

During his visits, the senior doctor would tell her that she was winning the fight against her unconscious mind, against the enemy within, the one that had been trying so hard to kill her, and she would lower her bottom lip into an uneven smile.

After two years, she slipped into a coma and died. It was far more time than anyone had a right to expect. A miracle, everyone in the hospital declared, even though Dr. Bek knew it was no miracle at all. It was the work of this doctor and the way he had convinced her mind to help her body.

"In Oslo, I learned that, in the fight against illness, the mind is the most powerful weapon at our disposal."

He tells me the Hospital patients were chosen not only because of our immunity, but because we had all endured trauma; we should have died a dozen times over and here we sit. We should be desperate to forget and yet our unconscious minds want us to remember, to stay alive. On behalf of the Hospital, private investigators studied our records—DCS reports, medical histories, court filings, credit ratings—in order to select the right sample, though Dr. Bek had the final say on who would come.

"Take you, for example." Behind the face shield his eyelids, laced with blue veins, flutter. "Abandoned on the steps of a hospital. In winter, no less. Raised in all those strange places, with all those strange people. Drugging yourself unconscious every chance you got."

Did he know our trauma would keep us from forming a cohesive rebellion? Keep us from doing more than standing around like dazed cattle? That we could be volatile, maybe even dangerous, but in the end have little faith in our ability to make anything better.

You aren't the first person to do experiments on me, I want to tell him, but maybe he already knows.

Dr. Bek stops. He releases a long breath and it sounds like something is being deflated.

"If I say you are a patient, you are a patient. If I say I am a doctor who will cure you, I am a doctor who will cure you. If I say there is a pathologist examining your blood, there is a pathologist examining your blood. At the hospital, this has been our philosophy, our way of reaching the unconscious mind."

I'm still sitting in the Venn chair, my feet planted on the floor, swimming with information. I realize two things:

First, Dr. Bek hasn't just been talking about Oslo. He has been talking about this Hospital too. They do not have a cure here and they are not in the process of creating one. Rather they are hoping that with the right encouragement, the right kind of help, we will be able to cure ourselves.

Second, I do the math. Dr. Bek's wife was still a young woman when she got sick, not so much older than me, and I understand that he is telling me this story about the kind of person, the kind of doctor, he has chosen to be, because he never got a chance to tell it to her.

■ ■ ■

That night, I dream of Jan Mayen. I'm standing on a tiny island in the middle of the sea, in sand the color of bone. There are people moving through this bone-colored sand with plastic bags over their heads and I think that one of them is Marcus. I try to find him by looking at everyone's palms, picking up one soft, warm hand after another and reading the lines, but they all look the same; I will never find him. In the distance, a volcano rumbles.

When I wake up, I'm not in my bed, but in our closet, hidden behind the legs of Louis's scrubs, panting in the dark.

. . .

Apart from my mother, there is only one other person I've searched for on the Death List. I checked for Marcus during my first week in the Hospital and could not find him on either list, not the one for the living or the one for the dead.

. . .

On my third meeting with Dr. Bek, there is no more talk of Oslo. The room feels colder. In the Venn chair, my skin hardens under my scrubs and I start shivering like I'm outside in the snow. This time, Dr. Bek doesn't start with a story, but by sliding a manila folder across his desk, toward me.

I look at the folder, so thin and ordinary, for a while before opening it. Inside I find sheets of paper with all the patient names, divided into two columns. I close the folder.

"There are two kinds of patients here," Dr. Bek tells me. "Those who are immune and those who have tested positive but remain asymptomatic. They will present sometime during the ten-month window." He touches the silver throat of his suit. "The hospital is the last home they will ever know."

I feel the chair sink into the floor, as though the Hospital is absorbing me into its structure, pulling me into that deep-down place where the buzzing comes from, where the incinerator burns. Dr. Bek's voice grows distant and I think maybe I am just returning from one of those in-between spaces I slip into sometimes and any second now I will blink and Louis will be there, tapping my wrist, trying to bring me back.

"I hope you understand why these lists must remain confidential," Dr. Bek continues, and suddenly the Venn chair is sitting normally on the floor and nothing about him is distant at all. "Any hope of success depended on them believing, first consciously and then unconsciously, in their own survival, in their ability to keep remembering."

The folder has become inevitable. I open it again and begin to read the names. Louis and I are separated: he is in one column; I'm in the other. My column is much shorter than his. Clustered around his name I see the names of patients who have died and then the print goes blurry and I think maybe I won't be sitting up in this chair for much longer.

"We've been trying to learn all that we can. The dormancy alone is a miracle. How can they stay asymptomatic for so long? Can the window be extended? Can they be cured?"

He pauses again. His cheeks are bright with sweat.

"We had hoped that the immune patients, like you, Joy, would help show the others how to live, present them with a contagious model of health, but that hasn't quite gone as planned, has it?"

I think of Louis roaming the Hospital, soaked in fluorescence, time ticking down inside of him, and feel my stomach rise.

"This is our last appointment," Dr. Bek says. "It ends in five minutes."

I slap the arms of the Venn chair.

"How do you know I won't tell everyone what you've done?" The folder is sitting in my lap and I'm afraid to keep touching the pages. They feel contaminated. "How do you know I won't run out there and tell everyone the truth?"

Dr. Bek's silver suit makes a strange whistling noise.

"It takes a certain kind of person to look into the eyes of another and tell them their life will soon be ending. Are you that kind of person, Joy?"

"Maybe," I say, because the truth is I'm still trying to understand what kind of person to be. "Maybe I am exactly that kind of person."

He looks at me, his eyes wide and patient behind the shield, like he is trying to teach me a lesson I am being very slow to learn. He makes a steeple with his gloved hands.

"It will not feel unnatural to keep the information I've shared between us. Some people would be burning to tell, but secrecy is your natural state. You are used to keeping them—secrets from other people, secrets from yourself."

■ ■ ■

After my last meeting with Dr. Bek, I find Louis in the fifth-floor hallway. I take him by the hand and pull him into the stair-well. He stands on the stairs, one step below me, so we are the same height, and I touch his face and his soft blond hair and think about how I am already missing him.

"Let's go back to that first month," I say. "I want to go back."

Time changes when you know you're running out. Now I want the slowness, the wet heavy thing, but the days are tumbling by. I tell Louis about my mother, about *Mysteries of the Sea*. In our room, I show him the photo. He stares at it for a long time, tilting it around in the light, and then tells me what he sees. We talk about leaving the Hospital and going south, to Florida. We talk about white beaches and endless sunshine and alligators and how we will find my mother there. We are becoming like the twins, only Florida is our Hawaii.

From a guidebook on the Everglades, Louis knows that alligators have been alive on the earth for millions of years. As I listen to him, I comb the air with my fingers and pretend I'm making my way through a sea.

That night, after Lights Out, we sit on his bed, in darkness, a sheet draped over us. We have decided to hold a séance, to see if we can reach the twins. We press our palms together and shut our eyes. We regulate our breathing. We try to enter a trance, but I keep getting distracted. His skin is warm. He has the clean smell of bar soap. How many breaths does he have left, how many memories? All the other patients look different to me now; I can see their pain hanging over them like a shadow. I keep thinking that maybe Dr. Bek is wrong. Maybe his data is mistaken. Maybe I am the one who is going to die and this is just another way of testing me, of trying to reach my unconscious mind.

"Did you hear anything?" I ask.

"Nothing." Louis shifts under the sheet. His palms slip against mine. He is so alive. "I think we have to go deeper into the trance."

"What if we can't?" Cocooned inside the sheet, so close to him, it's almost possible to pretend we are no longer in the Hospital.

I open my eyes. Our foreheads are touching. His eyes are still closed, his curved lashes dusting his skin. His lips part, preparing to answer. For the first time in weeks, I don't hear anything in the twins' room. I just hear him.

19.

In Allston, the Psychologist said he was training my brain waves. During our sessions, the Spanish music played on his laptop. He told me a man named Plácido Domingo was singing. He told me that he always wanted to live in Spain, where people sat under umbrellas in beautiful stone plazas and all the buildings were ancient and you could sleep through the middle of the day. When the music stopped, he asked me if I liked it and I nodded. He told me I could start it again with my mind, if I concentrated hard enough.

I was sitting on his bed. The white electrodes were stuck to my scalp. I thought as hard as I could about Plácido Domingo, who I had never heard of before. I tried to picture what he would look like and saw a man with a heavy black beard. Nothing happened.

"It's okay," the Psychologist said. "This is just practice."

Practice for what? I did not think to ask.

At the end of one session, he turned the computer around to face me. An image of my brain quivered on the screen. It was round and dense as a planet, the color a liquid green that kept shifting into yellows and blues.

"Imagine something happy," he said.

I thought of the rope swing in Ms. Neuman's backyard, the sensation of being airborne, and watched blue wash into the center of my brain. Plácido Domingo's voice returned.

"Now imagine something scary."

I thought of the white electrodes lying flat as leeches on my skull and his drawer full of eyeglasses. A watery red line swam around the front of my brain and the singing vanished.

"The trick," the Psychologist told me, "is to train your brain to think about the happy thing while the scary thing is going on."

■ ■ ■

He never explained himself to me, not in the way Dr. Bek explained himself to me, and maybe I should thank God or whatever for that.

■ ■ ■

During an Internet Session, I look up Plácido Domingo. I find the following: Plácido Domingo was born in Madrid. Onstage, he's played over one hundred and fifty roles. In the eighties, in Mexico, he pulled earthquake survivors from collapsed buildings. In this earthquake, he lost his aunt and his uncle and his nephew and more. There is a statue of him in Mexico City. I find a photo of the statue, a bronze figure standing with his arms raised. He has met the pope.

■ ■ ■

In the Hospital, I keep playing along with the examinations and the Community Meetings and the meditations. I try to be a good model of health, so good that my model might become contagious. Also: Louis cannot know what I know, because if he does then what I know will become real.

One night I show Louis the hole. We're naked and wrapped in our sheets. We keep the lights off. We sit in front of the hole, the sheets pooling white around us. A dull light rises from the opening. Louis leans over it and closes his eyes and I wonder what he is thinking or if the buzzing has walked inside his brain and taken away his ability to think at all.

"Do you hear that noise?" I ask.

He nods, eyes still closed. "It sounds like a machine."

"Sometimes I hear it through the walls." The sheets slide down my shoulder, and I am relieved at the sight of smooth healthy skin. "Sometimes I imagine I can say things and the twins will hear me."

He starts counting the knots of my spine. I feel the light pressure of his fingers moving up my back, toward the sensitive spot at the base of my neck.

We stay by the hole. We take turns sticking our hands into the opening and breathing the strange air. We feel the vibrations on our skin. After we slide the tarp back into place, Louis scoops me up like a bride and carries me to our room. In the morning, when a nurse comes for us with chilly alcohol wipes and cuffs and needles, the edges of our sheets are stained black with dirt.

20.

Louis gets his morning exam. I'm sitting on my bed and staring at the dates the nurses have forgotten to mark on the bird calendar, counting up our blank days like they are something that can be repaid. When I look over at Louis, he is doing the Romberg, only he's doing it differently than before. His back is to me and I can see his shoulders tipping to the right, a statue about to topple over.

N5 says to try again and I watch his body sway like he's being pushed by a wind.

She takes out her little flashlight and starts checking his skin. She looks under his sleeves and along his throat and down his back and inside his mouth. She's checking one of his legs when the light stops. She doesn't move to the next phase of the exam. She leans closer to Louis and all I can hear is her breathing.

He sits down on his bed and rounds his back, the bumps of his spine pressing against his green scrubs.

"There's an abnormality," she says.

She turns off the flashlight and packs her kit. She tells us to stay in our room and we nod dumbly. We don't need to ask where she's going. We know she's getting Dr. Bek.

When I hear the click of the door closing and look at Louis on his bed, hunched under the lights, his hands squeezing the edges of the mattress, I feel something inside me pop—a sharp sudden break, like a wishbone snapping. Microburst after micro- burst after microburst.

Louis keeps sitting on the bed. He doesn't say anything, doesn't turn to look at me. I go to him. I kneel at his feet and push up the leg of his scrub and there it is: a blister the size of a quarter on his shin, rough and silver in the center, ringed with pink. For a while, we sit wrapped in heavy silence.

"What's your name?" I ask him.

"Louis," he says.

I roll down the scrub. His feet are bare. I stroke the knobs of bone on his ankles.

"What's my name?"

"Joy."

"How long have you lived here?"

"Six months."

"How long have you been alive?"

"Three decades or thirty years. However you want to say it."

Three decades or thirty years or not nearly long enough.

"What do you want more than anything?"

"To be alone with you."

I kiss his knee. He puts his hand on the back of my head.

"You're going to be fine," I say.

■ ■ ■

By breakfast Louis has been moved to the tenth floor, where there are no roommates or even visitors. No activities or pilgrims or microwaves. I skip breakfast and I skip the Community Meeting, where I know his relocation will be announced. I sit in our closet, behind a curtain of scrubs, and remember.

In our room, Dr. Bek sat next to Louis, the mattress sinking under his weight, and asked him a series of questions. The basics, at first. Name? Age? Do you know where you are? His voice was warm and low inside his suit and did not sound like it was filled with lies. The more he went back—address in Philadelphia? high school attended? age at mother's death?—the more each answer became a stab of uncertainty.

When Dr. Bek asked how his mother died, Louis's eyes got quick and damp and I could tell he was searching for an authentic memory.

"Sick," he tried. "Sick for a long time and then she died."

Dr. Bek told me to get Louis's slippers. I set his slippers down in front of him and he looked at them like he had no idea what they were and Dr. Bek said, "Joy, help him," so I kneeled beside him again and pushed his toes into the cloth openings. His feet were heavy and cold. "Of course, of course," Louis said, and slid his feet the rest of the way in.

"I'll see you," Louis said before he rose from the bed. Every movement, every breath, was weighted with shock. I couldn't be sure he still knew he was talking to me and if he was, there was nothing in the world I could think to say back to that.

I stay in the closet through dinner. I don't get hungry. I feel like my life is a tent someone has folded up and carried away. I squeeze the empty legs of Louis's scrubs and go back to what the Pathologist's voice told us in November, before the snow came, when he said all we needed to do now was keep breathing.

I try to keep breathing.

After Lights Out, I lie in Louis's bed and find the part of the mattress that still has the shape of his body. I push my nose into his sheets like a burrowing animal. I wrap my arms around his pillow and hold on.

■ ■ ■

In the morning, after N5 has completed my exam and marked the day on the calendar, remembering the gesture for the first time in weeks, she starts stripping Louis's sheets. When the corners rise and I see the green mattress beneath, I rush over to the bed and yank the sheets away. She stumbles back. I bunch the fabric in my arms and run out of the room and down the hallway. I run like I'm making a break for it. Like I'm Paige trying to beat her fastest time. My hair blows back. My feet smack the floor. I pass patients from our Floor Group and somebody whistles. I burst through the double doors that lead to the Dining Hall. I lope around the empty room, slowing and winded, like a toy winding down. I stand on a chair and wrap the sheets around my body. The fabric stretches, turns translucent, and my elbows look strange through the cloth. I crawl under one of the long tables, like the twins used to do, and sit surrounded by the silver legs of the chairs and it hits me that I am alone, so totally alone, and there is no place for me to go from here.

■ ■ ■

I'm still under the table when I hear the Pathologist's voice on the speakers, telling me I'm wanted in Dr. Bek's office. By now I know he might not even be a real pathologist, that he is only a voice, a stupid human voice, and in the Dining Hall I have a premonition that this is the last time the Hospital will give me an order that I follow.

■ ■ ■

In Dr. Bek's office, there is something different about the Troll Wall poster: it has a little tear, right above gray cliffs, like someone has been jabbing the fog with a pencil. During our meeting, his computer keeps chirping and I keep thinking of birds. I tell him what I want and that my terms are not negotiable.

. . .

In the library, as I wait for news of Louis, I start a letter to my mother. I want to tell her about my life. I do not go in order. Instead I begin with the bus ride to the Hospital, the desolate view from the windows and the blond man sitting next to me. In Ohio, we passed a miniature golf course, dinosaur-themed. An orange plaster T. rex loomed over the abandoned green. "He used to be at the top of the food chain," Louis said. Those were the first words he spoke to me.

"What's that?" Rick asks from the library doorway. He's been in the Hospital for weeks, but still looks like he's just wandered out of the woods.

"A story," I tell him.

I think he's going to leave, but instead he comes into the library. He stands in a corner for a moment and I remember Curtis's stories and start to get nervous, start to anticipate a foul smell. He takes an encyclopedia from a shelf and pages through it.

"There are a lot of stories around here," he says.

I'm sitting on the floor, working with sheets of construction paper and a black crayon. The dark wax keeps smudging and the letter looks more like a ransom note or a deranged love letter than the story I want to tell. I don't have the right materials. I'm learning that in some ways life is all about having the right materials at the right time.

Three pages in, I stop and rip up the sheets.

"Tell me more about what it's like out there," I say to Rick. I tell him that I want to know what he saw, if he was afraid.

Rick sits next to me on the olive-colored rug and tells a story about where he grew up, which was not Oregon, but a town in Ohio, in the Mahoning Valley. For many years, his family worked in the steel mills on the river. As a child, he only knew the sky to be an ocean of gray smog. By the time he was a teenager, the mills had all closed and he learned that sky came in all kinds of colors. Without the mills, there was no money. The town's population started shrinking. Rick went out to Oregon, leaving behind thousands of empty buildings and abandoned mills lining the river like rusting ghosts.

"This town became sick," he tells me, turning over his palms. Brown scabs have stitched together the cuts on his hands. "Now that disease has spread and spread, so instead of only some places looking sick, many places look sick. That's what it's like."

"Tell me more about the Laws of the Road," I say next.

"You would do well out there." He points a finger at me. Dirt under the nail.

"Why's that?"

"Women never have a problem getting a ride."

When Rick leaves me alone in the library, I start to imagine the dark edges of the land that exist beyond the snow, waiting for those of us who will survive.

21.

At midnight, I meet Dr. Bek in the fifth-floor stairwell. His breath echoes and I imagine we're standing in the dark bottom of a canyon. He points a flashlight at the stairs. His silver suit makes me think of a deep-sea explorer. Of my mother. We start to climb.

To see Louis one last time, that was what I told him I wanted.

As we pass the sixth floor, he tells me more about his wife. Her name was Alice. She wanted to be an art historian. She did not want to live in Norway forever. She wanted to end up someplace warm, like São Paulo or Barcelona.

When we reach the tenth floor, my legs are trembling inside my scrubs. Dr. Bek taps a code into the keypad. At the end of the hall, white light slips through the bottom of a door.

In the final hours, patients suffer from radical changes in temperature—shivering under their sheets one minute, drenching them in sweat another. In the final hours, the brain swells, pushes against the limits of the skull. In the final hours, there is apnea, or temporary suspensions in breathing, and the stretches get longer until they stop being temporary.

Dr. Bek lets me into the room, but doesn't follow. The door clicks shut behind me, and I wonder how long he will wait on the other side.

Louis looks like all the rest. His bed is surrounded by a plastic tent. His IV bag is heavy with fluid. A thin white sheet covers his legs. His fingers twitch on the mattress like there's an instrument he's trying to remember how to play. The shape of his face has changed; it is round and glowing silver.

I touch the tent and the plastic ripples. "It's me."

He shakes his head. All the tubes shudder. In this room on the tenth floor, there is only one bed, but it is very long and wide and he looks so small on the mattress.

"Louis," I say again. "Do you know who I am?"

He blinks fast. His hands turn over and it looks like he's holding fistfuls of crystals. His chest stills and I wait for him to start breathing again. He has forgotten everything.

So I will start at the beginning. So I will tell him all about us.

"My name is Joy," I say.

He repeats my name in a slow slur, turning the word over in his mouth. I imagine the little black spot on my own memory eating away at my brain like a fungus, because that is what the sickness does, after all: it takes those dark stains that exist within us and melts them down into a lake of forgetting.

I watch fluid from the IV drip into a slender tube and decide that I will never leave him.

I reach for his chest through the plastic. He looks down at my hand like it's a foreign thing. He's breathing again, quick and grasping. His eyes are the color of a bleached winter sky. He can no longer speak, he can only listen, so I will have to invent for him something beautiful.

. . .

I want to ride a plane and look out the window and see water dotted with tiny green islands or blue mountains or maybe both. After the sickness, the thought of all those people sitting in rows, our fingers touching the same armrests, our breath circulating, fills me with alarm, so here is my solution: I am the only passenger, sitting in one of the middle rows, with no one behind and no one in front, the seat belt loose across my lap. Where are you going? Is there even a pilot? I ask the questions Louis would ask if he could, then I press my body against the plastic and tell him I do not know.

. . .

I first learned about flight from the Psychologist. In college, he spent a semester in Rome. First he went from Boston to New York, which took one hour, and then to Rome, which took nine hours. Did I know that a pilot and a copilot are forbidden to eat the same meal? That a 747 is made up of six million different parts? That "aerophobia" means fear of flying?

Back then I wasn't interested in flying. I wanted to hear more about Rome.

In Rome, the Psychologist heard Plácido Domingo's voice for the first time, on a radio. "It was the worst night of my life," he said, in an unusual show of vulnerability, "but his voice saved me."

I tell Louis this story too and wish it was possible to be saved by a voice.

22.

The night Louis died, I stayed in our closet. I did not move or eat or drink for two days. I only started again because N5 pulled me out of the closet, into a burst of light, and forced a straw between my lips. She breathed at me until I started sucking down a chalky milkshake from a can. In my meeting with Dr. Bek, I told him what I wanted, but he took away the sheets and would not be moved. I watched the white ball of fabric disappear under his desk. "Louis," he said, "is almost gone." He couldn't have met me in the stairwell, because he was drinking a bottle of cleaning solution on the first floor, his attempt at erasure. He survived, a miracle of the body or the unconscious mind, but was left weak enough to be confined to a wheelchair. When I heard this news I wondered if he told me the truth about the Hospital not as a way of reaching his wife, but as a way of saying good-bye. Of unburdening himself. Of settling up.

"Dr. Bek will require some time to recover from a very challenging evening." That was what the nurses told us.

Or was I there, with Louis? I can see everything so clearly.

This is the opposite of a memory trick, when you are trying to remember what you don't remember, not because you have forgotten, not because it has been hidden in some dark corner, but because it never happened. Remembering the false memory can make you feel like you are rewriting the past, reordering the laws of physics, which of course you are not.

All you are doing is telling yourself a story.

Now my room feels empty and the noise next door is back and I imagine the Hospital is speaking to me in a language I will never be able to translate. Dr. Bek has stopped holding Community Meetings. He has stopped taking our questions and talking about our specialness, about how we will soon be well. He stays on the first floor and I imagine his wheelchair rolling up and down the white hallway below us. The nurses have stopped coming for morning examinations. We see them slouching down the halls in their suits or sitting in the Common Room and staring at the dead TV. They don't enforce Lights Out, so the Hospital glows fluorescent day and night. Sometimes we hear muttering over the speakers, but nothing that can be called speech. When I walk the floors, I pass patients lying in the hallways, staring up at the white ceiling, and wonder what is going to happen to all of us.

At night, I smell that fresh grass scent. I hear footsteps in the hallway and a woman calling my name.

She's here, how could she be here, she's here.

In late February, I'm standing at the arched window and remembering the pilgrim who did the perfect cartwheel and then wandered out into the plains. I can see him trekking across the white field. I can see the winding trail of footprints he leaves behind.

The sun is setting. The horizon is the color of fire. Darkness is gathering along the edges of the field and creeping toward us.

We have seen so much from the windows of this Hospital.

Every day Rick tells me more about the Laws of the Road. If you need water, find damp ground and dig a hole. If you drink from a river, make sure it's moving fast. Grass is edible. Beetles and deer will bring you luck. At the window, I think about these rules and remember the pilgrim walking away from the Hospital and I think, Why can't that be me?

One night I see N5 sitting alone in the Common Room. There is no one else around. I sit next to her on the couch. I get so close I can feel her white suit rustling against my bare skin. She smells of rubbing alcohol. Her breath sounds like the ocean. I whisper, "What is the code, what is the code, what is the code."

She doesn't do anything for a long time. I don't give up. "What if you had a daughter? What if she got stuck in here?"

She picks up my hand and taps a series of numbers into my palm. I count the little pulses. The code is a date. The year of the date is 1980, the same year Dr. Bek went to work in the Hospital in Oslo, the same year he was married.

I don't say any good-byes. I take my mother's photo from its hiding place and go down to the basement. At the storage room, the code gets me in. I peel off my scrubs and put on my real-person clothes. Everything feels different on my body than it did before, the roughness of the denim, the weight of the sneakers.

I go to the door with the triangular window and enter the code. I hear the lock open. I push.

Outside I climb a short flight of concrete stairs. The cold is like being stuck with a needle. The air is thin and smells of tree bark. I pull my sweatshirt sleeves over my hands.

From the ground, I gaze up at the Hospital. It looks massive and impenetrable in the night, like even if I wanted to I wouldn't be able to get back inside. Light streams through the windows. On the fifth floor, my floor, I see a passing silhouette, a wisp of a person, and I wonder if anyone is watching. If anyone will ever tell my story. If anyone will remember.

BOOK 2

The dead have certain obligations. Is one of them
to remember us?

—Joy Williams, *The Quick and the Dead*

23.

After the Hospital, I run through stands of trees that have been turned into white skeletons by winter, the branches grabbing at my sweatshirt sleeves. I fight through drifts that swallow my knees and want to keep me with them forever. After the Hospital, I slip up a rise, clutching icy brush I can feel but not see in the night, frozen stems slicing open my palms. I slide down on my back and the rocks sticking out of the snow like horns scrape skin off my spine. I get snow in my hair and under my shirt and in my shoes and in my pockets and in my mouth.

After the Hospital, there is no one to warn me of the dangers, to protect me from the flaws in my judgment, and so I don't realize I am running across a frozen lake until the ice creaks. I stop. My lungs are burning. Ribbons of blood are hardening on my hands. The ice trembles underneath me. I have no idea how far I am from solid ground, if I am inches away from stepping through a gauzy circle of ice, into a deep and endless freeze.

After the Hospital, I watch dawn turn treetops and power lines gold, light up the ice-slick road that I will follow to La

Harpe. I see a deer leaping across a frozen stream and rushing into the woods. I feel every nerve curled under every fingernail. I see crisscrossing contrails in the tender peach-colored sky, even though there is no sign of a plane.

In La Harpe, the streets are rivers of brown slush. The sidewalks are ghosted. The tops of the buildings are wrapped in smoky fog. I don't see any passing cars, no way to hitch a ride. I find a covered bus stop on a corner. There is no posted schedule; the routes and times are a mystery. I fall onto a bench and feel the wild pulse of my heart, beating at a speed that might be fatal, but I am away from the Hospital, my mother's photo in my back pocket, and I remember everything that happened there.

■ ■ ■

The bus that slows in front of the stop groans and leaks exhaust. The windows are dark. The hubcaps are crusted in mud. Can it take me anywhere worth going?

The door pops open and a driver in a tan uniform stares down at me. He is a lean man with sunken eyes. "You plan on getting in?" he says.

"I'm considering my options."

"You're about to consider yourself out of a ride."

There are no other passengers. A long skinny aisle runs between the rows of seats. The rubber matting on the floor looks sticky. The driver says the bus is headed for Kansas City, which is a start. After I pay, I am down to twenty-five dollars in cash. I take a seat in the back and the bus lurches forward. The skin on my fingertips is waxy and gray, a color I have never seen on skin before.

I think about my infant self in the cardboard supermarket box, waiting to be found. I think about the burn of the cold on my tiny fingertips, all the pain I must have felt, the pain I was too young to remember.

Outside La Harpe we move through a white sea. The bus skids on the ice. I see another deer, but this one is dead, spread out on the roadside, its middle split open. The guts are a dark purple mush, the borders of the flesh bright red with blood. It looks like something in the wet middle of the deer is still moving, and I watch a snake slither out from the intestines and down the side of the road.

A list of what I know about dead bodies: after you die, your cells explode. After you die, your organs eat themselves. As a result, the bacteria in your body does not die at all; it keeps right on living. There are five stages of decay. They begin with bloat, end with bone.

I see green Christmas garlands twisted around a barbed-wire fence. I see an orange car rusting in a field. The tires are missing; the metal body is sinking into the land. Brown cattle rooting around in the snow. A windmill, the blades turning in a great slow circle.

On the bus, there is the feeling of passing from one self into another, like a ship moving from a bay into the vastness of open water.

I only know where my mother lives and that she is alive. Alive! I feel like shouting that word out the bus window. In Florida, when I find her, it is possible she will not be happy to see me. I know this. It is possible that whenever a strange young woman approaches, she feels a current of dread.

I have thousands of miles to travel. I don't know how many days those miles will take.

In time, she'll see that I'm worth keeping around.

"Do you know about existence affirmations?" the bus driver calls back to me.

I move up a few rows. The fog twists over the road in a way that makes me think it's not just air and water but something alive.

"I don't know," I say.

"If you affirm your existence daily, it will continue to be true." He drums his fingers on the wide black wheel. "Every day when I wake up I look at myself in the mirror and say, 'I am alive I am alive I am alive.'"

It sounds like this man is doing one of the Pathologist's meditations. I wonder what he would think of Dr. Bek and his theories about the unconscious mind.

In Paola, Kansas, two horses gallop into our path. One is white, the other sorrel. They seem to come out of nowhere. The driver hits the brakes and yanks the wheel. The bus shoots to the side. I'm thrown forward in my seat. I bite my bottom lip and taste blood. The horses slip on the road, heads raised high, manes billowing. Their running is frantic, without sense or direction. The bus stills. I press my hands against the window and think about how I used to dream of me and Louis leaving the Hospital together and boarding a bus just like this one and watching the landscape pass.

My hands leave twin palm prints behind on the window, the fingers bleeding into each other.

I lean my head against the glass and close my eyes, wanting to drift off, wanting to dream about anything other than the Hospital. I remember Rick's Laws of the Road, him telling me to never sleep in the company of strangers, but on the bus his voice gets smaller and smaller until it's gone.

When I wake, there are woods on either side of the road. I look out and see two black tires hanging from the branches of a tree, secured by thick hay-colored rope. The rubber circles sway on the branches. They look like nooses.

We break through the woods, surrounded once more by flat white fields. I see a young man in a flannel jacket, standing by an old hatchback on the side of the road. Louis, I think for a moment, touching the cold glass. He calls out and waves. The bus gains speed as we pass, spraying his pants with snow.

24.

The first sign of the city is the Missouri River, the water black and snaking in the night. A rail yard with tracks like thick veins in the ground and smokestacks netted in tiny orange lights. White loops of rising smoke. A tall silver skyline in the distance.

In Shawnee, we pick up a man wearing glasses so large and dark I think he must be blind. He sits next to me, even though the bus is still empty, and I consider the questions I could ask him, as a test. Do I look like I've always had this haircut? Do I look like I have a mother? Do I look like I have all my memories? Do I look scared? Does the skin on my fingers look dead?

In Kansas City, we pass an empty square and a bronze statue of a winged horse. In the Hospital, I imagined the cities were once again filled with brightness, the clatter of alive bodies, but this one looks dark and hollow, an underground system that's just been pulled into the light.

I decide to get off on Seventh Street. As I move down the aisle, I think of what I could say to the driver. I want to tell him those affirmations, those meditations, never worked out for me or for anyone else in the Hospital I left behind. I am still living not because of what I *thought* but because I *moved*.

"I am alive," I say instead.

On the street, I am dazed by the height of the buildings. It feels like being dropped in the center of a tall and intricate maze. On the corner, a man in a trench coat is selling hardback books titled *Does Death End It All?* I don't see a single person in a suit or a mask.

In a trash can, I find a pair of green gardening gloves, the palms stained with oil. They smell like gasoline. I put them on.

A block down, there's a motel called the Walnut. From the parking lot, the building is U-shaped and I count three concrete levels, each bordered by a railing. I find my way to a dim front lobby. The carpet, a pattern of red and gold diamonds, is musty and damp. I think of all the good our Floor Group could do in here, with our caddies of cleaning supplies.

No one is at the font desk. On the counter, there is a little ceramic dish of mints. I eat one and it turns into a sweet cloud on my tongue. A white plaque advertises a heated swimming pool, only "heated" is spelled "hated." I ring a buzzer and a man with a little black mustache zips out from behind the curtain, quick as a minnow. His skin is smooth and pale and rolled with fat.

"How much for a room?" I ask. My voice sounds hoarse and strange.

"Seventy," he says. "Call it the postdisaster discount."

I tell him I can't pay for a room up front. A fly buzzes around the man's head.

"We're not a shelter," he says.

"There are shelters? Around here?" A *shelter* sounds like exactly what I need, even though I know words aren't always what they claim to be.

The man shakes his head, starts shuffling papers. The fly shoots away and gets lost in the curtains. He's losing interest in me.

"I can get you the money." The words come in a rush. Of course, I have no idea about getting anyone any money. What about the duties of Floor Groups and proper procedures in the Dining Hall and tests? I'm not used to a world where the rules change as often as the weather, a world that runs on cash.

The man stops shuffling and looks at me. I notice a dot of blood in the corner of his eye.

"I mean it." I press my hands on the counter and am startled by the green gloves. Where did these hands come from? "You can trust me."

"Trust is out of style." The man fusses with the collar of his sweater. He lets out a little laugh. "Or was it *ever* stylish? I can't say that I remember."

I lean against the counter, because my body has gotten very heavy. I've never been to Kansas City before and the longer I stand there, in the murky light of the lobby, the less certain I become that Kansas City is where I really am. I can still feel myself walking the Hospital halls, my slippers sliding across the floors, my fingers moving over that patch of bubbled wallpaper, the cold on the windows.

I look again at the man. I do not know where to go or what to do.

"There must be something you need as much as money. I could wash dishes. I could clean rooms."

The man picks a ball of lint off his sweater. "What exactly are your skills?"

"Anything," I say. "I'm a fast learner."

"I'm no teacher."

"I can run for miles without stopping. I can memorize all kinds of lists." I point at the sign for the pool. "I can *spell*."

My unconscious mind is very powerful and it wants me to keep living, I do not tell him.

He taps a fat finger against his cheek, then pushes back the curtain and shouts for someone called No Name. I remember Ms. Neuman telling me and Marcus to never trust anyone without a proper Christian name.

. . .

No Name is tall as a giant. He has silver rings in his nose and in his bottom lip, one in each eyebrow. He's dressed in black jeans and a black hoodie and black sneakers without laces. In exchange for helping him, I will get a room for the night. It's unclear what he needs help with. In fact, he doesn't seem to think he needs help at all.

"I don't want her," he says when the manager introduces us.

"You were almost caught the last time." The manager hands No Name a sheet of paper, folded in half. "You need a lookout."

He jams the paper into his pocket. "You sure these are empty?"

"I'm sure," the manager says. "I just called them. Twice."

No Name stalks into a concrete courtyard, where shriveled brown plants sit frozen in clay pots. We pass a swimming pool that looks like no pool I have ever seen before. A giant pink clamshell hangs over it like a very beautiful awning. I stop and watch the water lap at the edges of the night.

"Keep up," No Name calls over his shoulder, and I forget about the pool and chase after him.

We walk along an open hallway, to a corner room on the ground floor. He slips a key into the door and we disappear inside. The room is dark. I move through a cloud of tiny bugs. I can't see them, but I can feel the itch of infestation move down a finger, across the back of my neck. One bug gets stuck in my eye. I'm supposed to stay by the door and listen for voices, footsteps. If someone tries to enter the room, I'm supposed to say that I work for the motel and there is a plumbing emergency under way inside and it is not a thing anyone would want to smell or see. He starts with the drawers by the TV and I catch the gold glint of a watch. The lights from outside wash the blinds in a soft glow.

"People always hide things in Bibles," No Name whispers in the dark.

He does a quick sweep of the bathroom and the closet and then we're off to our next room, on the second floor. He finds a wedding ring hidden inside a pair of socks—according to No Name, people are always leaving wedding rings in their room too—and a ten-dollar bill on the bathroom counter. We're about to leave when I hear footsteps coming down the hall and go rigid.

"Hey," I whisper, touching a finger to my mouth.

No Name flattens himself against the wall. I silently recite my lines about the plumbing emergency. We both wait, our breath drawn inside us, and listen to the footsteps pass. We hear them stop at the other end of the hall. A door opens and shuts.

"You're not terrible at this," No Name says when we're back outside and moving down another hallway, the lights above wavering like the ones inside the T cars in Boston.

"What's the closest you've ever come?"

"Once a woman came back to her room. I was in the bathroom when I heard the door and I had to hide in the shower until she left. She was walking around the room and talking to herself. She kept saying that she had done wrong. Wrong, wrong, wrong. If she found me, I knew there would be no way out, no way to explain. That was when it was decided I needed someone like you."

I whistle. My heels are rubbed raw. The insides of my pockets are still wet from the snow. "That's pretty close."

"I've come closer with other things," he says.

■ ■ ■

At ten, No Name announces it's time for a break. He unlocks a vacant room with a king bed. He sits down on the bed and takes out a pack of cigarettes. Soon the room is clotted with gray.

Smoking is not allowed in the Hospital, I want to tell him.

Sitting on the bed might suggest something I don't want to suggest, so I stay on my feet, by the door. I take off the gardening gloves and examine the grooves of dirt and blood on my knuckles, the black under my fingernails. Do I look like I escaped from someplace awful? Do I look like I ever had a home?

"What did you do before the sickness?" The red carpet is damp, like the one in the lobby, and I can feel a chill coming off the walls.

"Same kind of thing. Only bigger." He's smoking one cigarette after another and putting them out on the bedspread. The comforter is dotted with small, dark holes. I smell burnt polyester.

"What about during?"

No Name tells me that he was living here, in this motel in Kansas City, when the sickness came. Was there a better place to be? He had a bed, a shower, a TV, a telephone. If you knew where to look, there were endless supplies of bottled water, bar soap, towels, saltine crackers in plastic pouches. From the window, he could monitor what was happening outside. After the sickness ended, he decided to stay. He had been on the move his whole life—why not try living in one place? And then once the recovery began and travelers started filling the rooms, he and the manager saw an opportunity.

I ask No Name what he knows about Kansas City and he tells me this place is nicknamed the City of Fountains because there are hundreds of fountains. The cowboy boot was invented here. Kansas City is home to one of the world's largest roller coasters.

"Not just one of the largest in the country," he says, shaking his cigarette. "But in the world."

"Not bad," I say back. No Name seems to be fond of Kansas City.

"My turn to ask a question." He blows smoke from the side of his mouth. "How long are you sticking around?"

"Only one night. I have someplace to be."

Kansas City is just the first stop. Tomorrow I will keep pushing south.

"Someplace to be?" A pierced eyebrow pops up. He puts out another cigarette and the bed hisses. "Well aren't you fancy."

I hear sirens outside. I go over to the TV and try to turn it on, but the set is dead, defective, like the one I left behind in the Hospital.

"If I wanted a room with a TV, I would have gotten us a room with a TV," No Name says. "I'm real fucking tired of the news."

I ask him for a cigarette. He lights a fresh one and holds it out. I reach, but I'm standing too far away and he's not coming to me; I have to get closer. I take the cigarette and sit down on the floor and feel the wet of the carpet seeping into my jeans.

"So," I say, taking a drag. "What were things like before around here? How is it different now?"

He waves his cigarette and I follow the gray swirls. "What do you mean *how*?"

I want to tell him I've been in a Hospital for months and I have almost forgotten what it feels like to wear regular clothes and to breathe in city air and to stand in the tall shadows of buildings and to see people who are not patients, who have never been patients. I have almost forgotten there are people out there who smoke. I don't know what it was like a week after the sickness ended or a month after. I don't know if the emptiness and the rot is a new situation or if things have always been this way out here.

"I'm not very well traveled," I say instead.

"What's your theory?" he wants to know.

"My theory?"

"Of the sickness. Why it happened."

"I don't like to speculate," I tell him in place of the truth, which is: I have no idea. I let the line of ash get longer. I didn't really want to smoke. I just needed something to do. Outside the Hospital, conversation feels like a bright light in my face and I want to get away from the glare.

"Here's what I think." No Name kneels in front of me. His hood slips back and I see a red birthmark, vaguely Florida-shaped, on his temple. His cigarette has burned down to a white stub. "I think someone out there wanted very badly for another person to forget what they knew. I think someone started this whole goddamn thing just to make one person forget."

"That seems like a lot of trouble for just one person."

"Doesn't it?" No Name nods like we're agreeing. He puts out his cigarette and once again the bed sizzles. I'm starting to feel sick from the smoke. My body is not used to pollutants. I'm not sure how much longer I can stand being on break.

He takes out his list and calls the motel manager. He nixes one room and adds another.

"Back to work," he says after he hangs up.

What's your real name? I know better than to ask.

"I want the next room." My cigarette has gone dead between my fingers. My lap is dusted in ash.

"We'll see," says No Name.

■ ■ ■

When we hit our last room for the night, I get to do the stealing. I start with the dresser drawers. Empty. I move on to the bathroom, where I find a single pearl earring on the counter. The pearl is large and light, definitely fake, but I scoop it anyway. I wonder if the earring means this room belongs to a woman—if she is out here on her own, like me.

The first thing I ever stole was a comb. In Roxbury, I watched a girl run this comb through her hair day after day and coveted the pink plastic teeth. One morning she left the comb on her pillow and I took it without thinking, in a blaze of want.

I never felt bad for stealing cough syrup from the Stop & Shop. They always seemed to have too much of everything.

In the bedside drawers, I find a postcard stuck between the pages of the Bible. I'm about to call it quits when I notice a coat draped over a chair. The inside breast pocket holds two crisp fifties and a map of American highways, folded into a tiny square.

We examine our haul in the break room. We close the blinds and flick on the lights and dump everything on the king bed. We kneel together on the floor, breathless, sifting through our loot. The air is still heavy with smoke.

He counts the money: three hundred and seventy-five dollars. The coating on the fake pearl is peeling and faded. Neither of us want it; we took it for nothing. The postcard is a black-and-white image of waves breaking on a beach. The sky is caked with cloud except in the center, where flecks of light have burned through. Someone somewhere wrote an address and a message on the back, but the ink has bled.

No Name hands me a thin stack of bills. "This is for you."

A hundred dollars, plus the map.

I stare at the back of the postcard, trying to decipher the dark smudges. "I think this was addressed to someone in Virginia."

What an elegant, gentle-sounding name for a place, Virginia.

"Take it if you want." No Name pulls out his cigarettes and beats the bottom of the pack. "It's worthless."

■ ■ ■

In exchange for my work, I get a room on the third floor. I strip and hang my clothes in the little closet by the bathroom. In the mirror, my skin is chalk white. My bangs have grown down to my eyebrows. My legs are coated in rough fuzz. The hair in my armpits and around my crotch is a dark tangle. I rub the tender veins in my arms.

In the shower, I scrub myself with a washcloth until my skin is throbbing and pink, as though the cells hold memories I want to erase. I stand under the showerhead and let the water beat my shoulders for a while, waiting for someone to come and tell me that I'm taking too long or that it's time for a Community Meeting or Lights Out. Time to do the Romberg.

No one does.

It takes me a while to get the temperature right. For a while, the water either scalds or freezes.

I forget to put down a bath mat and leave wet footprints on the tile floor.

Once, in Roxbury, there was an outbreak of head lice and it was decided the cure was drenching our hair in mayonnaise and waving hot dryers over our heads until our scalps were burning.

I remember this when I see the gun-shaped hair dryer under the motel sink.

After the shower, I sit on the bed and line up the postcard and my mother's photo. They look right together, the captain and her sea.

I turn on the TV, hoping for *Mysteries of the Sea*, but instead an "outbreak retrospective" is on the news. A number of survivors have, in the last month, vanished. Some have moved across the country, abandoning jobs and mortgages and families, leaving behind only a letter to explain or just disappearing in the middle of the night. There are empty cubicles in office buildings and dogs tied to mailboxes and mounds of newspapers in their dewy plastic packaging on doorsteps. Others have committed suicide. Approximately five hundred people, to date. The news calls it a "microepidemic."

In an interview, a mental health expert explains that some survivors can't make sense of what they've lived through, of why they've lived through it, so they shed their life and assume another or shed their life and assume death. This man has a neat beard and a sweater-vest and I'm skeptical he knows very much about what it's like to live through unbearable things.

Images from the sickness come next: long lumps under white sheets; patients cowering behind plastic tents, tubes springing from their arms, skin brilliant with silver sores; helicopters sweeping cities; an army of yellow hazmat suits flooding a wide street. I don't want to keep watching, but I can't seem to make myself change the channel.

The final death toll was close to four hundred thousand, more than half the population of Boston. Now there is debate about whether the "microepidemic" victims should be added to that count or if they demand a count of their own.

A woman standing on a street corner, the wind whipping around her. A tissue crumpled in her hand. A flush is spreading down her nose and across her cheeks. She looks to be about the same age as my own mother. Her son survived the sickness, then dove off the Golden Gate Bridge. He left a note telling her he couldn't trust the world anymore.

What would Dr. Bek have to say about this man, about his unconscious mind?

She looks into the camera. A clear stream runs from her nose.

"When could we ever?" she says.

■ ■ ■

In the middle of the night, I get up and go down to the swimming pool. Under the clamshell, the water looks as soft and pink as a tongue. I smell the bitterness of chlorine. There's a crack in the concrete bottom shaped like a bolt of lightning. The white lounge chairs surrounding the pool are heaped with snow. No one else is in the courtyard. All the floors are silent.

Again I take off my clothes. I don't know what else to do with all this freedom.

The pool is barely lukewarm. The advertised heating feels like a lie. Like something to hate. My body is different than it was on land—lighter, more nimble, like all the blood in my veins has been replaced with air. My nipples are purple and hard.

In Somerville, I used to hear stories about the evangelical church baptizing new congregants in Foss Park. They had water that they had turned holy and they poured it over the person's head. They said a prayer and somehow that ritual was supposed to leave that person changed.

I always envied those people, envied the certainty of their faith, their ability to believe they were moving through life with a purpose.

If I stand upright, the water covers my waist, the rise of my stomach, and I feel the lethal chill of winter, so I sink down into the shadow of the clamshell. From there the clothing piled on the concrete edge of the pool looks far away.

I inhale, go under. I touch the lightning-shaped crack. I see the faded blue dolphins painted on the sides of the pool, flippers and noses bleached with time. I notice a freckle on my ring finger that did not exist before. My eyes are on fire from the chlorine and it is my choice to let them keep burning or not.

My choice, my choice.

Finally I get out and put on my bra and my jeans. I run back to my room, sweatshirt clutched to my chest, bare feet slapping the concrete.

I race past a woman standing by the ice machine in a nightgown, filling a plastic cup. When she sees me, the wet, shirtless girl running toward her, she screams and drops the cup and cubes scatter down the hallway, glinting like diamonds under the light.

In my room, I bolt the door and get in bed and wrap myself up in the sheets and the polyester comforter even though I know it has not been washed in a hundred years. Another little bug has gotten stuck to my collarbone and it leaves a dark streak when I wipe it away. I shiver and I shake until I have exhausted myself and fallen asleep, and a while later I wake certain of a presence outside my room. A presence that wants to get in. An intruder, the bolt of panic you feel before a strange man strikes you in the head or drugs you with chloroform, the nightmare that starts and ends and starts again when you wake in a basement, or never has a chance to start again because you don't wake at all.

The green numbers on the bedside clock say 3:05 a.m. and outside someone is pounding on my door. I am hazy with sleep, slow at first to register the sound. The knob is shaking so hard, I think it's going to fall off. I hear a boot striking, someone trying to kick their way inside.

In Mission Hill, the older girls kicked down bathroom doors while the younger girls were inside. This was one of the many ways they convinced us of their power. Every girl in Mission Hill learned how to finish peeing in twenty seconds flat, from squat to flush.

As I got older, I waited for that feeling of power to come alive inside me. I thought it would sprout on its own, like breasts or the downy hair on my legs. I didn't understand that it had to be claimed.

I creep up to the peephole and see No Name thrashing against the door. His face is warped through the glass, turning the proportions strange. His nose is a jutting ridge, his eyes are dark pools. The rings in his face glow silver. He's wearing the same clothes and his body is a black blur as he beats on the door. Something has happened to him since we worked those rooms together. He has changed, or maybe this person was there the whole time, smoking cigarettes and counting money in the break room, waiting to get out.

He stops for a moment. His mouth is open, his throat pale and tight. I can see that he's breathing hard. I wonder if he can sense that I'm right there, just behind the door. He wipes his lips with the back of his hand.

He licks the silver ring in his lip and then throws his shoulder against the door. The security chain jangles and I back away, afraid that somehow he can see me standing half-naked in my room and is already thinking, Come on, girl. Could you make this any easier?

I can't call the front desk because I know the manager will be on the side of No Name and will maybe even give him the key he needs to open this door, to make the jangling security chain the only thing between him and me. So I don't pick up the phone. I don't turn on a light. I put on the green gardening gloves. I get on my knees and crawl into the bathroom, moving slowly, my head animal low, and lock myself inside. The carpet leaves red marks on my knees. The floor is still wet from my watery footprints. I huddle in the tub. I cover myself with the bath mat. I rub away the dark streak on my collarbone. "Be still," I say. My new meditation.

I wait in there until the noise stops, and I go out into the room and see light slipping through the blinds like a rescue.

25.

At dawn, I walk to the bus station. All the floors are quiet. The pool sits empty. There is no sign of the manager or No Name. There is no man in a trench coat selling books. I'm still wearing the gardening gloves. The city looks abandoned in the early-morning light.

Down the street from the motel I find an empty lot with circles of ice as large and dark as oil slicks. There are spidery cracks along the perimeter of one circle, a sharp plunge in the center. Farther down I see clusters of brick factories with tall glass windows and slender chimneys. What kinds of lives are happening here? The sun is a pale gold disc in the sky.

I board a bus bound for Birmingham, Alabama. I wonder what I will do or what will be done to me the next time I need cash.

In Columbia, Missouri, we collect more passengers. A man in bifocals sits down next to me and digs a ringing cell phone out of his pocket. "Fuck the guilt," he says to the person on the other end of the line. "It's no way to live."

He hangs up and turns the phone over in his hands.

I sink into my seat and watch the slim points of tree branches bend in the wind.

The bus stops. The passengers change. The man in bifocals disappears into the day and a nun sits down next to me and starts talking about the immortal soul. She says we worry too much about the body, about where we take sacraments and pray, but the immortal soul isn't inside us, isn't in the body.

"Where is it then?" I ask her, and she says it can exist anywhere, that we have to go in search.

I wonder how it's possible for the soul to live outside the body. Will I find it on my mother's island? Will I see it drifting over the water like smoke?

The nun gets off in Jefferson City. At a rest stop, I buy chips and a Coke from the vending machines. I nearly miss the bus from spending too long touching the warm buttons, trying to remember how to choose.

We pass a small airport. The tarmac is a jumble of machinery, rusting engines and squat white trucks and carts with black wheels. A little green plane sits at the end of a runway, the wings heavy with snow.

After the airport, the landscape turns rural. In the fields, sprigs of brush stick up through the snow. These fields are surrounded by disintegrating wood fences, panels that have fallen to the ground like dislocated body parts. A steel grain silo. More brown cows, scruffy and sick-looking and weaving through the winter muck.

I see distant lines of trees, the silhouettes slight and charcoal black, like they've been burned. I see power lines, the cords sparking and swaying in the wind.

A mist rolls in and covers the trees. The windows fog. It feels like we're driving through a cloud.

I unfold the map of American highways and follow the lines that will lead me south. From Birmingham, I'll ride down to the

Gulf Coast, pass into Florida through the Panhandle, and keep going.

When I look up from the map, I notice a man three rows ahead. I don't remember seeing him get on in Jefferson City. He's sitting in the window seat. He's staring out and I wonder if he is seeing anything through the fog or if his view is as dense and white as mine and he too is pretending that we are no longer on earth.

No one is sitting next to him. He is alone, like me.

I remember the masked man standing on the street corner in Chinatown and the masked man I followed all around the Stop & Shop in the middle of the night. I remember wearing the vampire mask in my basement apartment and thinking that if I never took it off I would just slowly suffocate under the heavy sweet smell of the rubber.

I fold up the map and tuck it into my pocket. I leave my seat and sit down next to this man. He is wearing a rabbit mask. The round eyeholes are surrounded by swirls of white plastic fur. The ears are a pair of white points, the cheeks mounds of pink. The lips are plump and rosy. A nice healthy rabbit. He looks like a cartoon character or a make-believe bandit—except I am touching the pointed ears and he is not yelling or telling me to get away. Behind the mask he is breathing deep and slow.

He's wearing black pants and a puffy maroon coat with a hole in the stomach, so the cotton stuffing spills out. I watch him reach into his lap and push the yellowed guts of his coat back inside.

I remember him showing me how the life line on my palm ran long and deep. I remember the white tuft of hair, which I know is hidden somewhere under that rabbit mask. I want to reach inside and find it. I remember the Real-Life Ghost Stories and the hair dye on our fingernails and Latin homework and the sweaty smell of his boy body in the bathtub.

I remember.

He pulls off the green gardening gloves, one at a time, and looks at my hands.

The bus slows. The air is thick with fog. Something inside me collapses, goes warm and soft, and there is a wet heat on my face. Never have I wanted someone to remember me as much as I want to be remembered now.

"Marcus," I say.

. . .

In Charlestown, Ms. Neuman liked to play the Powerball lottery. Marcus and I would sit on the floor, just beyond the light of the TV, and braid the shag carpeting. We would watch little white balls jump around in a plastic bowl and a man in a tuxedo call out the winning combinations. Ms. Neuman always played the same numbers. We didn't know what those numbers meant to her; we only knew that she never won a dime. Once Marcus whispered a set of numbers to me, the bloodied lips of a zombie mask brushing my ear, and then I saw that same sequence appear on the TV. He did it again, a month later. Here Ms. Neuman had spent years trying to guess right and Marcus had done it twice in a row. That was the first time I realized his mind didn't work the same as everyone else's. The second time was when he woke me in the middle of the night already knowing Ms. Neuman was unconscious on the floor.

. . .

We don't say anything for the longest time. We stare straight ahead and watch the fog begin to lift and the road unfurl like a scroll before us.

I'm the first to speak, to ask how he found me. Marcus has no way to explain. After the sickness ended, he started traveling the country by bus, moving from one city to another to another until he ended up here.

"I wanted to get out there," he tells me. "I wanted to see."

He has passed through Ohio, Illinois, Indiana, through places called Cuba and Brazil and Lebanon. Cities named for countries. He felt a westward pull, though he never made it as far west as Kansas.

A list of what he has seen: a helicopter crashed on the white edge of a field; an abandoned watchtower, the clock hands stuck at noon; a replica of the Statue of Liberty, only instead of standing on an island and holding a torch, this lady was outside a church and holding a giant wood cross. He has seen hitchhikers and shooting stars and a bleating goat tied to a fence and a nightfall that closed around him like a fist. A woman sitting on the side of the road, a sleeping bag draped over her shoulders. A gas mask discarded in a parking lot.

For both of us, these long hours on buses have shown us more of America than we have ever seen.

We pass a field with humps in the snow, like there is a creature living underneath all that white.

When Marcus wants to know where I'm going, what I'm doing here, I look at him and say, "I have a mother."

I catch a road sign for Indianapolis, which doesn't seem right at all. According to my map of American highways, we should be seeing signs for Fayetteville and Little Rock and Jackson, but then again what do I know about cross-country bus routes.

A damp snow starts falling. It covers the yellow highway lines.

"You have a mother? Since when?"

"Since two months ago."

"Where is she?"

"Florida," I tell him. "Shadow Key. That's where I'm going."

"I've never been to an island before," Marcus says.

I look down at his hand. I reach for his fingers and squeeze. His skin has the same soft feeling I remember from childhood.

Soon there is another river, wide and glossy with ice. A light fog hovers over the river and it looks like the water is breathing. The trees on the banks are stooped and gray. They have an ancient way about them.

I see a distant bridge and wonder when's the last time somebody jumped.

"What about you? Where are you trying to end up?"

"Nowhere," he says.

· · ·

In Dayton, it becomes clear that all along this bus has been going in the wrong direction, that it has no intention of taking me to Birmingham. I go up front to talk to the driver and he tells me this bus is going east and has always been going east and he doesn't know where I got my ideas about Birmingham. I ask about the next stop and he tells me it's Harrisburg, Pennsylvania, unless I want to be let out on the side of the road, in which case he will be perfectly happy to oblige.

I have a feeling this driver does not believe in existence affirmations.

"We're going to Pennsylvania," I tell Marcus when I return to my seat, and I am squeezed tight by the fear that the forces of nature are trying to drag me back to Massachusetts, to Somerville and the Stop & Shop, and away from my mother.

It takes us three hours to get out of Ohio, to cross over the Pennsylvania state line. We pass signs for Pittsburgh, a city divided by a river, and after a while the highway tapers into a narrow road bordered by forest. I look into the trees and see dark darting things through the branches. This road leads us to a town where the streetlights are burned out and the power lines are

drooping and the earth beneath the sidewalks has swelled, pushing up the concrete squares so they look like rising waves. We
pass a block of little houses with rusted awnings and crumbling
foundations. White sheets with black x's cover windows. Yellow
notices hang from doors.

The bus stops in the middle of the road. The sky is a swamp
of gray. I look toward the front and see that the driver has a map
of his own. He is frowning and turning it this way and that.
After a while he takes out a cell phone and clicks around. Eventually he puts away the map and the phone and we start moving
again, but now there is no mistaking that we are lost.

We pass smoking hillsides, as though great fires are raging
behind the rises. At a stop sign, I look to the right, to the road
that extends east, and see that the asphalt is rippled and brown
weeds have shot up between the cracks. A fallen tree blocks the
path. The roots are black and frozen. White steam, thick as the
hillside smoke, pours out of the metal grates in the ground.

We pass signs that read DANGER: TOXIC GASES PRESENT and
WARNING: GROUND PRONE TO SUDDEN COLLAPSE. Outside, dusk
is falling.

"My god," the woman sitting behind us says. "We're in
Centralia."

Marcus and I twist around in our seats and ask what she
means by Centralia and the woman tells us that this used to be a
mining town but many years ago the landfill caught fire and the
fire spread through the network of mines underground. Those
underground fires couldn't be put out and there were problems
with poisonous gases and sinkholes, just like those signs said. She
stabs at the air above her. The town was condemned; the underground fires never stopped burning. This is not damage done by
the sickness. This we did all on our own.

"Centralia," the woman says again. "It's famous, this place."
She touches her window. She has a faraway look in her eye.

I am terrified by the idea of sinkholes, of being consumed by the earth.

Marcus and I sit back down in our seats and look at each other and I wish one of us knew what to do. I keep watch through the window and when we pass another block of condemned houses I think I see a woman standing on an icy lawn, waving at us through the smoke. She is wearing some kind of soft wrap or maybe a bathrobe and she is barefoot like that one pilgrim I saw from the Dining Hall window in the Hospital.

"Look," I say to Marcus, but the bus is moving and the smoke is getting thicker and there is no way to tell if she is still there, if she was ever there at all.

The other passengers start objecting to the driver's course of action. The ones who have been asleep wake and open their mouths like animals trying to lose a strange taste. When they look out the windows, at the hot smoking ground, their muscles shed the looseness of sleep. They grab the backs of seats, knock on windows, call up to the driver. "Go left!" "Go right!" "Turn around!" "Get us out of here!"

The driver hunches over the wheel. The bus starts going faster.

We roll onto an unpaved road. A clunking sound and we're back to slow.

White dust blooms around us, luminous in the headlights. I smell rotten eggs and feel heat coming up through the floor.

"The other way!" someone shouts from the back of the bus.

The driver sends us in reverse, the tires crunching over gravel, and starts down another road. By then we are surrounded by nothing but night and all the things that night is capable of hiding.

26.

During an Internet Session in the Hospital, I found a video of my mother talking about the day she almost died. She was diving and rose too quickly. She knew all about decompression sickness, but she saw a spar wedged in a reef of brain coral and she was young and she got excited. During the ascent, her interval stops weren't long enough. On deck, she knew something was wrong. Her legs felt thick and numb. She heard a strange ringing, like bells were sounding on the ship, and said, "Where are the bells?" Her crew looked at her and turned over their palms, as though to prove they weren't hiding the sound in their hands. *What bells?* All she wanted was to lie on the cot in the lower cabin, but she didn't even make it down the stairs. She slumped against the wall. She clawed at the wood paneling. She wet herself inside her dive suit. She felt a sharp pain in her knees and elbows and in the bones in her feet; the pain spread like a rash, into her hips and spine. They were in the middle of the Atlantic, hundreds of miles off the coast of the Dry Tortugas. She knew how to prevent this, she had been trained, but she had forgotten and now, because of that one mistake, that one moment of forgetting, she was slipping away.

Mud sliding down a mountain in springtime, as Dr. Bek once said, his hands making that little dive.

She remembered the white stretcher that carried her out of the stairwell, the hands that fastened the straps. The circle of freckles, the knuckles soft with hair, the scar on the thenar, the crooked ring finger. All these hands working in harmony, as though they belonged to the same body. The smell of salt.

In her memory, the orange coast guard helicopter was noiseless. She only remembered the water churning white beneath her and the sensation of being lifted and then lifted higher and the ocean looking like an enormous blue disc that stretched on into eternity.

■ ■ ■

In Harrisburg, Marcus gets off the bus with me. He has no place to go. I have no one else to go with. The choice to leave this bus together, to get away from this lost driver, who took all night to find Harrisburg, into the light of the day, is so easy it doesn't feel like a choice at all.

The morning is pale and cold. All the buses are going west or north; nobody seems to want to go south. When I say "Florida," the drivers look at me like I've asked if a bus can swim across the ocean, if a bus can take us to Hawaii. Finally we get on a bus headed for Charleston, West Virginia. It takes eight hours to get there and by the time this new city is in sight, the afternoon is winding down into dusk.

We pass yet another river, the Kanawha, according to the signs, and a bronze statue of a man with a sword. All cities, I'm learning, are filled with their monuments.

With the money I earned in Kansas City, we get a room at an

Econo Lodge. The lobby is cluttered with fake ferns, as though someone wanted to give the appearance of entering a jungle. At the front desk, there is a stack of brochures that tell us about the history of the Econo Lodge. The Econo Lodge was founded in Norfolk, Virginia, by a man named Vernon Myers and his son, Vernon Junior. They were the first motel chain to put beds on boxes instead of legs, an innovation in motel management at the time.

I close the brochure and have a funny thought: does anyone care about history anymore?

Our room is small and dark and smells like chlorine, even though there is no swimming pool. I'm tired in a way that feels permanent. I take off my sneakers. My toes are swollen, the pads tender. On my soles I find blisters filled with white fluid and think about the barnacles hugging the bottom of my mother's ship. If you open barnacles up, do you find something soft inside?

Our room has double beds with forest green comforters and headboards that are slabs of honey-colored wood. In the center of each headboard, there is a lattice cut of a bear walking through a forest. We sit on a bed, facing each other, and Marcus tells me about an exercise that can help you find a person you are looking for. It goes like this:

First, close your eyes and picture a movie screen. You are sitting in the audience, in the dark of the theater. Imagine this person appearing on the screen. See her face. Second, imagine a phone booth in the corner of the screen. See the doors to the booth open. Hear the phone ringing. Third, see yourself leaving the audience and entering the screen. See yourself answering the ringing phone. See yourself saying, Hello, where are you? Imagine you are hearing this person speaking back.

In this imaginary theater, I sink into the seat and wait for my mother to appear.

"How did it go?" Marcus asks when I open my eyes.

I don't tell him that I couldn't get past my mother's face on the movie screen, couldn't get to the booth and the ringing phone. My imagination is only feeling so cooperative.

"It went," I say.

In the evening, Marcus wants to walk, to move: on the buses, we sat still for unnaturally long periods of time. We have energy stored inside us. We go out into the streets and watch clouds slip across a fat moon.

At this hour in Boston, on the brink of dusk, the windows in the buildings would start to shine bright as jewels. Here the skyline is low and the windows stay dark.

We wander down a broad empty street, the river, the Kanawha, on one side. We find our way to a white building with columns and a domed roof. It looks like an official building of some kind, powerful and secretive. I've forgotten the gardening gloves and my hands are cold. We walk up the steps and stand between the columns and look out at the river winding through the powdery blue light.

We continue on, under an overpass, the concrete pillars stained with bird shit, where we can hear the low hum of traffic. We find a little park with a fountain in the center. The tops of the trees are flat and dark like mushroom caps. They cast large shadows on the ground. The ice-crusted grass has become a net for trapping cigarette butts and the metal tongues of beer cans. The fountain is dry. Green pennies are stuck to the bottom. The paint is cracked and tiny weeds are forcing their way through the concrete. We climb into the base of the fountain and look out at the world around us.

"I was in a Hospital," I tell Marcus. "I didn't think I was ever going to leave."

I stand there and absorb the force of that feeling. It is a physical recognition, a warm pressure in the center of my belly. In the Hospital, in the unending cold of winter, I began to believe that I would never again see another city or park or monument or river. I began to believe that version of my story, but that version turned out to be wrong, because here I am in the capital of West Virginia, with Marcus, on my way to find my mother.

I should be free of that feeling now, hundreds of miles from the Hospital, but the shadow of it hangs over me, like there's a part of me that is still locked up and will never be anything but locked up.

"You got out." Marcus rubs his plastic lips. "You'll always get out."

"I got out," I say, hoping to convince that locked-up part of myself.

I jump onto the edge of the fountain. I place my hands on my belly. I feel the warm pressure building. I stare out into the night and scream and am stunned by my own loudness. Marcus jumps up beside me. He grabs my hand, hot and slick, and we scream together. I see our voices rising into the trees and getting tangled up in the branches, making nests of sound.

Eventually we walk away, calling out everything we know about rabbits. Rabbits are excellent at leaping and digging and running. For their entire lives, their teeth keep growing. They can live everywhere except for in Antarctica. They can infect people with rabbit fever, a disease that makes the patients sweat and itch. They like the dark. They do not like to be alone.

Just when the city is starting to feel like it belongs to us, the city sets us straight.

We are away from the park, wandering down a narrow side street, when a mob of people dressed in black, their faces painted a ghoulish white, rush out from behind the corner of a building. A cavalry of acrobats, I think, even though I know enough to know "cavalry" and "acrobat" are not two words that belong together.

We stop in the center of the street. These people are charging toward us and before we can escape, we are in the thick of the pack. I see holes in their black shirts and patches where the white paint has faded, revealing the humanness beneath. Wild eyes. Beneath us the asphalt rumbles. Marcus is carried away from me. I see the yellow fluff spilling from his coat. We cast our arms forward like swimmers in a roiling sea, trying to fight our way back to each other.

These people don't stop or speak or try to take us with them. They run with animal indifference, like those horses in Paola. I don't know who they are or what they have decided to be.

For a second, I am tempted to follow them.

Marcus disappears from sight. I tumble toward the edge of the group. I try to break free. My toes get stomped on, a jab to my tailbone makes me howl, the vibrations of their running moves like electricity through my body. I tuck my chin to my chest and push my way through.

There is a moment that must be like the eye of a storm, where the noise of the footsteps is so loud, so overwhelming to the senses, it becomes a kind of silence. I turn inside the dark swirl. Mouths open, feet strike asphalt, and I can't hear any of it. I see an orange helicopter hovering over an ocean and the white froth of the water below and my mother on a stretcher, sealed inside a world where there is no noise and all the hands working the straps belong to one body and the borders of the ocean are not borders at all, because they are endless.

■ ■ ■

The stampede leaves our hearts pounding and our hands shaking and that warm pressure in my belly is being replaced with something as cold and hard as stone. Marcus's rabbit mask has gotten twisted on his face. An eyehole has been displaced to a temple.

I watch him put his features back in order. We stand on the empty side street until the vibrations have dripped out of our bodies and the asphalt has gone still under out feet.

We start back to the Econo Lodge, but we get lost. We go down street after street. In the dark all the buildings look the same. For a while, we run like the people in black, but eventually we get tired and fall into a stumbling walk. Who are we kidding? We find ourselves under the same overpass, back in the same park with the mushroom trees, back inside the fountain, circling and circling. This time we don't jump inside and scream.

Panic creeps in, winds its way around my bones. What if we are searching like this forever? What if morning never comes? In the park, Marcus closes his eyes and tries to see our street and our motel and the way back, but his imagination is not feeling cooperative either.

We wander down a street where all the traffic lights are a dull red. We see a little white building called Johnny's Luncheonette, a gas station called Stop & Go. Instead of being tucked into the pumps, the nozzles are all lying on the ground like they were once an alive thing that someone has killed. The inside of the station is aglow with light.

Behind the counter we find a man in a Kiss T-shirt. His chin is barbed with dark hair. He has a lazy eye. We tell him that we're lost.

"What are you trying to find?"

"The Econo Lodge. Washington Street."

A plastic container filled with vials of black rocks sit on the counter. The man picks one up and shakes it. W. VA COAL is painted across the vial in small red letters.

"This isn't real coal," the man tells us, one eye drifting toward the door. "But it sure looks real, doesn't it?"

Marcus and I are starting to think this man in the Kiss T-shirt is not someone who can help us, but then he starts drawing a map on a brown paper napkin. He tells us we're close to where we want to be. He sketches out a tight maze of streets and adds arrows to show us where to go.

"Have you seen those people with painted faces running around?" I ask the man. "What are they?"

"Oh, those people," the man says, shaking his head.

We wait, but he doesn't give us anything more.

We thank him and head back out into the night.

"Mountaineers are always free," he calls after us.

We have no idea what that means.

We follow his map back to the white building with the domed roof, but then we get turned around again. We end up sitting on the steps of the building and blowing hot air on our fingers. I can feel the blisters growing inside my sneakers. We watch the sun rise over the river and soak the water in light. We set out again with our little gas station map and this time we don't walk for long before we find ourselves, as if by magic, standing right outside the place we are supposed to be.

. . .

In our motel room, I get into one of the beds. The curtains are thick and block the rising sun; in here it is endless night. Marcus is sitting on the other bed and scratching the skin behind his mask.

I turn on the TV, where a reporter is chronicling all the ways people have tried to find cures. One man concocted an antidote from household cleaning supplies and poisoned his entire family. After the sickness ended, they were found lying in a circle on their living room floor, feet pointed at the wall, heads pointed at the center of the circle, like they were playing a game or doing a meditation exercise or taking a nap from which they would, at any moment, wake.

Next door a man is shouting. The noise is too much. My mother seems very far away. I feel the world grow duller, feel sound melt into a fuzz, and it occurs to me that this might be what it's like when you begin to die.

When I wake, Marcus is kneeling next to me and holding a finger under my nose. He blinks at me from inside the rabbit mask. My feet push at the empty space at the bottom of the bed. I feel slow and thirsty, like I have been away on a very long adventure I can no longer recall.

"Are you alive in there?" Marcus says.

I sit up and the sleep peels away like sand falling out of my hair.

"You've been asleep for twelve hours." He pulls his hand back. "Ten hours is a coma. I was starting to get worried."

I look at the bedside clock. Already another day is slipping past. Outside the Hospital the rules of time are confusing to me. Maybe in my sleep I was swimming toward that new self I know is out there.

The TV is still on, but muted. A camera pans across a purple mountain range, an advertisement for a special kind of oxygen-enriched air. This air is called Super Air and it promises to help you get what we all want: more time on earth.

"Yes," I say, for the second time since leaving the Hospital. "I am alive."

■ ■ ■

When I was alone, the act of calling my mother's number, of pressing that particular sequence of buttons, seemed impossible. With Marcus, I feel braver.

Still, I don't call right away. He walks me through the phone visualization exercise again and this time I get as far as the booth and the ringing; I just can't get myself to walk on the screen and answer. We each take showers and we wash our shirts in the sink and dry them with the hair dryer in our room, which is long and white instead of dark and gun-shaped. In the bathroom mirror, we stand side by side and look at our reflections. I can see my nipples through the thin cotton of my bra and I don't feel exposed and I don't feel ashamed. Marcus's body is still boyish. His torso is pale and hairless except for the soft ring around his bellybutton and the freckle over his right nipple. With his masked face I think he looks like a wrestler and tell him so.

"What would your wrestling name be?" I ask. "Marcus the Marauder. Marcus the Murderer."

"Marcus the Monster!"

"Marcus the Monsoon!"

"Rabbits are vicious," he says.

We laugh and in the mirror our stomachs ripple.

I'm so starved that my body feels like it has been emptied, like I contain nothing but dust. We get dressed and go outside, driven by hunger, and find the same white-faced mob standing on a street corner and passing out sandwiches wrapped in tinfoil and Styrofoam cups filled with cold coffee. The day is the color of slate. We drink the coffee and chew the stale bread. Marcus slips everything under his mask with an expertise that makes it look like a magic trick. These provisions are free and right now anything free feels like a blessing.

When we ask these people if they remember us from the night before, if they remember nearly running us the fuck over, the bright white faces stare back, uncomprehending. When we ask them what they're doing out here, they tell us that this is their city and they are saving it. When we ask them why they run in the night, they tell us they do it because they are so glad to still be among the living.

Inside the motel we pass a woman cleaning the fake ferns with a sponge, and when she sees our sandwiches, she points the sponge at us and says, "Goddamn those people. They are terrorizing this city." She tells us the sandwiches are probably poisoned. We each ate two sandwiches apiece and we don't know what to believe. What if the acrobats are part of some kind of cult? What if they are trying to incite mass suicide? In our room, we sit on a bed and hold our stomachs. We suffer no ill effects.

Calling my mother is the last thing I do before we leave. I pick up the phone and listen to the dial tone. I start pressing the numbers. The phone rings and rings. I count to twelve and hang up.

"No one's there."

"Try again," Marcus says.

The phone rings three times before someone answers. They don't say anything, but I can hear them breathing on the line. Is this my mother? Does she know who I am?

"Hello," I say.

There is just breath and breath and breath.

■ ■ ■

On the road there are certain things we learn to count on. There are the water fountains with the rotten egg smell and the low-pressure ones that force your lips too close to the spout. The rough brown paper towels we use to clean our faces and necks and armpits and between our legs in the bathrooms, except for when the dispenser is empty and what you want is a wet crumple on the floor. In that case, we use toilet paper or little white napkins or go without. There are the bathrooms that are clean and the ones that look like a tiny apocalypse. In Horse Cave, Kentucky, I see a cardboard core of a toilet paper roll soaked in blood. There's the thin gas station coffee we doctor with sugar and cream. The vending machines that eat your change and the ones that give you double Cheetos, which feels like cosmic balance. The shifting configuration of the riders, like a party where the pool of guests keeps getting made over, except no one is talking or laughing or having any fun. There is the smell of exhaust, the smell of unclean bodies, the smell of hot dogs roasting on gas station counters, the skin crisped and gleaming, the smell of the tall boys passengers crack open late at night. The road is alive. There are people in rest area parking lots, filling up tanks, spreading maps across hoods. There are Jehovah's Witnesses handing out pamphlets and telling us that God cares about the individual burden of our suffering. There are cars and pickup trucks and semis rolling alongside us on the highway. Everyone is trying to get somewhere.

27.

In Memphis, the bus drops us on the outskirts of the city. We have been riding for nine hours, passing through towns with names like Cattlesberg and Hurricane and Coalton. We are down to seven dollars and fifteen cents.

We passed the Olympia State Forest and signs for Dinosaur World and I thought about the books in the Hospital library, about asteroids and epidemics and continental drift. In Black Rock, Arkansas, we passed a lake with a tiny forest in the center. I looked into the dense dark trees and wondered what kinds of things might be living in there. In a gas station bathroom, I saw a sign that said USE THE RECOVERY POSITION, with a drawing of one person standing over another and rolling them onto their side.

Somewhere in Tennessee, on I-40, the driver pulled onto the shoulder and got out. What is wrong with these drivers? He stood in the cold, staring at the barbed-wire fence and the snowy field beyond it. The wire points on the fence looked like tiny stars. I watched his breath rise above him in white clouds. The passengers cupped their hands and peered out the frosted windows, waiting for something to happen.

Marcus and I rapped the panes. A few people went out and tried to see what was going on. A woman wanted to get the keys and drive the bus herself, to leave this man behind, if that's what he wanted, but the driver wouldn't hand over the keys and no one seemed willing to take them by force.

After two hours, the driver got back on the bus and continued down the highway. No one knew what changed within him, why he stopped in the first place or why he decided to keep driving.

Is there any greater mystery than the separateness of each person?

Now the sun is sinking, another night-soaked arrival in a strange place. That is the pattern of our days, not clock time, but the cycles of light and dark. For a while we walk along a river and Marcus tells me about how, before the sickness, he bounced around shelters in Cambridge, played chess for cash in Harvard Square. He beat the mental patients and the teenage geniuses and the punks and the professors. He had an uncanny ability to predict his opponent's next move. For a while, he belonged to a group at a community center that was supposed to teach its members life skills, but when they got together all they did was stand around and hug each other.

"You mean like sex?" I say, not wanting to imagine all those lost people groping each other on some musty basement carpet.

"No, I mean like this," he says, and wraps his arms around my shoulders.

In darkness, we climb a steep hill. We find train tracks to follow and hope they will lead us somewhere, to lights, to people, but everything we pass looks deserted. A string of little houses with screened porches and soft, sunken roofs. Impenetrable thickets of bramble and tree. An abandoned barn.

I remember waiting for the T one night, at a stop where the

trains went above ground, and seeing a man with a backpack trudging up the tracks, into the distant dark. I shouted "Watch out for the trains!" and felt ridiculous for warning him of such an obvious danger. Didn't I know the worst dangers weren't the obvious ones?

We leave the tracks and head in the direction of the barn. We get snagged on roots, brush against the rough trunks of trees. There is no light anywhere around us.

"Fucking shit," we say.

We are lost. There is no getting away from that. We decide to sleep in the barn. At least it is a structure, with four walls and a roof. We walk through a doorway that is missing its door, into an enormous space as dark as an underground cave or a black hole in outer space or the Hospital at night.

The floor is blanketed in frozen leaves. As we go down, they crunch like tiny bones.

I dream about the Hospital. I'm alone, in one of those white hallways, the window a distant arch at the end. I'm standing under a speaker and the most terrible noise is pouring into me. It is Dr. Bek's rasping breath, only much louder than before, like a team of hazmatted people are standing around a microphone and speaking into it. In the dream, I have been in this hallway, listening to this noise, for many years. I want to stop the noise, to knock the speaker off the wall, to tear out the wires, but I have no way to do such a thing. I don't have any of the right skills and that seems like the worst part, my inability to save myself.

When I stop dreaming, I'm grabbing at leaves and daylight is streaming through two coffin-shaped windows and large hawkish birds are perched on the wooden beams above. I can see light coming through the holes in the walls. I hear a rustling in the corners and the wind outside.

I sit up. A pebble falls out of my ear. Leaves are trapped in my hair. My mouth feels like it's full of gravel. Dirt is stuck to my arms. There is a sloshing in my stomach. One of the hawkish birds swoops down and lands on the ground. It pushes the leaves around and then flies away with a small squirming thing clutched in its beak.

I shake Marcus awake.

We get up. We look around. We touch the walls of the barn, searching for liquid, condensation, melting ice. We are that thirsty. That desperate to get what we need to survive. On the walls, there is no liquid, just dust that sticks to our fingers. It hurts to walk, to bend down, to look up, to breathe. Outside we find small patches of snow and we eat them. I take off my gardening gloves and scoop the ice into my palms and lap at it like a dog. The snow has rocks in it and tastes like dirt.

■ ■ ■

When we leave the barn, the afternoon sun is low and fading, like all the color is being slowly sucked out, and we realize we are on the edge of a property. From a distance, we can see an old house on a hill, a two-story with a dormer roof and a sagging wraparound porch. The dark splotches on the roof where shingles are missing look like water curving around land on a map. The white paint is peeling. The front door is knobless. A neon yellow skull has been graffitied in the center. A tall metal frame stands to the left of the house, as though the structure was abandoned mid-renovation.

A young woman is on the porch in a nubby sweater and corduroy pants and rubber boots. I appreciate the soft look of her clothing. On the road softness is something I miss.

There is something strange about her body, something misshapen, and it's not until we reach the edge of the front yard that I see the white angel wings hanging from her back.

She waves to us, this woman.

We cross the yard, through the mud and slush. We watch the woman pet her wings. We tell the woman our names. We say we're looking for a place to sleep. We ask if she can help us.

The woman's name is Darcie. She has freckles on her eyelids. The tips of her front teeth are stained caramel. She lives here with a man, Nelson, and they call this place the Mansion. She tells us we can stay for as long as we like.

"The Mansion always has room," she says, opening the door.

Inside she gives us water in Mason jars. There's grit floating in the bottom, but we couldn't care less. We hold our jars with both hands and gulp the water. I close my eyes and feel the cool slip down my throat. I chew the grit when it gets stuck in my teeth. Exhaustion has brought on strange pains in my face: aches in the jaw, along my hairline, in the spaces between my eyes.

There is no sign of this other person, this Nelson. The Mansion is warm and quiet.

"Where did you come from?" Darcie wants to know.

We're standing in a dim kitchen, and I can make out a big metal sink and long windows. White candles, burned to waxy nubs, on the sills. An old boxy refrigerator. The door is ajar and I catch the scent of rot.

A blue tile floor streaked with mud, like a sky with a storm rolling in.

"From the west," we reply.

Darcie rests a fist under her chin, like she's giving careful thought to our origins, to what it means to have come from the west. Two downy feathers fall from her wings and into the shadows below.

When we ask where she came from, she tells us that she cannot remember.

■ ■ ■

Darcie gives us a room on the second floor. This room is empty except for a bare mattress with a white sheet. The floorboards are swollen. The walls are peeling. A window overlooks the back-yard, a small sprawl of land surrounded by a halo of leafless trees and then dark woods, the rounded treetops stretching into the beyond. On one wall, we find a series of stick figures drawn in pencil. The figures are taking shits and fucking and choking each other. LIFE WHO NEEDS IT someone has written below them in big jagged letters.

Once we're alone, the sky turning dark outside, Marcus asks how I'm feeling and I tell him I'm feeling sad.

I sit down on the mattress. "I thought we would have gotten farther by now." When I left the Hospital I thought I would just keep going and going, all the way to Florida. I didn't foresee be-ing so thoroughly beaten by the elements, for my mother to still feel so far away.

"Here's something," Marcus says. "In a bathroom in West Virginia, I saw a sign telling people to not use toilet water for drinking. There was a drawing of a man dunking his head in the toilet with a big red X over it."

I laugh and tell him about the recovery position sign I saw in a bathroom, and then he grabs my waist and we take turns roll-ing each other onto our sides, into the position of recovery. The skin on his arms is cold and gummy. My intestines twist around.

We should be exhausted, tranquilized with sleep, but instead we keep assuming the recovery position. After all, we have so much to recover from. Finally we settle down on the mattress, still quivering with laughter, nearly delirious. We lie on our backs, the sheet tucked under our arms, our feet sticking out. The mattress fabric is printed with pink and green flowers, the stems faded. I pull off the gardening gloves. My fingertips are pruned.

"Right now I don't feel like I will ever be able to move again," I tell Marcus.

"Tomorrow," he says. "We'll feel better tomorrow."

We fall asleep on our backs, our feet hanging over the edge of the mattress, heels touching the floor. We do not dream.

In the morning, Marcus and I wake curled on the mattress. In our sleep, our bodies have taken on new positions. We are facing each other, legs tucked, full of aches and hunger. My tongue is stuck to the roof of my mouth. My stomach makes a rumbling so loud it startles me. The soles of my feet are so blistered and bruised, it looks like they're evolving into something not quite human, concentric circles of dead skin, bright purple blotches.

My toenails are sharp.

I lie awake for a long time before I feel capable of moving. I face away from the window and watch a black beetle scuttle up the wall and think about how this house could be our recovery position.

We find Darcie at the foot of the stairs. Her hair is long and blonde, dark at the roots, the ends tangled in her angel wings. She wants to know about our dreams, but we tell her that we didn't dream anything or at least not anything we can remember.

"Just you wait," Darcie says.

In the Mansion, it is dry. In the Mansion, we have a place to sleep and it does not cost money. There is food. A mushy piece of fruit. A can of cold tomato soup, opened with a pocketknife, the blade dull with rust. On the second floor, a claw-foot bathtub that can be filled with the rainwater Darcie and Nelson collect in black plastic tubs.

Out there we don't know what will happen to us. The cities are strange, the bus drivers unreliable. We have been temporarily slowed by the needs of the body, the body that doesn't care that my mother is still far away in Florida, that she is still in need of finding. The body that only cares for food, water, sleep.

In the kitchen, we each eat a piece of brown bread and a sour orange. Marcus peels his orange carefully and eats one wedge at a time. I don't take off the skin. I bite right into the peel and juice spills down my chin.

After we finish, Darcie tells us that she wants to give us a tour.

In the living room, one side of the wall is papered with gold leaves. The other side is bare plaster, marked with lines of rust and brown clay that look like streaks of shit. Silver lamps, black with tarnish, sit on the floor. A red velvet armchair with a fist-size hole in the seat stands in a corner. The fabric at the bottom of the chair sags. More holes in the floorboards, the edges splintered. In the center of the ceiling, a skylight. The clouds above are gray and swirling. The fireplace is made of beautiful blue marble, the hearth packed with sticks and leaves and ash.

"This house will play tricks on you," she says.

We keep looking around. Rain clicks against the skylight. The ceiling darkens and swells.

Darcie bends down, picks up the thin string lying on the floor, and pulls. The trap door that opens is the size of a dumbwaiter. She crouches inside it. Marcus and I move toward her, inspecting. Up close her feathers are dingy and frayed.

"See?" she says from inside the door, raising her hands. She is a woman of average size, but her hands are small as a child's. "Tricks."

Next we go into the kitchen, to the corner where the walls don't meet in a smooth line, but are separated by a slim column, like a body with an extra feature: a sixth finger, a surplus molar. There's a small hook on the wall, something you'd hang a coat on, and when Darcie pulls the hook, the column, which is some kind of mechanized door, slides open. There is the scent of cedar, a wave of dust.

The last thing she shows us is a little alcove off the living room with shelves built into the walls. The shelves are filled with books of all kinds: hardbacks in their dust jackets, grocery store paperbacks, linen-bound ones that make me think of the books in the Psychologist's bedroom. Marcus and I move around inside the alcove, examining the spines. I pull out a paperback titled *Twenty Thousand Leagues Under the Sea.* On the cover there is a submarine descending into the ocean, into the tentacles of the octopus waiting below. When Darcie turns away, I slip the book into my pocket.

Back in the kitchen, a door slams and a man skids into the room. He looks young, like the rest of us, except his hair and eyebrows have already gone silver. His eyes are quick and violet. I can see blue networks of veins and arteries in his wrists and along his pale throat, evidence of a working body. He's wearing a poncho made from a black garbage bag, the plastic beaded with rain.

"Nelson," Darcie says.

Nelson is holding a toy gun. It has a red handle and a metal barrel. He looks at me and then at Marcus, looks carefully at his rabbit face, as though he's trying to decide which one of us to shoot first.

"These people, they're going to stay with us for a while." Darcie moves her shoulders in a way that makes her look like a bird fluffing its feathers. Orange pulp has dried around my lips.

Nelson aims the toy gun at me. "Bang!"

I put my hand over my heart, pretend to fall.

"Cops and robbers," Darcie says. She smiles and claps. "Nelson loves to play cops and robbers."

*   *   *

On that first morning, the four of us sit on the sticky kitchen floor, holding strips of white cloth soaked in rainwater. We shove the cloth into our mouths and scrub our teeth and gums. We don't say anything. We watch each other disappear into our own strangeness. Hands stretch cheeks, air gushes through nostrils. We scrub and grunt. I can see Marcus's hand pushing around under his mask. I haven't cleaned my teeth since I left the Hospital, haven't done more than swirl tap water around in my mouth. I taste blood on my gums, I feel a warm drip on my bottom lip, but I don't stop for anything.

28.

Darcie and Nelson have much to teach us about survival and we are interested in being taught. They know how to purify the rainwater they collect by boiling it on the gas stove. They show us how to make garbage bag jackets of our own and how to take a bath in the claw-foot tub. The porcelain bottom is padded with rust. The first time I clean myself in there, I look down into the red water and think I'm bleeding.

They pull up weeds and eat them. Their favorites are dandelion and thistle and fat hen. They have learned the hard way about what will make them feel sick and what will make them feel well. In the alcove library, they show us a book with drawings called *Wicked Botany*. We turn the pages and I see black-and-white illustrations of spade-shaped leaves drawn in meticulous detail, fibrous roots, blossoms dangling from stems like tiny bells.

They seem to know a lot about the state of Tennessee. Shelby County has more horses than any other county in America. Murfreesboro is the geographical center of the state. In Tennessee,

204 • LAURA VAN DEN BERG

there are over three thousand caves. Lake County is the turtle capital of the world. There is a replica of the Parthenon in Nashville.

I memorize these facts about Tennessee and repeat them to myself on the nights I have trouble sleeping—which is every night.

One afternoon, they lead us away from the Mansion, down a wide dirt road that runs behind a water tower and an abandoned trailer park. Someone has painted an enormous red smiley face on the tower. The trailers are being consumed by moss and vine. The windows are rectangles of green fuzz. They look like they're being absorbed into the earth.

The water tower and the trailer park are surprises in the landscape. In my imagination, we have been situated in the middle of nowhere, with nothing around for many miles. My internal geography adjusts, makes room for these new details.

We have been in the Mansion for three days, time slipping by like a river over stones. In his Laws of the Road, Rick did not mention how long you should stay in any one place before you move on.

On the dirt road, Nelson starts telling us about the twin paradox, one of Einstein's thought experiments.

"Imagine a pair of twins," he begins, kicking up dust.

This part is not hard for me to do.

One twin is sent on a journey into outer space. The twin experiences a slowing of time and when he returns, he appears younger than the twin who stayed behind, which is the paradox. But in fact two have become three: the twin who stays home, the twin who leaves, and the twin who comes back. The twin who leaves is not the same twin who returns. That is a physical impossibility. Nelson says the experiment has to do with how we change. We go on a journey and we are never the same person when we come home.

I imagine Current Me sitting next to Stop & Shop Me on an MBTA bus. Current Me looks at her with tenderness, touches her cheek, tucks her hair, her still beautiful hair, behind her ear. There is so much this Stop & Shop Me does not yet know. Together the Mes look out at the other passengers and the construction rising from the ground and the people playing pool in Laundry World and the evangelical church, swollen with song. They stop at a red light and that is when Current Me leans in and whispers, One day all of this will be gone.

"I'm doing my own experiments," Nelson says.

I've gone missing inside myself. I focus on the rhythm of sneakers hitting dirt, the little shocks of energy, and find my way back.

"What kind of experiments?" Marcus is walking beside him, hands deep in his pockets. I notice a dark smudge on his rabbit nose.

"I'm going to find a cure," Nelson says.

"Is there anything left to cure?" I ask. Deep dirt trenches run along the sides of the road. They look like they've been created by a machine.

"There is everything left to cure," Darcie says.

We walk by a small construction pit. An orange cement truck is parked next to it, along with low stacks of metal beams, yet it seems like the actual construction never started. There is just a cavernous hole in the earth.

We keep going until we come to a small post office, a square brick building with an American flag and a sign that reads MICHIE TN out front. There is nothing else around. No other houses or stores. The window shades are drawn tight.

Is that where we are right now? Michie?

"There are people living in there." Nelson points at the windows. "People with means."

"People who aren't invisible like us," Darcie says. "We are against people with means."

Ever wanted to test your own level of invisibility? Write out your obituary and see how many people you are survived by.

We go around to the back of the post office, to the large Dumpster pressed against the brick. We watch Nelson and Darcie climb into the Dumpster and stand knee-deep in trash. Darcie's wings bob on her back. Nelson fishes out a withered apple and tosses it to Marcus. A plastic bag holding a quarter loaf of bread, the crust spongy with green mold, follows. A jar with a few spoonfuls of peanut butter inside. I get to hold the jar and can already feel the thick nutty paste on my tongue. There is something gummy on the label and little black bugs are crawling through it. They get inside the gardening gloves and nip at my hands.

Nelson finds a pack of sparklers too. The package has a cartoon of a white wolf on the front. He draws a sparkler from the pack and sniffs it, then passes it to Darcie. I think of the slender antenna glowing blue on my mother's ship, the St. Elmo's fire.

"Abracadabra." Darcie waves the sparkler over her head. "Hocus pocus."

Even when she's smiling, her eyes are glassy and rolling, like she's not really thinking about the *here* but about all the fearful things off in the distance, on the edges of the land.

What kind of spell is she casting?

■ ■ ■

That night, we light the sparklers in the backyard. We're all wearing garbage bag jackets. Underneath the plastic, Darcie's wings are a dark mass. Nelson ignites the first sparkler with a match, nudges the tip of his against the rest. Four globes of light that make our faces glow. I catch Darcie in profile and for a moment she looks like the girl who attacked me in the bathroom in Mission Hill, but then the light changes and she turns back into herself again.

Tricks, I think.

Nelson is the first to break from the group, yelping and bolting toward the trees. We run around the yard. We slip in the cold mud, leaving behind arcs of gold.

Earlier, on the second floor, I opened the copy of *Twenty Thousand Leagues Under the Sea*. The spine creaked. The pages were crusted with water stains. I read: "In the very heart of an extinct volcano, the interior of which has been invaded by the sea, after some great convulsion of the earth. Whilst you were sleeping, Professor, the Nautilus penetrated this lagoon by a natural canal, which opens about ten yards beneath the surface of the ocean."

A great convulsion of the earth, or at least our American corner of it. Isn't that what we have all lived through?

I closed the book and stuck my mother's photo and the postcard between the pages.

In the backyard, I can feel the space between past and future growing larger, like we have been crossing a river by hopping from one little island of rock to another and now the distance between the islands is expanding and we know that if we miscalculate our next jump, if we fall into the water, the river will twist itself around our ankles and drag us under. So for now we are staying still, Marcus and me. Still.

My sparkler has burned down to a black nothing and the heat stings my fingers. I drop it and the light fizzles. The magic is over, at least for tonight. Soon I lose sight of Darcie. Only Marcus and Nelson are still burning. I stand in the massive shadow of the Mansion and watch Marcus cut through the darkness. His mask is a streak of white, his body slender and quick. I hear the zap of his sparkler going out and his rabbit face vanishes, like we are lights that are being turned off one at a time.

As I listen to us move through the yard, the crunch of slush, the sucking sound of shoes on mud, I think about how this is what our childhoods could have been like if it had been all kids and no parents or people pretending to be.

· · ·

The twin paradox isn't Nelson's only theory. He lives at the very top of the Mansion, in the attic bedroom, a cramped space with a low roof. Up there I see few signs of it being a place where a person actually sleeps. It looks more like a laboratory: cloudy beakers, a long pair of metal tongs, an eyedropper, a cutting knife, goggles scattered across the floor, the lenses scratched and fogged.

A small oval window, like a porthole on a ship, overlooks the gray-green front yard, the grass lightly marbled with snow. From the window I can see the scaffolding. Nelson tells us that he knows the dimensions of this room so well, he can work in here at night, going by feel.

Three white bowling pins and a black ball are jammed into a corner. "Bowling helps me concentrate," Nelson says when he sees me nudging the ball around with my toe.

"Concentrate on what?" I ask.

"Darcie had the sickness," he tells us. He's not wearing his garbage bag jacket, just a white T-shirt, sweat dark around the underarms, and gray pants. I can see that his body has been stripped to the essentials. Every part is sharp and shadow thin. "But I got to her in time. She forgot, but she didn't die."

Darcie is sitting in a corner, her angel wings smushed against the wall, and picking mud out from under her fingernails. "It's true. He found me on the side of the road in Cordova, in Tennessee, and brought me here."

She gathers the mud on a knuckle. Once she has made a little dark lump, she eats it.

"Darcie is what we call *lucky*," Nelson says.

She tells us that the memories had been pouring from her for days, like a chemical you sweat out. She didn't know how to stop it, how to hold on to what she knew. She didn't know where she was headed or where she had come from or why she was wearing angel wings or if the road she was walking could even be called a road. Surely she had the sickness. Surely she should have died.

"There are other things that can make you forget." I look at the horseshoe-shaped burn marks on the floor. Every time someone moves, the boards creak and I imagine the house keeping track of our whereabouts.

"But what are the odds?" Darcie gathers her hair on one side of her neck and pulls it like a rope. "What are the odds of forgetting for some other reason during an epidemic of forgetting?"

"It's true." Marcus picks up the tongs. He makes them open and close like a beak. "What she's saying about odds."

"In the Mansion, she started to remember." Nelson taps the side of his skull. "We got the blood flow redirected, got those capillaries snapping again. Got her consciousness back."

My unconscious mind is very powerful and it wants me to keep living, I do not tell them.

When we ask Nelson what he did before the sickness, he says that person is gone. Not forgotten—just gone. He picks up a pair of goggles and puts them on, like he's ready to get to work. He moves with the authority of a person who is used to being in charge of other people, while Darcie has the meek manner of someone who has never known what it's like to have power over another person and maybe not even over herself.

"Where did you get all this stuff?" I bend down to touch a beaker. The inside is crusted with salt.

"We found it in the basement," Nelson says. "Has Darcie shown you the basement yet?"

Marcus and I shake our heads.

"Darcie loves the basement," Nelson says. "That's where she thinks she can talk to God."

29.

Our nights are filled with games.

Here are the rules for cops and robbers: the cops cop and the robbers rob. Marcus and I get to play the robbers, which I like. We're naturals in the role. Have I ever been a natural at anything before? We run away from Darcie and Nelson and the toy gun, screaming. It feels good, all that running and screaming. Sometimes Marcus grabs my hand and I think we're escaping for real, to a place where we will find my mother. I imagine us running outside and the woods parting and spotting her island among the trees like a pearl in an oyster, waiting to be found.

When we get caught, Darcie and Nelson press us against the wall and twist our arms behind our backs. I taste the chalkiness of the plaster, get dust up my nose. It is the best kind of capture, because nothing happens; there are no consequences for our stealing. No stern warnings, no fines, no jail. We are released into the night, to do it all over again.

Hide-and-go-seek, that's another one. Darcie always wins hide-and-go-seek. We check every room in the Mansion, all the secret compartments, until we finally give up and tell her to come out. If she doesn't come out right away, Nelson gets impatient and starts banging around the house, slamming doors, kicking over carpets, tearing up and down the stairs. In the dark, his silver hair glows. He smacks the wall and we hear plaster crumbling. He tells her to come out right fucking now or she can just forget about ever being fully cured.

"I was in the basement," Darcie always says, even though we've already looked down there.

In the Mansion, Marcus and I are starting to become very curious about this basement.

There is no electricity, but there is an oil lamp that we light and carry around with us at night—or rather, Nelson carries it around. "Whoever has the light has the power," he sings. Sometimes, after the games end, we drink the alcohol Nelson has cooked up in his lab. He says it's made from yeast and table sugar, but I only know that it sloshes around in a green bottle and burns when I drink it. It smells sweet like the Robitussin and after it goes down, faces turn into bright blurs, like the world is a wet canvas someone can't stop touching.

In the Mansion, our nights are long. We have started going in reverse: winter is leaving, yet our window of daylight keeps growing smaller. During these windows, we are busy. We are busy stomping through the woods, pulling up dandelion and chickweed and creeping charlie. Thistles with thorny leaves and soft purple flowers. We are busy measuring our water supply. We are busy suffocating cockroaches by coating them with the lye Nelson stores in his lab. The roaches flop over onto their backs, tiny legs kicking. We watch until the kicking stops. We are busy standing in the Dumpster and picking out what the people with means do not want. We go to bed near dawn and wake just before sunset. We are turning nocturnal. We are no longer in sync with the outside world, with the patterns of nature, but aligned with the rhythms of this house.

■ ■ ■

As it turns out, Darcie doesn't think she can talk to God in the basement.

In the basement, there is a steel door and behind that door, a tunnel. The floor is cool dirt. The walls are dark and smooth. The ceiling is rounded and just high enough to walk upright. You can go thirty steps before the tunnel ends, cut off by a stone wall. The wall is old and the rocks are coming loose. No one knows what's on the other side. It is in this tunnel that Darcie hears the voice of her mother, who is dead.

I wonder if the people who built this house intended the tunnel to be a safe room or fallout shelter, a place to go when the world ends.

"Dead from the sickness?" I ask Darcie, who shakes her head.

"She died a long time ago."

She tells me and Marcus about the tunnel in the living room. Nelson is upstairs, working in the attic. We can hear the bowling ball knocking down pins. Clunk, clunk, clunk. Darcie is balled inside the trap door, her chin resting on her knees. Her hair is tucked behind her ears, her roots black and oily. It's dusk. I look up and see tiny crystalline stars through the skylight.

"How do you do it?" I ask. "How do you hear her?"

She shrugs. Her wings rub the floor.

"It's private," she says. "It's mine."

"My mother is gone," I say, choosing to not elaborate on what I mean by gone.

She looks at us. She chews her upper lip.

"His too," I add, nodding at Marcus.

"Like I said, it's my tunnel." Darcie sniffs. "Besides, it's not as simple as walking in and saying hello. There's an entire ritual."

"We can learn," I tell her.

"You can watch." She pauses, looks across the room. "And that's as close as you're going to get."

In the basement, the ritual starts with Darcie putting four drops of a sweet-smelling liquid under her tongue. It's something Nelson has given her, to help her remember, to help her become fully cured. On her own, she discovered that if she takes the drops and goes into the tunnel, she can hear things. Like voices. Like her mother's voice.

"The first time it was an accident," she tells us. "I didn't even know there was a tunnel down here. I was just doing what Nelson said I should do. I was just wandering around and trying to remember."

The liquid in the eyedropper is clear as water. It looks like a serious drug, like GHB or ketamine, which I have never taken before, because *being* dead and wanting to *feel* dead are not the same thing. In Mission Hill, I heard stories about girls getting drugged with GHB and waking up half-naked in backyards and in parks and in parking lots, always outdoors it seemed, only they didn't call it GHB. It was Cherry Meth or Easy Lay or Grievous Bodily Harm.

"Hm." I flick a finger at the eyedropper. "I've seen the end of *that* movie."

"What movie?" Darcie says.

I'm scared of this liquid, but just because it is not something I would have taken before, in the land where there was an endless supply of cough syrup and no mother to reach, doesn't mean I wouldn't be willing to do it now.

"You sure you don't want some company in there?" I do the same finger-flick at the steel door.

"In the tunnel, there is no such thing as company," Darcie says.

She squeezes the liquid into her mouth. Next she takes off her clothes. She pulls her sweater over her head, unzips her pants. She has nothing on underneath. She doesn't blush or turn away. She is not shy around us. I can see the fine bones in her back and the strange shape of her kneecaps. Her nipples are pinpricks of brown.

It's cold in the basement. Cobwebs sag from the ceiling like dead skin.

We can't help it. We stare at Darcie.

"I told you there was a ritual," she says, as though that explains everything.

We watch her open the steel door and slip inside the tunnel. She's gone for a long time. I look at Marcus and imagine him naked in the basement. I see his long thighs and the tight mass of his balls. The strangeness of a masked face against all that hairless skin. I pick up the eyedropper and look at the residue inside. It smells like nothing.

"I want to go in there," I say to Marcus.

"I remember my mother well enough," he says. "I don't need to hear her voice."

"Speak for yourself," I say.

In a corner, we find a plastic baby doll with a missing arm and a dark bow-shaped mouth. We take turns putting on Darcie's wings. I walk around the basement with the weight of them on my back. We wait for the door to open and for Darcie to come out and tell us all about what she's heard in there.

When the door finally creaks open and Darcie spills into the basement, she's crying. Her hair is stuck to her cheeks. She crosses her arms over her stomach and shivers.

"What's wrong?" we want to know.

I pick up her sweater and try handing it to her. Above us there is the rumble of falling pins. "Did you not hear her?"

"Sometimes you don't hear what you wish you would," Darcie says.

• • •

One night, in the living room, Darcie tells us about this idea she has for a city with only one building. When we point out that a city with only one building can't really be considered a city, she says we don't understand.

We are taking turns drinking from the green bottle. The oil lamp is stationed on the floor and I watch an ant crawl through the circle of light. It looks injured.

"Everything cities have would exist in this one building." Darcie reaches into the fireplace. She finds a stick and starts drawing her city in the air. A large moth touches down on a lamp shade, then flies over to a window and beats the glass with its wings.

"The building would be so tall, it would reach the stratosphere. That's between the troposphere and the mesosphere, in case you didn't know. It would hold millions of people, no, billions, billions of people, and roads and schools and police stations and museums and train stations and airports and restaurants."

"That sounds crowded," Marcus says.

"It's a stupid idea for a city." Nelson reaches for the bottle, his pale arm thrusting into the light.

Babylon, I think, imagining a stone tower ascending into the clouds. Where have I heard about Babylon before?

"No one would ever be lost," Darcie says, as though she hasn't heard our misgivings. She gets the bottle next.

"Imagine this instead," Nelson tells us, taking over.

He tells us to imagine getting so tangled up inside yourself that you would do anything for a way out. To imagine the lure of forgetting, of wiping it all away. He tells us that what separates us from animals is not logical thought but our ability to set our own traps. What if we could get away from all that? None of the infected remember how they contracted the sickness—how could they? The sickness was designed to erase who we were. Who could say how it all started?

"It started with Clara Sue Borden." I slurp from the green bottle and feel the words turn to syrup in my mouth. "Everyone knows that. It started with California."

"Imagine," Nelson says, raising a finger. "That this is something we did to ourselves."

Rain beats the skylight. I hear scratching in the walls.

"Take Darcie here," he continues. By now Darcie has forgotten all about her city with only one building. She is lying on the floor. The tops of her wings are brushing her ears. Her mouth is open. Her eyes look wet and empty. "The trick was getting her so far outside herself that she was able to stand back and see that she could still remember, could always remember. That she could see that she was well."

On the floor, Darcie does not look well.

"I went to an official place, to try and talk to official people, but no one wanted to hear about it."

"Where?" I put the green bottle down. I feel a shiver of curiosity.

"Where what?"

"Where was this official place?"

"Far away. Someplace far away and cold." Nelson claws at his arms. His skin is dotted with little red sores. "Those official people didn't want what I knew, so now Darcie gets to have it."

She rolls over on her back, crushing her wings. Feathers shoot out from underneath her arms.

Nelson starts talking about the rash of postepidemic suicides.

Arlington Memorial Bridge, Tobin Bridge, Rio Grande Gorge Bridge. Bayonne Bridge, where the jumper self-immolated, so that when she leaped she was a burning ball of light, so there would be zero chance of survival. He tells us the sickness is over and everywhere people are using bridges not for crossing but for jumping and what are we supposed to think about that.

"So, as I am illustrating, there is still a lot to be cured."

The bottle is almost empty. Nelson spins it around in his hands.

"How have you done such a good job of keeping up with the news?" I want to know.

I don't want to admit that I've been thinking about all the suicides and disappearances too, trying to calculate how much damage a person can take before it becomes unsurvivable.

"The people with means," Darcie mumbles from the floor. "They play their radio way too loud."

Nelson tells us about his old job, at a facility that cared for people who didn't belong in a hospital, but didn't belong on their own either. Assisted living, you could call it. I wonder if that's the kind of place Ms. Neuman ended up in.

At this facility, they had a patient who woke every morning coated in bruises. The doctors checked her out and worked up her blood; no one could understand the cause. The facility installed a camera in her room, thinking they might catch one of their own staff mistreating this patient, but instead on the footage they watched this woman get up in the middle of the night and ram her body into the bed posts, the dresser corners, the closet door. The whole time she was doing it to herself.

I think of the cutters in the homes, the girls who sliced themselves up in the night and came to breakfast with long red cuts on the undersides of their arms, the skin hot and raised. Those were the girls who wanted to get noticed, to show off how much pain they could take. The ones who didn't wore long-sleeved shirts in the summertime and used loose razor blades to sever the skin between their toes.

I think about those girls and Dr. Bek and the hospital in Oslo, about how it all connects back to the unconscious mind.

Nelson finishes the bottle. He stands and steps out of the light. I raise the lamp and watch him do one perfect cartwheel.

I keep holding up the lamp. I feel myself melt into the floor.

He lands light on his feet. He takes a small, swooping bow.

"Imagine," he says, "that we are just a nation of people with a deep desire to die."

· · ·

In our room on the second floor, alone with Marcus, I open the book and read to him: "The sea is everything. It covers seven-tenths of the terrestrial globe. Its breath is pure and healthy. It is an immense desert, where man is never lonely, for he feels life stirring on all sides."

Terrestrial, I keep thinking, still woozy from the green bottle. The word feels strange inside my brain.

Is the sea still everything to my mother? Is she still pure and healthy?

"Yes," Marcus says, and I realize I've been speaking aloud.

Marcus has started adding to the drawings on our bedroom wall, only in his drawing there are no people. He uses a pencil he borrowed from Nelson's lab. From the mattress, I watch him sit alongside the wall, like he's in a canoe, and squeeze the pencil tight. Next to the person taking a shit, he is sketching a sailboat. It is empty of passengers and floating on waves shaped like teeth.

I have gotten used to him sleeping next to me, gotten used to the weight and warmth of another body. He smells like a city after a rain. His left foot jerks when he dreams. Sometimes we wake with our legs twisted together or our hands touching, damp and warm, or with his rosy rabbit lips pressed against the back of my neck. Every night we are close, but I am his sister still.

When I'm alone in the Mansion, I find myself standing at the top of the basement steps. I think about the cold and the nets of cobwebs and Darcie filling the eyedropper with a liquid that has no color and no smell. I think about how Cherry Meth sounds like it could be candy and how the Mission Hill girls said there was a stretch of time when it felt glorious, like someone had given them an amazing gift and they were going to dream forever. How can Darcie be convinced? I look at the dark stairs and wonder what it would be possible for me to hear down there, to remember.

■ ■ ■

I have the dream about me and my mother swimming in the ocean. I smell grass. There is no land, no fear, no limit to how long we can hold our breath—same as before. Only this time my mother swims up behind me and lashes her arm around my chest and hauls me under the water. Suddenly I have limits. Suddenly my air is running out. I twist and I kick. I bite her muscled forearm. I try to get loose, to turn in the water and see her face or what her face has been replaced with. She holds me under until the shadows at the bottom of the sea start rising toward me. I feel the cold on the soles of my feet and when I wake my feet are cold like they've been soaked in ice and I'm breathing fast and in the dark of our room it's Marcus who has lashed his arm around me. He is holding me as tight as my mother did in my dream, only he is saying, "Easy easy," and I know he isn't trying to sink me but bring me up.

■ ■ ■

One week it feels like spring outside and our games move into the yard, a race through the woods behind the Mansion, the halo of bare trees the starting point, the creek at the bottom of the slope the finish. We line up in the shadow of the house and Nelson shouts, "Go!" and we all take off. The slush is melting, uncovering the world that has been sleeping beneath, a vast map of root and mud and branch and leaf and weed. Nelson is fast, and for a while he's right beside me, but then something in me shifts and I'm gone. My steps grow longer. I feel my body gaining speed. I bounce through the mud, over fallen logs. I smack against the ferns. I skid downhill. I leave everyone behind.

I don't stop when I hit the creek. I splash through and continue up the bank. At the top of a small rise, I finally stop and turn around. Nelson is sloshing through the creek. In the distance, I can see the pale flicker of Darcie's wings. I wait to see Marcus winding through the trees, wait for the white flash of his mask, but he stays invisible.

Nelson comes up the rise first. He bends over and grabs his knees, gasping.

"You weren't supposed to win," he says after he gets his breath. His sneakers are slick with mud.

"You should have run faster," I say back.

I am still looking for Marcus. I forget about Nelson. I stand tall on the rise and make Xs with my arms.

"Where is he?" I ask Darcie as she climbs the rise, struggling under the weight of her wings. She says that she doesn't know, that he was ahead of her and then she lost sight of him. She thought he would be up here by now, waiting with the rest of us.

I stop waving. I pull my sweatshirt sleeves over my hands.

"I'm the slowest." She holds up her palms. "I can't be held responsible."

I remember one of the Pathologist's meditations: A PANICKED HEART IS NOT A WELL HEART.

I try to listen.

We wait for the sound of footsteps moving through the trees. We wait to see a figure crossing the creek, the water spraying silver around his ankles. I pace on the rise. I chew my nails. No one comes.

"Uh-oh," Darcie says.

I run back into the woods. I weave around the trees like I'm on an obstacle course. I race around the trucks, kicking up leaves. I fall over the roots. Fuck the Pathologist and his meditations, because now the panic is a cold burn in the pit of my stomach and I can feel it poisoning me, making my heart unwell. I reach into bushes. I look behind fallen logs. The land feels emptier than it did before and I have this terrible feeling that I have lost him, that I have lost Marcus, all because I didn't stay with him, all because I decided I wanted to be the fastest, to win, and now he has disappeared into some unfindable place. I say his name and then I call his name and then I scream his name, because my voice has to be loud enough to reach into that unfindable place and pull him out.

The woods are getting darker and I am running wildly and I don't know how I will ever stop with Marcus in that unfindable place until I run right into something solid. The force knocks me onto the cold ground, wind pushed out. I touch my forehead and feel the wet of blood. Two figures are standing over me, watery, like I'm looking through the glass bottom of a boat. Behind them I see a tall tree. I squirm on my back. All language is trapped in my throat. They kneel beside me, one on either side, and touch the blood on my forehead and tell me that the woods will never give me what I want if I don't know how to ask.

Darcie and Nelson take me back to the Mansion. I thought it was the middle of the night, but when I look up I see that the sky is starting to fade into dawn. I don't want to go back to the house,

I want to keep looking, but Nelson insists that to find is not an act of will, but an act of submission.

"The trick to finding is to stop looking." He is leading me by the elbow. His grip is not gentle. I want to shake free, but don't trust myself to walk on my own. The energy in my body wants only to charge through the trees and to scream and to bleed.

"What bullshit," I say to Nelson. "What absolute bullshit."

To be looked for is to matter.

Every girl on every missing persons flyer has mattered more than me.

"Think what you want," he says, squeezing. The blood on my forehead is drying into a sticky red line.

In the living room, we discover Marcus sitting in front of the fireplace and I feel the burn in my stomach turn hot. He has been right here, in a very findable place! How could he have left me alone in the woods? I get away from Nelson. I stomp my feet and plaster slides down the wall and makes white poofs on the floor, like tiny bombs are detonating.

"What's the matter with you?" The terror I felt in the woods, how can I even begin to explain that to him. "I thought my fucking heart was going to stop."

Marcus sits with his shoulders rounded, like a child in time-out. He tilts his head, so I can see the white edge of his mask, and pushes the stuffing around inside his coat.

"I don't like races," he says without turning around.

I feel Darcie's eyes on me. She runs her tongue over her stained front teeth. She smoothes her feathers.

"Maybe the tunnel has something to teach you after all," she says.

30.

I should be cold in the basement, but after the eyedropper I feel warm inside. I undress in front of Darcie and Marcus, stepping out of my jeans, wrestling out of my sweatshirt. That moment when the sweatshirt comes over my head, the seconds of blindness followed by the return of sight, feels like another kind of passage. I do it all slowly. I want them to see me, to remember.

Darcie watches. She pulls a feather out of her wings and chews the quill. Marcus stares at the doll with the missing arm.

On the road, the weight has fallen away. I'm surprised at how small I am without my clothes, board straight except for the bulges of breast and belly. I pinch my collarbone and the sharp lines of my hips. I feel the veins on my stomach.

The liquid has no aftertaste. It disappears on my tongue. I try to think Cherry Meth and not Grievous Bodily Harm.

Darcie leads me into the tunnel. She closes the door behind me. I start walking. My toes grind into the dirt. In the narrowness of the tunnel, I begin to feel thirsty and dizzy and like I am not still inside a house but wandering into some distant land.

A wave nearly knocks me down. A wave of *what*, I'm not sure, but it makes me hot and sick. I stop walking. My stomach lurches. I want to get close to the ground and put my head between my knees, but the cold of the dirt drives me away.

What if all of this is wrong? What if we have gotten lost?

I can imagine these questions, but I am in no way equipped to answer them, because my brain is a blue jellyfish that has crawled out through my ear and is hovering somewhere along the roof of the tunnel, happy to finally be free of the body.

"Come back here," I say to the jellyfish. I snatch at the air above and scrape my knuckles on the top of the tunnel.

Echoes.

Deeper inside, the cold hits. I start to shiver. My teeth clank together. The cut on my forehead pulses. I feel a sharp ache in the bone, like something is trying to burrow into the soft matter. Grit on my heels. I want to turn around, to run back to the door, but it's like the path behind me has disintegrated and now the only way to go is forward.

I reach the end and touch the stone and the empty place where a stone used to be. The blue jellyfish brain returns for a moment, the tentacles twisting around my hair, before floating away again. I turn and find that the path back is still real and solid and I picture Darcie and Marcus standing behind the steel door, waiting.

I'm halfway there when I hear the voice—faint at first, like the tendrils of language you catch through static on a radio. I stop walking. I listen to the gradual swell of sound. The voice is singing something. It sounds like a nursery rhyme. I make out the words "billy goat" and "ax" and "wooden leg."

I smell burning rubber. Another waves comes.

I lose all sense of the minute and the hour, become trapped inside some strange pocket of time, like the watchtower with the stopped hands that Marcus saw from a bus window. I try to find ‑

the source of the singing, but it's everywhere, in front and behind and on my skin and in the air and in my plasma. There is no getting away from it and I'm not even sure I want to get away, because maybe this is my mother speaking and maybe I will want to crawl inside this voice and live there forever.

My high keeps stretching on. I feel vibrations under my skin. My eyes are running, but in a way that almost feels good, like a toxin is being released.

"Don't leave," I say in the tunnel, reaching into the emptiness in front of me.

The voice disappears. Like my mother, it doesn't give a damn what I want.

■ ■ ■

In the basement, I lean over and vomit on the floor. My body acts without warning, a sneak attack. The liquid splatters up the naked insides of my legs. Marcus throws my black sweatshirt over my shoulders.

"What did you give me?" I cry out to Darcie.

She is supposed to go in the tunnel next. She still has her clothes on, but from the look in her eyes, the expanding pupils, I can tell that she has already swallowed the liquid.

She stands in front of me, on the edge of the vomit. She grabs my chin and lifts my face, so we're looking each other in the eye. "What have you been eating in the woods?" she says back.

I'm squatting and hunched, my lips wet. "Nothing you haven't been eating."

She lets go of my face and steps away, disgusted. Now her basement is going to smell. I wipe my mouth. Another wave is coming. I clutch at my stomach and feel something move inside me.

...

I keep going into the tunnel. Every time, I hear the singing. Every time, it fades into nothing. I don't understand what I'm doing wrong. Once Darcie comes out crying so hard, she starts hiccupping. Marcus and I crowd around her and I pull her naked body close and feel her jerk in my arms, like something is trying to kick its way out.

Marcus has become a kind of facilitator. He folds our clothes and screws the eyedropper on the vial and waits on the other side of the door for whatever we bring back with us. I wonder what he and Darcie talk about when they're alone and waiting on me. I wonder if she asks to see his face and if he shows her and if they come up with their own theories of the sickness, their own ideas about who or what is to blame.

"I'm scared of rabbits. Aren't you scared of rabbits?" I heard Darcie say to him once.

"Rabbits are afraid of everything," he replied. "That's what makes them dangerous."

Away from the tunnel, "billy goat" and "ax" and "wooden leg" keep playing in my mind. I arrange and rearrange the words like puzzle pieces, wait for them to start making sense. I lie on the mattress and smell that grass scent and look at my mother's photo and try to remember. I am moved by the idea of her singing to me, but troubled by the question that must follow: why did she stop?

Sometimes, when I'm in the tunnel, I can picture her so clearly, I trick myself into thinking she's right there, standing against the stone wall, and all I need to do is reach out and touch her.

If I think about the tunnel for too long, the Psychologist walks into the scene, with his electrodes and his Plácido Domingo records, and wrecks everything. These two people don't belong together, I try to tell my memory, my unconscious mind, but it never listens and I have to put my mother's photo away. I stay on my back and press my stomach, searching for the source of those distressing waves, and listen to the pipes in the Mansion groan.

The liquid from the eyedropper is not at all like guzzling Robitussin in the bathroom of the Stop & Shop. It makes the laws of gravity disappear. It makes my brain a blue jellyfish. It doesn't blur the world, but vanishes it. I understand what those girls in Mission Hill meant when they talked about thinking they were going to dream forever, if that kind of absence can be called a dream.

In the Mansion, on my lesser days, I think I want to dream forever too.

■ ■ ■

In our room, on the second floor, Marcus and I come up with our own games to play.

A new version of hide-and-go-seek: we hide *Twenty Thousand Leagues Under the Sea* around the bedroom and close our eyes and guess where it is. Before we guess we are supposed to relax our thoughts, to not *think* about where the object might be but *feel* it. We are supposed to find its energy and follow that current with our mind. Does it feel hidden under the mattress? Does it feel hidden in a corner? Does it feel hidden in a person's hands? Does it feel sweaty? Does it feel hidden outside the window? Does it feel cold? I guess right 50 percent of the time, because there are only so many places to hide the book.

Once I pretend my mother is hiding somewhere in our room. I shut my eyes and try to feel her energy. Is she under the sheet? Standing in the corner? Behind the door? Is she sitting in the windowsill, admiring the shapes of the trees? Is she underwater or on land? Is she anywhere near me?

. . .

The next time I'm in the tunnel, I hear the twins.

At first, everything is the same, dark and strange and cold, but then instead of the singing, Christopher is there, or his voice is there, and telling me all about the origins of my name. Old French and Latin, popularized by Puritans in the seventeenth century. They believed it meant to be "joyful in the Lord."

"Are you joyful in the Lord?" It sounds like he's speaking from the bottom of a stairwell, his voice tinny and small.

I stop. I can't go forward or back. The path around me is disintegrating again.

Where are you? I want to ask. What's it like there?

"Everything was okay at first," Sam says, and I wonder how I asked the question without asking the question. "But now." He stops and I know he's waiting for his brother to finish his sentence, like he used to in the Hospital.

"But now," Christopher says, "we are just so bored."

31.

The grand obituary, that is another game. We play it in bed at night, when we should be sleeping. We don't share it with Darcie and Nelson. Here are the rules: we make up a name. This is the person who is getting the obituary. We go back and forth, adding detail after detail, until we have made the grandest obituary imaginable.

"Erica Hall," I begin.

"Of Dover, Massachusetts," Marcus says.

"At one hundred and thirteen years of age."

"Passed away peacefully in her sleep, in a room overlooking the sea."

"She battled no diseases. She felt very satisfied with life."

"She felt she got plenty of time."

"She is survived by three daughters and nine grandchildren."

"She was the mayor of Dover and during her tenure she did everything right."

"She put Dover on the map. Dover would not be Dover without Erica Hall."

"She fed the homeless."

"She believed in God."

"She was a champion tennis player."

"She traveled the world. To Africa, even."

"She will live inside the hearts of all Doverians forever."

I think about an obituary I once read in the newspaper, written by a woman who knew she was dying, so instead of leaving it to someone else, she wrote out her own, to be published after she was gone. In the obituary, she talked about how for a long time she was angry about dying, since she was only fifty and never smoked and it all seemed too soon, but by the time she wrote her obituary she wasn't angry anymore. All she wanted was to share what she had learned about life.

I still remember the last lesson on her list: death will always take us by surprise.

In this game, Marcus and I are not allowed to use our own names. We will never be the recipients of a grand obituary.

My mother might.

• • •

The next time we're all in the basement together, Darcie goes into the tunnel first. Marcus and I are sitting on the floor, our backs against the wall. I'm anxious for my turn to take the drops. I rest my head on Marcus's shoulder. I roll my tongue around in my mouth. A lump of nausea grows in my stomach. We don't hear Darcie moving in the tunnel, don't hear the door opening, and even though there are no clocks in the Mansion, no way to be certain about the time, we start to feel sure she's been gone for many hours.

We crack open the metal door. It feels wrong to enter the tunnel clothed and clear-headed, to go against Darcie's rituals. To interrupt whatever it is she might be doing. The light from the basement illuminates the opening of the tunnel and I can see little black bugs squirming on the floor. We lean inside. We call Darcie's name. There are no echoes; the tunnel swallows the sound of us.

We slam the door. We hear footsteps above and shoot up the dusty staircase. I'm thinking we're going to have to tell Nelson that Darcie is no longer in the tunnel, that she has vanished into that unfindable place or maybe her mother's voice has eaten her or maybe she's had too much Grievous Bodily Harm and is collapsed by the wall with the stones hanging out like loose teeth and we were just too chickenshit to go in there and find her.

Nelson is in the living room, wearing his goggles. He is kneeling in front of the fireplace, trying to get a fire going. After it catches, he picks up a pair of tongs and uses them to push a beaker into the heat.

He isn't the only one in the living room. Darcie is there too, fully dressed, her wings on her back.

"It's going to rain soon," she says.

We stop in the doorway. I grab on to Marcus's arm. I shake his jacket sleeve. His rabbit face bobs. We saw her go into the tunnel. We waited on the other side of the door. No one came out.

"How did you get up here?" I ask.

She turns and looks at us like she doesn't know who we are.

I hear a crackling in the fireplace. I smell burning leaves. The room is suddenly very warm.

I watch Darcie by the window. I watch her tap her finger against the glass. I wonder if the real Darcie is still somewhere in that tunnel, if the woman who has materialized in the living room isn't even her, but some kind of double.

• • •

Darcie is right about the weather. It pours rain for the rest of the day. Upstairs I sit on the floral mattress and listen to water drip on the floor and keep reading about the sea.

I remember my mother speaking on another video I found during an Internet Session, the feeling of her voice being branded into my memory: *In another life, I could have been an oceanographer. I love the sea. In another life, I could have been a pirate. I have a mercenary side.*

Do I have a mercenary side too? I think I must, with all that stealing.

In our bedroom, I list the things I still do not know about myself.

Later I try to match the voice that lives in my memory to the voice I've been hearing in the tunnel, but one is a speaking voice and one is a singing voice and how can I possibly compare those two things?

I look up and Darcie is standing in the doorway. I put the book down.

She sits next to me, her wings drooping over the edge of the mattress. I stroke the soft feathers. She smells of mildew and I know that I probably smell that way too, like something damp and old. I check for signs that it's really her—the freckles on her eyelids, the stained front teeth—but I don't get far before she starts telling me about her mother.

"I remember everything about her now," she says.

When Darcie was a child, her mother would leave her alone for days, and when she returned, the scent of smoke trapped in her hair, she would say that she had met a little girl who was a far better little girl than Darcie. *It's a miracle I ever came back for you,* she would say. *Why should I want to come back to a lesser little girl?*

"I'm cured or getting close to it." She lies down beside me. She squints and tries to slip an index finger in my mouth. I press my teeth together, blocking her. Her skin has a bitter taste.

No one has ever touched my teeth before.

"How did you get out of the tunnel?" I ask. "Where did you go?"

"I don't know." She pulls her hand away. Her face darkens. She looks like she's about to cry. "I was there and then I wasn't."

Fragments of the song drift through me. I can't decide if Darcie is lying or telling the truth. If this house is a perfectly normal house and she is the one who likes to play these tricks.

My mother's photo is between us on the mattress. Darcie picks it up.

"Who is this?" she asks.

"I'm still figuring that out."

"I don't ever want to go down there again," she says, still looking at the photo.

32.

A list of things the girl hates about Allston: the old Twin Donut sign; Frederick Law Olmsted's Ringer Playground, where sometimes people get murdered; the frozen yogurt place on Brighton Ave. that is always out of vanilla; the martial arts center on Harvard Ave. where people who are not her get to learn about self-defense.

. . .

The girl stands on the Psychologist's bedroom floor. She is not wearing any clothes. What are clothes? she sometimes thinks, to try to make it all feel more normal. If clothes do not exist in this world, how can she be expected to wear them?

He is kneeling in front of her and dabbing white electrodes on her skin. Where have all these electrodes come from? There's one on each nipple, one on her knee, a constellation of them on her stomach, all round and cold. The Psychologist is dressed as usual, in his khaki pants and blue collared shirt. His socks are striped like the coat of a tiger. She remembers the wing-shaped sweat marks on his stomach. She remembers his hot rotten breath.

"One hundred billion neurons," he tells her. "All of them have to be trained."

She is older than she was the last time she saw herself, but not as old as she will be on the farm in Walpole. This is the in-between.

They are alone in the house. The room is silent. There is no Spanish singing, no Plácido Domingo, and she almost misses him. She misses the familiarity as they move into this strange and terrifying new phase.

The first time they did it this way, he took off her clothes one piece at a time. Her socks were the last to go.

His glasses keep sliding down his nose. He slips an electrode inside her. He sits back on his heels, wipes his forehead with his wrist. This stage is finished. He goes to his computer and she waits for the tiny pulses. Forget her mind. She waits to see what this will do to her body.

A whale sound comes on. She has heard the same wet moans and snorts on a marine life video she saw in school. He tells her she is controlling the sound with her mind. He tells her to keep thinking about the happy thing. To do as he has taught her.

She imagines her hands batting at a ball, trying to keep it high in the air.

Even after the electrodes are peeled away and her clothes returned, she knows the evidence of these sessions will remain; it will cling to her, it will never leave, and there will be no other option except to live her life exactly the way she will end up living it, with a memory that is like a tunnel where you can only get so far before you are blocked by a wall.

One day she will knock that wall down. One day she will be ready.

For months they do this and he tells her that her brain is

being forever changed and she believes him. She can feel it happening.

Here is one way she is changing: she is being trained to believe happiness is not real, but a thing that exists only to cover up the ugly.

Here is another way: color is starting to look different—the grass, the sky, the red Twin Donut sign she hates. More precisely, color is disappearing. When she looks at the sky, the borders are a white fuzz, like a drawing someone has started to erase.

■ ■ ■

When they are in their separate rooms at night, she hears the blare of his TV. She hears the action movie actors shouting and the bombs exploding and the screeching car chases—Doesn't this keep his parents awake? Why don't they complain?—and later when she finds herself living in a Hospital, when she hears people scream in the night, instead of What the fuck? a small part of her will think, There is something familiar here.

What kind of upbringing does it take for any part of being hospitalized in the middle of nowhere during an epidemic of historic proportions to feel at all familiar?

Her kind.

Something else about this girl: when she is older she will forget the cautions against the burning stove and the steaming soups and the busy streets and being outside after a certain hour of the night; instead of warnings she will remember heat singeing her fingertips and the tip of her tongue. She will remember the whoosh of the car coming around a corner, into the space that held her seconds ago. She will never wait for cross signs or for anything to cool or put her seat belt on. She will stand on the edges of T platforms, in easy reach of a homicidal pusher or a suicidal impulse. She will forget her coat in the dead of winter.

She will forget all the warnings, because another small part of her is always thinking, What else can you do to me? Who knew how important all these small parts would turn out to be.

Another thing: one evening, when this girl is all grown up, she will see a woman with a child on the T. An ordinary sight, but it is rush hour and the passengers are all pressed together and somehow this woman has put herself between the child and the bodies of these strangers. The child's face is pressed against the woman's stomach. Her tiny fingers are hooked around her belt loops. The T stops and more passengers get on and the woman pulls the child closer and covers her with her coat.

The grown-up girl will see this and feel a rage that could shake the train right off the tracks, into the river below.

■ ■ ■

Once he takes the girl to Revere Beach. It is warm outside, but not yet summer. May. She is supposed to be in school, but he explains that he talked to her teachers and got permission. He says that he knows all the teachers at her school.

In the car, he lists the things they will find at Revere Beach: kites shaped like dolphins, chocolate ice cream, roast beef sandwiches, hungry seagulls.

They keep the windows down. They listen to a baseball game on the radio. The thunder of the crowd. The clink of a bat striking a ball. He does not say why he is bringing her to the beach, if it is a reward or another part of his experiment or if it has something to do with her changing brain.

"Will Plácido Domingo be there?" she asks.

He laughs and changes the station.

A folk song comes on. The rhythm is soothing but there are words like "ax" in the song that are not soothing at all.

Through the windshield, the sky has that faded look.

On the way, they stop at a drugstore and he buys her a purple bathing suit with a ruffled waist, the first bathing suit she has ever owned.

At the beach, he tells her that he doesn't want to go into the ocean. He doesn't like to swim. He just wants to watch her out there, in her brand-new bathing suit. He sits in the hot sand, in his pants and one of his sea-colored polos. He wraps his arms around his knees.

She swims out. The farther she goes, the more his figure looks like a small, sad lump, like something forgotten on the shore. She can only see the vague shape of his body. She can't see his face. He begins to lose his power over her.

She's treading water when she gets the idea to escape. This is her chance. The water is calm. She is a good, strong swimmer. One of the best at her school. She just needs to slip past the buoys and keep swimming until she finds a boat or a coast guard or divers. Anyone who can help her.

She swims the breaststroke. She counts her breaths. She gets past the buoys. The sun is hot on her back. The chop picks up. Her arms start to feel heavy, like someone has tied bricks to her wrists, but she doesn't stop. She knows this is the kind of chance that doesn't come twice.

She hears a shrill whistle. She turns in the water. There are figures standing on the beach, waving. She keeps swimming.

She hears the whistle again and again. By now there is nothing but water around her. She treads and looks. There are no boats, but maybe if she keeps going.

She keeps going.

The ocean turns icy. The waves start rolling over her. She comes up for air and gets a mouthful of brine.

When the lifeguard hooks his arm around her, she says "no,

no, no." She bites his wrist. She plunges underwater and pretends that she is hidden, that the ocean is camouflage. She watches his legs kick at the darkness below.

He came from land, so he cannot be trusted.

The lifeguard hooks her again and they start swimming back to shore. His chest is hairless and cool. Her arms are jelly. She can't get away. She knows this is the end. There is not and there will never be a woman to cover her with a coat.

He keeps bringing her in. She feels like a fish on a line.

On the beach, the Psychologist is waiting with a soft towel. He wraps it around her shoulders. Sweat is rolling down his cheeks. His gaze is murderous. He thanks the lifeguard for saving his little girl. He even tries to give the lifeguard money, as though to demonstrate how valuable the girl is to him, but the lifeguard turns it away.

"The kids never swim where you tell them to swim," the lifeguard says. He looks at the money and then down at the girl. He shakes a thick finger at her. "You might have an Olympic swimmer on your hands there."

"I'll bet you're right about that," says the Psychologist, tucking the money back into his wallet. "I'll bet you've seen it all."

The girl shivers under the towel. She knows they will never come to the beach again. She knows she should apologize, but she has not yet learned how to apologize for things she is not sorry for.

The girl rides back to Allston in the trunk.

■　■　■

Again they are home alone. This time skinny black wires—they remind the girl of snakes—connect the Psychologist's laptop to the TV in his bedroom. The familiar sound comes on and the Psychologist tells her to concentrate on her happy thing, to concentrate harder than she ever has before, to not let other thoughts trespass into her mind. She listens to the bellow of the whales and thinks as hard as she can and then one appears on TV. A whale! Right in front of her! Blue and massive and crashing through the water. The eye of the whale is small and savage and its body is crusted in white shells, a deep-sea monster for sure. The whale disappears and the Psychologist tells her that she lost her concentration, that she made it leave.

She's naked again, the white electrodes stuck all over her body.

She gets back into the right headspace. It's like standing on one foot and fixing your sight on a specific thing until you find your balance, except the balancing is happening in her mind. She wants to stop and listen to the whale. She wants to see it spout water and gulp fish, to see what it's like to be a fearsome creature of the deep (could she ever learn to be a fearsome creature of the deep?), but this time she knows the whale is not there for her.

This girl stays awake at night remembering the sensation of swimming out, away from the sandy coast of Revere Beach, into the cold dark of open water. She keeps rewriting the endings. Keeps telling herself stories.

In one, she joins a band of pirates. In another, she grows gills and learns to breathe underwater. In another, she is picked up by a wealthy couple who have always wanted a child. In another, she drowns.

She stares down at her bare toes. She digs them into the carpet. In his bedroom, these alternate endings are the happy thing she thinks about.

When she looks up, she sees Mr. and Mrs. Carroll, which is not possible. She blinks and they're still there, frozen in the doorway in their gray guard uniforms. She didn't hear them come home. She didn't hear anyone coming up the stairs. Mr. Carroll is holding a six-pack. His shirt is untucked. Mrs. Carroll is reaching for the wall. Her lipstick is a red smear on her mouth. They are still wearing their museum nametags.

They aren't usually home until after dark, so either the Psychologist has gotten confused about time or Mr. and Mrs. Carroll have changed their schedule. She doesn't know what is true.

She also doesn't know how long they've been watching and now there is something about their watching, about seeing their expression take on the wrongness of what is happening and reflect that wrongness back at her, that makes her feel like her organs are being rearranged. Her liver and her lungs switch places. Her spleen is in her elbow. Her heart is in her knee.

Mr. and Mrs. Carroll make no move to help her.

The whale vanishes from the screen.

The Psychologist is busy recording new data on his laptop. He doesn't yet know that his parents are in the room, that they are approaching from behind, slow and slack with shock, and very soon this girl will be sent away.

She sees them coming. She sees the wrongness grow. Piss runs down her legs and darkens the carpet. She feels the hot liquid curve around the edge of her foot.

She sees herself in the trunk of the car. The air was too hot and thick to breathe. It turned to cotton candy in her lungs.

She is going to pass out on the bedroom floor and wake up on a farm. It sounds impossible, but that is what is going to happen.

She will never understand what the Psychologist wanted from her, the nature of his experiment, but she knows what he took and that he kept taking it long after she left Allston.

His parents keep getting closer.

The Psychologist keeps clicking away.

"Look at you, my little monster," he says. "Look at what I've trained you to do."

33.

A theory on why we stop remembering: there is a part of our story that we do not know how to tell to ourselves and we will away its existence for so long that finally our brain agrees to a trade: I will let you forget this, but you will never feel whole.

. . .

What is a memory but the telling of a story?

. . .

In middle school, I went on a field trip to a whale watch at the Stellwagen Bank National Marine Sanctuary. When we saw the first sign of a whale, the spray of white, the great V-shaped tail smacking the water, I screamed in terror and did not know why.

. . .

In high school, I kicked a boy in the chest when he tried to touch between my legs.

. . .

It was never my mother in the tunnel. It was always him.

. . .

Does this mean he's dead?

. . .

Ask me if I feel bad for hoping he is. Just ask.

. . .

When I stop remembering, I'm not in the Mansion. I'm standing in the woods, breathing fast. The land is heavy with silence. The tree branches are reaching toward each other like fingers and through them the sky is the opposite of faded. It is such a deep shade of blue that it almost looks unreal, like a screen that could be split open. I don't remember leaving the Mansion and walking outside. I don't remember crossing the yard and moving past the halo of bare trees. The woods feel like shelter.

The ground is damp and the heels of my sneakers are sinking into it. I stand on a mass of tree roots, like a person seeking high ground. The woods smell faintly of smoke. I listen to the rushing sound of the creek. I wrap my arms around the trunk and think of Marcus and feel my heart begin to slow.

A bird with a yellow chest flies from one branch to another, on the run from something. The ferns have left little wet handprints on my jeans.

Now it's like this: you look at yourself in the mirror and watch your reflection take off a mask. You look hard at all the wrongness in this new face, you look hard at the ways that wrongness has shaped it, and you have to decide if this new face is something you can live with.

If you decide no, you dissolve into yourself. If you decide yes, a small thing inside you is set free.

34.

In the Mansion, there are animals all around us. I've seen the scurry of whiskered rats, snakes in the grass, possums with spindly white tails stalking the backyard after dark. I've seen birds in the trees, the ones that sit hunched on the broad low branches, buzzards or something related. There are alive things in the house too. I keep hearing the tick tick tick of nails on the floor, a scraping in the walls. It's only a matter of time before one gets stuck inside.

In Charlestown, Ms. Neuman was always setting out cages for mice. Once they were in the cages, she would feed them cheddar cheese with poison inside. If Marcus and I found a trapped mouse sniffing at the bars, we carried the cage outside and let it go.

In the living room, when a raccoon gets stuck inside the trap door, Nelson says it will make a great tool for an experiment. The four of us stand around the closed trap door, having been drawn into the room by the sound of the animal's thrashing. I can feel the raccoon racing around beneath us. I can feel it slamming against the walls. A pulse, an aliveness, rises from the floor.

"You probably aren't aware that the history of animal experimentation goes back to the Greeks," Nelson tells us, sensing our hesitation. "That the rhesus monkey helped find a vaccine for polio? That heart valve replacement surgery was tested on dogs?"

I can see that Nelson thinks of the Mansion as a kind of Hospital, its inhabitants the patients, and I do not need another Hospital or another doctor trying to pry his way inside. I've had it with scientific inquiry.

"We should let it go," I say.

"Yes," says Marcus, who has always had sympathy for trapped things. "I vote to let it go too."

"Who said anything about voting?" Nelson stands on the trap door and crosses his arms, unwilling to give up his prize. Earlier he was outside. His pants are streaked with fresh mud. "You just got here. You don't know how things work."

Somehow, in the middle of all this, Darcie continues with her remembering.

"I was in a basement," she says, loud enough to get our attention. We stop arguing about what to do with the raccoon and look at her. She's pulling feathers out of her wings. "I was living down there. I couldn't get away. I was tied to something."

"When?" I ask her. I don't know if she means the basement downstairs or some other place, if she was in a basement before Nelson found her on the side of the road in Cordova. The raccoon is whining now, a shrill plea.

"Sometime before. I think." Darcie's eyes widen and she looks like she's about to tell us more, but then she stops and sinks down into the velvet chair, her wings bursting over the arms. She's holding fistfuls of feathers. There are bald spots on the ridges of her wings.

"See!" Nelson claps his hands. "She's remembering. She's getting fully cured."

Marcus and I look at each other. We're not sure we like this idea of what it means to be cured.

"Oh no," Darcie cries. She drops the feathers and pushes her face into her hands. "Oh no."

A Real-Life Ghost Story, I think. That's what she's remembering now.

The animal claws around inside the trap door. The floorboards shudder. Darcie runs upstairs and into the bathroom. We chase after her and find her sitting in the rusted tub and rubbing her arms like she's washing herself, even though there's no water.

"Don't kill it," she says when she sees us huddled in the doorway. She leans back in the tub and rests her black-soled feet on the porcelain edge. "Don't you dare kill it."

"But what about progress?" Nelson asks.

She closes her eyes and shakes her head. For the moment she is the one with the power.

We decide to leave the raccoon alone for now.

■ ■ ■

That night, there are no games. No drinking, no copping and robbing, no hiding, no tunnel. Instead we vanish into our separate corners. Darcie stays in the bathroom, pretending to wash herself in the tub. Nelson retreats into the attic and soon after I hear the bowling ball rolling across the floor, the clatter of pins. The raccoon stays locked inside the trap door, thrashing. Marcus and I are in our room. I'm reading on the mattress. He's sitting silent on the floor.

My body is leaden. I am sleeping more and dreaming less. I am unsure if this is progress. The waist of my jeans has started digging into my stomach, leaving behind a mark that looks like a second bellybutton.

We don't speak. We don't draw. We don't play hide-and-go-seek or grand obituary, at least not aloud. I know we're not supposed to use our own names for obituaries, but silently I do them for my eight-year-old self and my Stop & Shop self and the self that is still locked up in the Hospital. All the little selves I want to kill and bury deep.

In the middle of the night, I wake up alone. The room is dark. From the cold of the mattress, I know Marcus is gone. I push open the window and climb into the sill. I drink in the mineral smell of the night. The moon is a white sphere in the sky. I watch the light shift, the pattern of shadows on the ground. I think about how easy it would be for me and Marcus to slip out of this house and away.

Marcus steps into the backyard, carrying a burlap sack. His steps are long and slow. From the way he's holding the sack in his arms, I know it's not empty. He walks past the halo of trees and stops at the top of the slope.

The raccoon is dead. It suffocated under the floor or bashed itself in the head. It did not survive us. Marcus stops walking and I think he's going to take out the dead raccoon and dig a grave or leave it for other animals to eat, let it return to the earth, but then he kneels and opens the sack and the raccoon leaps out, fully alive. In the moonlight, I can see the little black paws, the fluff of tail. The animal stands on its hind legs. Its head jerks left and then right. It opens and closes its mouth, tasting the air. It darts into the woods and is swallowed up by the night.

Marcus rolls up the burlap sack and slings it over his shoulder, but he doesn't come inside right away. He stays there long after the raccoon is gone. At first, I think he's just getting some fresh air or contemplating our current situation, how much longer we can stay in this house with Nelson and his experiments, with Darcie and her memories, or maybe even having a memory of his own, but then he kneels and starts pushing the dirt around with a stick and I know it's something else. I almost call to him, but I can tell he's really concentrating, that whatever he's doing feels important. He is looking very hard at something in the ground.

. . .

When I lose sight of Marcus from the window, I start to worry about him disappearing again. I don't get back into bed. I sit at the top of the stairs and wait for the door to open and close, for movement on the floorboards. At the foot of the stairs, he stops and watches me, his mask glinting. I see the burlap sack. I smell the dirt and sweat. I hear him breathing. He moves toward me one step at a time. On each new level he pauses and I think of my mother coming up from a dive, the interval stops. I stand and open my arms, and maybe it is because he did not disappear this time or maybe because he is taking so long to reach me or maybe it is all the remembering that makes a welling in my body, a pressure behind my eyes, that unmistakable feeling of being on the verge of tears that are going to come so full and so hot you think you are going to flood the house.

. . .

Nelson blames Darcie for releasing the raccoon. In the morning, we hear shouting from our bedroom and go downstairs, into the kitchen. Through the window we see that Nelson has Darcie cornered on the front porch. He is telling her that he is trying to do something meaningful and she agreed to help him but of course she can't really understand what that means because she has never done anything meaningful in all her sorry life.

We watch from the kitchen window. The sink is filled with Mason jars. A line of red ants marches up a dirty wall. My scalp itches.

"You know this about yourself." Nelson has her pressed against a railing, the wood dark and soft with rot. "You know this is true, now that you can remember." Darcie is shaking her head and doing her hiccup-cry. Her back is bare.

We go outside, looking to break up the fight. We stand in front of the knobless front door, the neon yellow skull. When Nelson sees us he shrugs and takes a step back, casual, like this is all a misunderstanding. "Go away," Darcie says, and at first I think she's talking to Nelson, but then I realize she is looking at us.

We're about to tell Nelson that Darcie is not responsible for the raccoon going free, that we are to blame, but then we notice a gray haze all around us, settling over the house and yard like a fog.

We walk into the yard. We see a wild bloom of orange.

The ground squishes under our feet. We follow a path of footsteps through the mud. New grass has started coming up along the edges of the lawn, a sparse green fringe. The buds on the tree branches are tight as fists. I smell chemicals. I smell death. A wind blows the heat toward us and I feel it on my stomach and on my face. Swirls of ember and ash. A charcoal taste in my mouth.

We stop in front of the burning thing. The feathers are gone, but I can still make out the metal frames on the ground. They are glowing with fire. They are melting into nothing. Darcie's angel wings, alight on the front lawn.

35.

That night we leave the Mansion under the cover of a moonless sky. I take only what I brought with me. I can't be sure if the pages of the book are tainted with the trickiness of the Mansion, so I leave the sea behind. We stay away from the train tracks. We go out the back of the house, into the woods, down the slope. We follow the creek in the opposite direction, through a wet, brown valley. We stay close to the low rush of water.

There was a comfort to staying in the Mansion and watching the outside world recede, but after I started remembering, after Marcus showed me what he found in the woods, I thought of Ms. Neuman telling me I could be any kind of person I wanted and the thought of choosing wrong scared me more than being back out on the road.

In the woods, I am not as fast as I used to be. My breasts ache, push against the thin cotton of my bra. I feel the downward pull of gravity. I have become heavy and slow. I can no longer deny the signs, can no longer deny the newness in my body, which is swollen and tender with Louis's child.

Eventually the woods fall away. Eventually we find Memphis. Another river, another bridge. A strip of neon signs for BLACK DIAMOND and KING'S PALACE CAFE and GUS'S FRIED CHICKEN. The lights sting my eyes. We see a man in a wheelchair. He is wearing a sweatshirt that says GOD BLESS AMERICA and spinning himself in circles. We see people wandering the streets, masked by night. They stand under the signs with lit cigarettes, the smoke rising and disappearing into the above.

We go into a Bojangles' for water and toilets and in the bathroom I find a woman lying on her back under the sinks. Condensation is dripping from the pipes and hitting her in the face. A tiny syringe is sticking out of her arm. I stand over her. She is blinking very slowly and sliding her head back and forth across the linoleum. There's wet toilet paper all over the floor. The tiles are a sick shade of green. I remember the RECOVERY POSITION sign, remember practicing the action with Marcus, and roll the woman onto her side. She is heavy and hard to move. Her skin feels like putty. I run out of the bathroom and tell the man behind the counter that he has a problem in there.

Back outside I take breaths so deep my lungs burn with oxygen.

We board a bus and don't stop. There will be no more motel rooms, no more houses, no more detours. No more chances to become lost. This is our thinking now. At rest stops, I slip into bathrooms and vomit into toilets. I slosh water around in my mouth and wipe my face with wads of toilet paper and try to understand how my body is changing.

On the bus, a woman sitting across from us is reading a book titled *Almost a Psychopath*, and I wonder where the line is.

In Tupelo, Mississippi, I look at myself in the mirror of a gas station bathroom. I look hard. I am surprised by the length of my hair. The dark tips brush my shoulders. I can tuck my bangs behind my ears. The evidence of Raul's sheepdog haircut, the evidence of that locked-up person, is almost gone.

I comb my hair with my fingers and remember the feeling of his hot, rough hands moving over my scalp.

In the light of the bathroom, I see lines on my face. They almost look like scars except I've never been cut by anything but time.

When I meet this child, will I want to do what my mother did? Will I want to leave it behind?

On the bus, Marcus takes off his rabbit mask and puts it on me. The elastic band digs into the back of my scalp. It's night again. I can feel the heat his skin has left on the plastic. I concentrate on the movement of the bus underneath, the light that cuts in and out. I feel like the bandit now.

I don't think so, I decide, touching my stomach. I turn my head and watch the landscape pass through a window. I don't think I'll be that kind of person.

At a gas station in Tuscaloosa, I'm in line to pay for coffee. We are almost out of cash. A little black TV sits on a stack of blue milk crates behind the counter, the volume blaring. In the Mansion, there was no TV—how long has it been since I've seen one? The news is on. I hear about a virulent strain of the flu that has put a town in Texas in isolation. A rash of suicides by cyanide in Michigan. A woman quarantined at the Boston airport because she was showing signs of the sickness. A false alarm, but it makes a person wonder: what will we do if it comes back? An infant found abandoned in a sewage pipe in Virginia. I add that to my list of things a mother can do that are worse than leaving.

A new headline, "Kansas Project Exposed," snakes along the bottom of the screen.

"Stop," I say even though no one in the line is moving. I ask the cashier to turn up the volume.

"Do you want us all to go deaf?" he says, but does what I want anyway.

The broadcaster says news outlets are searching for details about a hospital near La Harpe, Kansas. Inside this hospital authorities have discovered eighty bodies. There were eighty-four people in the hospital when I left, which means four more must have died of the sickness after I was gone. These bodies were found tucked in their beds, slumped against walls, in hallways. According to the preliminary reports, the patients and staff appear to have died within twenty-four hours of each other. The cause is unknown, but the theories include: experimental vaccine, toxins in the water or food supplies, psychosis brought on by excessive winter, mass suicide. Casualties of the microepidemic.

There is a still of Dr. Bek in a simple white doctor's coat. Without the silver bulk of his suit, he looks frail and old. His eyes are different than I remember. They are a darker shade of blue, impenetrable as lake water.

A camera moves across the exterior of the Hospital. It looks just as it did when I arrived and just as it did when I left—tall, fortresslike, surrounded by the plains, the land white with snow. I try to imagine the vast emptiness inside. The silent halls. The bare mattresses. The dead TV in the Common Room. The microwaves in the Dining Hall. The hole in the twins' room that leads to nowhere.

If I had stayed, they would be talking about my own death, which would have been anonymous, a small shift in the total. The difference between eighty and eighty-one.

I drop the coffees. Brown liquid sloshes across the gas station floor. The cashier stands up from his stool and shouts.

I bolt outside and behind the gas station, into the stench of Dumpster garbage. I lean against a concrete wall and I can almost feel Louis coming up behind me, his hand on my spine, but then the ghost of his touch disappears and I am alone.

I close my eyes. I can hear Marcus calling my name.

I get sick behind the gas station. I am sick of the road. I am sick of TVs, of the news they keep bringing. I bend over and my body heaves and this time I know it's not from the child.

. . .

At night, we pass through Montgomery and Columbia, edge out of Alabama and South Carolina and into Georgia. While the rest of the bus drifts, I creep to the front, where a sleeping man has left a backpack by his feet. I unzip, reach inside, find a wallet. I take all the cash, moving once again inside a blaze of want. We will need money to get all the way to Florida. We will need money to find my mother. These are the facts. I tuck the bills into my back pocket and return the wallet to where it came from.

At first light, the man is still asleep and I'm counting the bills in the back of the bus. I'm expecting to see tens and twenties, but these bills are hundreds, crisp and clean, the cleanest bills I've ever seen. I count and recount, disbelieving. The sleeping man had two thousand dollars in his wallet.

I wake Marcus up. I watch him come to life behind the mask. Two thousand dollars is enough to cause a problem. There will be consequences once the man realizes his money is gone. He will come around to all the passengers. He will take his case to the driver. He will demand to know.

When the bus docks at a rest stop in Macon, we get off. Down here the air is wet and warm. I smell gasoline. The parking lot is filled with semi trucks. The drivers are standings outside, leaning against cabs, chewing toothpicks, the brims of their baseball caps pulled low. As we pass, they turn to stare at Marcus in his mask.

We walk up to a driver in a red baseball cap and a T-shirt that says PROUD TRUCKA. His jeans are too tight around the crotch. I look at the back of his semi and wonder where he's headed, what he might be hauling. He watches us watch him and spits a white glob on the asphalt.

"You want some company out there?" I ask.

The man stands back and looks us over.

"What's with that mask?" he asks.

"Childhood," we say.

"Rabbits stink," the man says. "Rabbits can be scared to death."

He rubs his hands together and spits again. I hear honking, the rumble of engines, as some trucks begin to pull out of the lot, back onto the open road. He jingles his keys in his hands. He tells us to get inside.

36.

"Florida!" the man says when we tell him where we're going. Marcus is up front, rubbing one of his rabbit ears. I'm in the back, trying not to feel sick. I spread out my map of highways and follow the lines that lead south. If I puke on this man's floor mats, I know we'll be out of here.

"Here's what I know about Florida," he tells us.

His mother grew up in Nassau, the biggest city in the Bahamas. Years ago, when she was dying, she told her children that she wanted her ashes scattered in the water surrounding the island. This man and his sister drove from South Carolina to Miami with an urn strapped down in the backseat. In Florida, they planned to rent a boat, but private charters were too expensive, so instead one night they got on a party boat called *Bottoms Up*, bound for Nassau.

"You should have seen it," the man says in a sleepy drawl. "People were taking Jell-O shots and dancing and glow-in-the-dark hula hooping and screaming 'Eat my dick!' whenever we passed another boat. And then there was my sister and me, stone-cold sober, holding this urn filled with our mother's ashes."

When the island was in sight, they opened the urn and let her go. A drunk bumped into them while this was going on and they dropped the urn in the ocean, which wasn't part of the plan, but that was okay, they decided in the end. Let it go. Let it all go.

"So," he says. "That's my story about Florida."

I can tell from the way he talks about his sister that she is dead too, but I don't ask.

Next the man tells us his theory of the sickness. He thinks it's something the government did to weed out the weak, the citizens that have been holding this nation back, the citizens they no longer wanted. To harm America in order to save it. A controlled burn, like firefighters do with forests, except of course this did not stay in control.

"Save America from what?" I ask. Earlier he shared a jar of peanuts with us. Now my mouth is dry and my fingertips are pebbled with salt.

He does not answer. My sister was not weak, I know he is thinking.

"I was standing in my yard in Greenville when I saw these planes pass over," he tells us. "There were six of them, all military, and they were spraying something on the fields. A light, fine mist. I went inside and closed the blinds. I stuffed towels under the doors. I sealed up the cracks. When I saw those planes, I knew in my heart this sickness was something they were doing to us."

He does not answer. He pounds his fist against his chest. The semi drifts toward a silver guard rail.

We did it to ourselves or someone did it to us: that is how all the theories break down.

A heavy rain is falling and we can't see the road ahead or the highway signs or other cars. The windows look like they're melting. The darkness around the headlights is immense. We have no way to monitor our situation, to know if this man is really taking us to Florida or someplace of his own design.

Later I watch Marcus sleep. His hands are folded in his lap. His head lists to the side. I can still see the boy inside him when he sleeps.

I wonder if he loves that boy or if he wants to kill him and bury him deep.

The rain keeps coming. Lightning cuts the sky. Each time it looks like an explosion. The radio is on. I listen for something more about the Hospital, but there is only talk of the weather, which has turned strange everywhere: snow in Los Angeles, tornadoes in the mountains of Vermont. Volcanic activity in New Mexico, in the Sierra Blanca. A sinkhole that swallowed an entire neighborhood in Delaware. The station changes and someone is talking about a prehistoric forest that has been discovered in a faraway country, filled with petrified trees that have been dead for thousands of years. Trees are lucky: they do not have to worry about what they leave behind. I put on the gardening gloves and lie down in the cab. It is just me and this man, alone in the night.

"No one is waiting," I think I hear him say. The rain makes it hard to tell. It sounds like we're stuck inside a car wash.

"What?" I say, sitting up.

"What?" he says back.

. . .

In the woods behind the Mansion, Marcus took me to the spot where he set the raccoon free, just past the halo of trees, behind a large bush with shriveled berries hanging from the branches.

The soil had been turned. We bent down and I saw the smooth milky edge of a bone. We were afraid to touch it; we used sticks to nudge it out of the dirt. It was unmistakably human, long and knobbed at the ends, a femur or a tibia. We pushed the bone back into the earth.

"There's more down there," Marcus said. "A lot more. A whole person, maybe."

I leaned back on my heels. I crossed my arms and held on to my elbows. We didn't say anything for a while. We just stared down at the soft ridges in the soil.

We didn't know where the bones came from or who they belonged to, if the sickness or old age or Nelson or something else was to blame. It didn't matter. We knew there wasn't a cure for anything in the Mansion, or at least not a cure we could ever want. We knew it was time to stop being lost.

As I looked at the turned soil, I thought about how, if it weren't for Rick, this was how the twins might have ended up, a secret in the earth for someone to find.

■ ■ ■

When we wake, the truck is parked in a field. I hear the swoosh of cars passing on the highway, but I can't see the road. Marcus and I sit up at the same time. We yawn, stretch stiff arms, look around. I rub my face, brush rough crystals from the corners of my eyes. I roll my head in circles and listen to my bones crack. My neck is sore.

The rain has stopped, but recently: there is still water beading on the windshield. The engine is off and the keys are missing from the ignition and the driver is gone. His door is hanging open and when we get out, we find a cluster of footprints around the semi and a trail of flattened grass, leading out into the field.

Maybe the truck broke down. Maybe he needed to find a

place to piss or jerk off. If we knew his name, we might have called it.

Instead we follow the trail into the field. We cannot resist the dewy grass or the lush canopy of trees in the distance. All that aliveness.

In the canopy, we hear a rustling and look up. There are children in the trees, maybe a dozen. Some are nestled in the treetops. Others lie flat against the branches, their slim legs and arms wrapped around the wood. They are wide-eyed and silent, waiting for the danger to pass.

Did the driver look up and see these children too? Is this what lured him away?

We wave at the children. They don't wave back.

"Come down," Marcus says. "We won't hurt you."

The children don't move from the trees. They have heard this line before.

37.

We start back to the highway. We pass the truck. There is still no sign of the driver. According to the road signs we are near Birmingham, back in Alabama, and now signs for Birmingham mean we have been going in the wrong direction, just as wrong as Centralia.

From the road, we try to find our next ride, and it is just as Rick said. One person is easy to pick up, especially if that person is a woman, especially if the driver is the kind who does not see a woman standing on the side of the highway, but prey. Two people is more complicated, especially if one of them doesn't want to show you his face. There is an air of danger about us. Together we might make a plan. Together we might have the power to overtake.

For a while, no one stops or even slows down. We drift a little too close to the highway and a car honks. A man with a beard rolls down the window and shouts something about rabbits that gets lost in the air. We stumble back into the bed of rock and thin green weeds.

We're picked up by a choir bus. It's an old GM, shaped like a bread box, the pink paint stained with rust, something from another century. Inside we find a flock of men and women in white robes. The only empty seats are in the very back. As we walk down the aisle, these people reach out and touch us. Their fingers are hot.

They tell us they are traveling across America. In each state, they stop someplace and sing. They started in Maryland and have been working their way through the south: Virginia, the Carolinas, over into Kentucky and Tennessee. After Florida, they are heading west, all the way to the salt flats of Utah and the deserts of California and then north, to Alaska.

They tell us about the highway that leads to Alaska. It runs just over 1,400 miles, passing through British Columbia and the Yukon and the Delta Junction. It ends in Fairbanks, near the North Pole. Do we have any idea how cold it is in the North Pole? The highway was built in 1942, during the war. Before, you could only reach Alaska by water, which made the state feel like it was not part of America, but free to be its own country. From the windows of the bus, they expect to see bears and caribou and wolves.

They want to keep going past Fairbanks, to a place called Deadhorse, on the Beaufort Sea. They tell us they will sing to the animals, if there's no one else to listen. They will not be afraid of the wild.

In Georgia, in Valdosta, they pull in to a rest stop. They get out and stand in the center of the parking lot, on a mound of brown grass, and sing. Marcus and I watch from the bus windows and I remember the first pilgrims who came to the Hospital, the sound of their voices rising up to our floor. The air is blue with dusk.

At night, back on the bus, they keep singing. They clap and stomp. Even the driver rocks in his seat. They sing "Let the Praise

Begin." They sing "If God Is Dead." The bus windows are cracked open. I smell exhaust. It is a relief to know there are people out there who will always choose living.

I turn to Marcus. I put his hands on my stomach and ask him to tell me what he feels.

38.

At first, Florida is a kingdom of green. We pass through the forests of Tallahassee, the trees draped with moss, and the gentle hills of Ocala. In the center of the state, the land flattens and we settle into another network of gray highways. I don't sleep. We drive through the darkness and I count the headlights of the other cars and wonder what all these people are searching for.

In Miami, the dawn sky is dramatic, with rafts of enormous pink-bellied clouds. Do clouds ever die? It seems like clouds must get to live forever.

A list of things that must get to live forever: clouds, volcanoes, fossils, certain insects, the sea.

The bus weaves through the shadows of skyscrapers and crosses a drawbridge with tiny limestone guard towers. A canal runs under the bridge, the water a brilliant green. A tugboat called *The Jean Ruth* slips under the bridge and putters out toward the Atlantic. The colors of Miami are nothing like the colors of the other places we have been. They are lime, they are butter yellow, they are citrus orange, they are candy pink. A shade of blue that is like the most beautiful clear sky. I imagine my mother living inside this landscape of color. I see her as a silhouette on a balcony, a figure on a bridge, a body on a boat deck turning to face the sun.

The singers have taken us as far as they can. At the bus station, across the street from a strip mall, we learn the next bus to Key West isn't leaving for six hours. The day is ours. We are dazed by the new colors and the heat and the palm trees, the leaves long and fringed, and the fat iguanas dragging themselves across the sidewalk. What is this place? We've never seen anything like it before.

"It's a girl," Marcus told me on the bus.

In the night, I started another letter to my mother. I've been collecting scraps of paper, carrying around the pen I pinched from a gas station in South Carolina, in Troy. I want so badly to tell her about my life, about the kind of person I am becoming.

We go over to the strip mall and peer inside the windows. One plain face and one rabbit face stare back. Everything is closed. In a store, we see a group of mannequins jumbled together on the floor. Their heads are arranged at strange, deadly angles, their limbs twisted together. I want to set these mannequins right, to free them of each other, but the door is locked and we have to keep walking.

We pass an empty parking lot with a small pearl-colored carousel, the kind of thing you'd see at a fair, languishing in a black pool. We climb onto the carousel and stroke the five white horses with gold saddles. Their nostrils are pink and flared, their eyes wide and afraid. There there, I think, petting a muzzle. The sixth horse is missing from its station. I imagine someone carrying it away on their shoulders and another person watching from a distance, unable to see the human body holding the creature up. They only see the white horse with the rich gold saddle riding into the city and believe themselves to be in the presence of magic. They are wrong, this theoretical person, but they will believe it anyway.

We follow a broad sidewalk that leads us deeper into the city. We pass a church made of yellow stone with a pair of blue archways, a white cross perched on the roof. A group of young people are standing under the arches. They come over and offer us little paper cups filled with apple juice, which we are in no position to refuse. We drink the juice in a single swallow. They want us to come into the church and watch a video. They tell us there is more apple juice inside.

In a small, dark room in the back of the church, we sit on a carpeted floor and watch their video. The video tells us the sickness was just a test, a way for God to find the true believers. There is another sickness coming and this time it won't be a test. It will not burn out. There will be no recovery. Only those on the side of God will be saved.

God is watching, the video tells us. God is seeing everything.

There are clips of the sickness and preachers preaching the Word and people collapsing into prayer, into the ecstasy of salvation. Somewhere inside the church incense is burning. I watch these preachers chant and sweat. I watch the life fire up inside them and wonder how many are still among the living.

I was never supposed to make it this far. I was never supposed to make it out of childhood. Out of Kansas.

Fuck all of you, I can't help but think. I outlived you all.

When the video ends, the young people want us to stay and talk. They want us to tell them how we feel about what we've just seen, but they have no more apple juice and so it's time for us to go. These poor young people, I think as we wave good-bye. They have no idea who anyone really is.

I'm still a young person too, I know that, but I don't think I will ever again feel young.

39.

From Miami, the bus follows Highway 1 until we are just riding a thin strip of concrete extending across the Atlantic, until we are surrounded by ocean. The sky is knotted with cloud. We see the hulking silhouettes of cargo ships. It rains again and the water around us turns dark and roiling. The bus shakes on the highway. I keep working on the letter to my mother.

The bus driver has the radio turned up and I catch something about more snow where there is not supposed to be snow and E. coli in a New Hampshire town's water supply and fires on the plains of Nebraska that can't be put out, because no one can identify the source.

Ghost fires.

I have started to think of the sickness not as a single, contained catastrophe, but as part of a series of waves. We are still burning. What will be the wave that puts us out? I feel the heat of my mother's photo in my pocket and try not to think about what might be coming next.

Marcus is no longer wearing his mask. The scarred skin

around the damaged eye looks like melted wax. He left the mask in Miami, the rabbit face floating in the water. I didn't ask him to explain. I know what it's like to want to leave part of yourself behind.

I am shedding too. I left the gardening gloves on the choir bus. I don't need them anymore, now that we are away from the cold.

In Key West, the palm trees are storm-battered. Green fronds have gone missing, bark tongues flop away from trunks. The ocean is clearer and I can see dark masses of seaweed floating in the water like continents. The beach is not a smooth white crescent like the one in Miami, but a narrow sandy strip, rough with broken shells and driftwood, guarded by a concrete seawall.

We pass a graveyard with stone mausoleums sitting on the grass like little houses. A row of folding chairs and a tent are set up in one corner of the graveyard, the mark of a service that has already happened or has yet to begin.

We pass the Key West weather station, an L-shaped concrete building with a radar dish. I imagine people scurrying around inside, going crazy trying to keep up with the changes in the atmosphere. We pass a museum devoted to shipwrecks. I wonder if any of my mother's finds are in there. I picture us standing on the decks of wrecked ships, climbing the lookouts, crawling through the cool dark of the hulls. We pass an elementary school painted with red hibiscuses, houses standing on cinder blocks, houses surrounded by faded picket fences that make me think of shark's teeth, a house with a tree growing through the roof, the thin branches twisted together and dripping with brown, hairlike moss. We pass a Laundromat where all the dryer doors are hanging open like mouths awaiting permission to speak.

Wild roosters peck at the sidewalks, their red tail feathers swaying. A calico cat stands on its hind legs and watches the passing bus.

Imagine a world where the animals are slowly taking over.

Imagine a world where the weather does whatever it pleases. Blizzards in summer. Heat waves in winter.

Imagine a world where you can go to a store and pick out a new person to be. You can buy that person off the rack and just *become* them. A new face, a new name, a new soul. In this world, it is that easy.

Imagine a world where ghosts get to stay real.

Imagine a world without mothers.

The bus stops at Mallory Square, a brick marina lined with skeletal palm trees. A road sign announces MILE MARKER ZERO. We have reached the southernmost tip of the Florida highway. The bus is full. We are not the only ones who wanted to get far away from the mainland, far away from wherever we were before.

The passengers scatter into the streets. The bus speeds away. Above us electrical wires crackle. There is something thrilling about being on the coast, on the edge of the land.

The lone boat at the marina is a party boat, just like the one the man in the semi told us about, only this one has a different name. It's a white double-decker with BOOZE CRUISE painted across the side in red letters. When we talk to the captain, we learn that we are the only interested passengers. There is no schedule, no set route. You simply pay and tell him where you want to go.

I give the captain a hundred dollars and tell him Shadow Key.

The party boat captain is barefoot. The tops of his feet are tan. His toenails are pitted and yellow. He's wearing ragged denim shorts and a white captain's hat and a white shirt with gold buttons. He tucks the money into his shirt pocket and tells us that he used to have a boat called *The Lion's Paw*, but he lost it in a storm and now he has this one instead. The old boat was named after a children's book about three orphans who run away together and live on a sloop.

"Do you know it?"

We shake our heads.

"It's a beautiful story," he tells us.

The *Booze Cruise* does not have a story.

Marcus takes my hand and we climb aboard. The boat sways. We launch from the marina, into a white spray of water, a biting wind. I wonder if there will be whales. We look out at the stony beaches and the rock fingers that jut into the water, dark and pocked like volcanic rock or what I imagine volcanic rock to be.

A child in yellow shorts stands at the end of one of the fingers, waving.

We wave back. We don't know if we will ever return.

The wind lifts my hair off my shoulders. I lean against the railing and feel the spray on my face. I taste the salt. I listen to the churn of the engine. When I look back toward the marina, the wake is a wide white tail behind us.

A green cooler stands against the helm. Back when the *Booze Cruise* was a real party boat, I imagine the cooler was filled with ice and beer. When we look inside, it's empty and dry. Lit up tiki torches have been staked in the deck corners. Sweet smoke curls into the sky. The fire flickers in the wind, but finds a way to keep burning. A song about margaritas plays over a speaker. It is not a song that does justice to the gravity of our moment. I touch the slight roundness under my sweatshirt and think about the months that lie ahead, the ways my body will become alien to me.

I imagine me and Marcus stepping onto my mother's houseboat, my hands cupping my stomach, and offering her another path. I imagine all of us grabbing this new life and living it and living it and living it.

We wander to the upper level. We sit down. The blue vinyl on the seats is peeling. I pull back a gummy strip and try to see what's underneath. I feel the vibrations of the engine against my thighs. The margarita music is louder up here and I think about the Pathologist's voice crackling over the Hospital speakers, dripping into the rooms and hallways, all the lies he told us.

"I can't stay up here," I say to Marcus. He touches my forehead like he's checking for a fever. I want to kiss him. I go back down to the deck, stern side.

A mist rolls across the water. The sky is marble. The clouds look like mountains. Birds hover above. Birds with orange feet and black wings. Birds with white feathers and slim elegant beaks. I feel a pang in my chest, like a muscle is cramping up, and want to believe that one of the birds is Louis, that the end is not really the end but a chance to become something new. The birds make big swooping circles. I watch until I get dizzy.

We enter a pocket of fog and it is like navigating through one of those mountainous clouds. My hair is damp. A cold creeps up my belly. The fog turns thick as smoke. I breathe it in and my heart surges and the world grows empty.

40.

I remember everything I do not want to remember and everything I do.

. . .

I remember the boy I loved and never saw again.

. . .

What is a baby but a ghost turning real inside you?

. . .

I remember the flyer of the missing girl in the T station. I see the masking tape on the post. I see the frayed edges of the paper. I see her face and I see her face turn into my own. I imagine myself picking up a phone and dialing the number. A woman answers. I imagine her voice is familiar.

. . .

This girl you're looking for? I hear myself say. Yes. Yes. I've just seen her.

. . .

I remember my theory of the sickness: for the immune the flaws in our memory protected us. Take me. Already my mind had washed away what it could not stand to remember. The sickness circled me and took a whiff and decided that my own memory was already doing the work it wanted to do, the work of forgetting. That I was already too far gone.

. . .

When the fog lifts, I raise my hand from the railing and point at the thin line of coast ahead. "Land," I say to no one.

. . .

There is a rumble that sounds like an underwater earthquake. A freezing wind. A sudden purple sky. Lightning that looks like a creature thrashing behind the clouds. An ocean that is blue electric against the darkening horizon.

A curtain of water surrounds the boat. The distant coast disappears. The tiki torches go out with a hiss. The music stops. My body is filled with the drumming of the storm. I turn around and look for the *Booze Cruise* captain inside the helm. I see a silver spinning wheel and the pale blur of his hands moving over it.

The nose of the boat dips down. My clothes are heavy and dripping. I slip to my knees. I spit water. Ocean gushes from my sneakers. The cooler slides across the deck and crashes into the railing.

A tiki torch leaps from its holster and does a suicide jump into the water.

The roar of the engine mixes with the thunder of the storm, a big hurtling ball of noise. The boat rocks back and forth. Water spreads across the deck, slick as oil. I see myself swimming out in Revere, the waves rising over my head. I see those same waves growing larger and rising over this railing and swallowing us up. I am sure the boat is going under.

■ ■ ■

What if the boat disappears inside the storm? What if my mother is the one sent looking? What if the boat sinks to the bottom, never to be seen again? What if we turn into mystery, myth?

■ ■ ■

Maybe I wouldn't mind becoming a myth.

■ ■ ■

The storm is a squall, quick and brutal. It leaves me drenched and gasping. I grab the stomach of my sweatshirt and squeeze out the water. The ocean is murky and churning. I imagine sand and seaweed and fragments of shipwrecks being dredged up from the bottom and scattered.

My mother says water is neutral, that it doesn't have wants, but what about these storms that want you and everything you have? That want your life? I add this to my list of questions to ask her.

We drift closer to the island. I see a faraway line of boats. One of them is my mother's houseboat. She is tucked inside, dry and warm, unable to shake the feeling that something is closing in. She stands up and goes outside. She begins to wait. She feels my energy traveling toward her. This is what I imagine.

Again the sky rumbles. The captain keeps turning the silver wheel.

"Land," I say to the child.

I see a silhouette on a boat deck, a slight still point in the distance. This I am not imagining. I will the figure to be a woman.

A ship horn bellows. The dark clouds slide over the party boat, satisfied with what they've done here, in search of new destruction. The water clears and I see a darting school of fish, a tangerine flicker.

I keep expecting the figure to turn, to vanish, to reveal itself as a figment of the mind, but she stays.

I feel a rage that could sink this boat faster than any storm.

I make the choice and feel the small thing inside go free.

"My name is Joy," I say, practicing.

The woman is a dark speck at first, an idea of a person, but slowly she takes shape. I can make out the straight line of her legs, the curves of her shoulders. Whoever she turns out to be, I will ask her my questions and see how she answers.

Where will I even start? Here is where I will start.

I will ask her who she is and what she remembers. I will ask her if I seem familiar and how long has she been waiting and did she ever give me a name. I will ask her what she knows about consequences and when she tells me what she thinks she knows I will tell her she has no idea and then I will say, Fuck the guilt, it's no way to live. Do you know the secrets of your unconscious mind and the parts of yourself you want to kill and bury deep and can I help you with that shovel? Did you really think you could ever bury me? Do you think it is possible to love someone you don't know and do you think it is possible to love a ghost and are you really missing if there is no one there to look?

I'm here, I will tell her.

Look.

ACKNOWLEDGMENTS

Thank you:

To Ragdale, the Virginia Center for the Creative Arts, the Studios of Key West, and Spiro Arts for the time and support.

I've worked on this book in a number of different places—North Carolina, Pennsylvania, Baltimore, Utah, Virginia, Illinois, New York City, Boston, Key West—and each landscape made its mark. I'm especially grateful to Key West for the ghosts and the stories.

In the early stages, I consulted *Killer Germs* by Barry E. Zimmerman and David J. Zimmerman and *Flu* by Gina Kolata, later turning to sources that shined a light on our current American dystopia—especially Andrea Elliott's "Invisible Child" series for *The New York Times* and Matt Taibbi's "Apocalypse, New Jersey: A Dispatch from America's Most Desperate Town" for *Rolling Stone*.

To Mike Y., for letting me crib from his Twitter feed.

To the Writers' Room of Boston, for the space and the view.

To Courtney and her excellent apartment, where this book was finished.

To the American Academy of Arts and Letters for the extraordinary show of faith.

To Don, Jess, Robin, Tarfia, Karen, Lauren, Ted, Shannon, Porochista, and Jane for the company on the path, which would have been so much darker without you.

To my early readers, Josh, Matt, and James, for helping me find my way through the woods.

To Mike S., Nina, and Meghan for the support and guidance when it was urgently needed.

To Elliott, for writing alongside me.

To Sarah Scire. To Sean McDonald. To Nayon Cho and Abby Kagan. To Delia Casa and Nina Frieman. To everyone else at FSG who helped this book come into being. Thank you.

To Emily Bell, for keeping the path alight with her fierce vision and impeccable editorial eye. For her trust and her friendship. I owe you the world.

To Katherine Fausset, for the exceptional privilege of being able to call you my agent and my friend. You are simply the best. Thank you as well to Stuart Waterman and everyone else at Curtis Brown.

To my family, for believing.

To my grandmother, whom I miss.

To Paul, for everything, always.